THE VINDICTIVE VINES
A Djinn and Tonnick Mystery

Steve A. Zuckerman

ISBN: 9781712238721

For Kay and Haskell.

Thanks to Faye and George Gilpatrick at Rancho Ventavo Cellars for their support and winemaking expertise, which helped make this book possible. Special thanks to Michelle, my muse and editor extraordinaire.

"Anger is an acid that can do more harm to the vessel in which it is stored than to anything on which it is poured."

Mark Twain

CHAPTER ONE

Napa Valley, California. 1865

NO ONE KNEW WHERE the Harper sisters came from, nor how they ended up owning a large parcel of farmland north of George Yount's vineyards. At first glance, Merrilee and Rosalee appeared to be in their late fifties, but in truth, they were far older. The rumor floated around the small, nearby town of Napa, was that the spinsters were well monied, as they paid cash to have the two-story clapboard house built on the frontage of their hundred-acre spread.

From all accounts, the two sisters were nice enough, but reclusive—although that could be attributed to their common disability, as both were wheelchair bound. As such, neither of them did their own shopping in town, instead sending money and a list of supplies to Grayson's outfitters regularly. Martin Grayson's son, William, routinely delivered the sister's monthly orders to their farmstead as part of his regular route.

A talkative and friendly young man, William was always happy to carry the staples into the sister's kitchen, all while regaling Merrilee and Rosalee with the latest news. It was on one of these occasions he mentioned something that interested the sisters enough to garner more than their usual polite, perfunctory responses.

"So, you know there's this feller I deliver to, name of Watkins... Ain't that a funny name? Well, ya know, he's tellin' me he's fixin' to make wine otta his grapes."

"That's nice," Merrilee responded. "Our grapes 'round here are good for the table or raisins, but not so much for wine."

"True enough," agreed Rosalee, looking out the front window. They had many rows of grapevines growing on their land, and the fruit, though plentiful, contributed little financially.

The two were watching and listening as William hauled a sack of flour into their pantry.

"Yes, Ma'am. But this feller been cuttin' roots n' such together an' says he's got it figured out."

"Cuttin' roots?" Merrilee asked.

"Uh, huh," said William. "He says he's making som'thin' call infidel wine. I'm goin' to his place next with the sack o' beans he ordered."

"Do you mean 'Zinfandel?'" Rosalee asked.

Neither of the Harper sisters was attractive by any measure. Their thin bodies appeared frail, dwarfed as they were by their matching, oversized wheelchairs. William, like everyone else who knew them, assumed they had been born handicapped or deformed. Even in the warmest weather, both women wore blankets on their laps that hung down, concealing their legs and feet.

The sister's familial resemblance was unmistakable. So much so, that they might have been mistaken for twins at first sight. Both wore their jet black hair wound tight in a bun atop their heads, contrasting prominently with their wrinkled, porcelain white skin. Other features they had in common were their narrow faces and sharp beak-like noses jutting above the thin, blood-red lips that framed their unusually wide mouths.

Most notable were the women's small beady eyes, sunken and set wide apart. Those inky irises, as black as their pupils, were dark, shiny marbles that never seemed to stop wandering—except on those rare occasions when something caught their interest, as they did now.

"Could'a been. It was some kinda wine," replied William hesitantly.

"From Zinfandel grapes?" asked Merrilee.

She fixed her penetrating stare on the young man.

"Yeah, that's it," answered William, tearing his eyes away from hers.

He thought the ladies were nice enough; nevertheless, something was unsettling about the pair that always made him nervous in their presence. He rushed off, welcoming the opportunity to retrieve the last bag of cornmeal from his wagon.

Rosalee turned to Merrilee. "If he's got a way to make decent wine, we would do very well."

"Yes, indeed," Merrilee said. Her wry smile looked out of place on her otherwise stern features. She pushed back at a flyaway strand of hair with one of her long, curved fingernails. "Europe's grapes are all dying... As the oracles at Delphi had predicted."

Rosalee returned Merrilee's grin, which looked no better on her than it had on her sister.

"There's coin to be made then, isn't there?" she replied, observing as Merrilee tucked the errant bit of hair back into the bun on the top of her curiously oblong head. "One can't have enough coin, can they?"

"So true, sister," agreed Merrilee. "That has never changed."

When William returned carrying the sack of cornmeal, Rosalie asked him to wait a few moments. Merrilee had rolled over to the desk to scribble something on a piece of paper. When she had finished, she folded it and sealed it with wax before presenting it to the lanky delivery boy.

"Here, William," Merrilee said, handing him the note and a large coin. "For you... To deliver this note to Mr. Watkins."

William looked down at the coin, and his jaw dropped in wide-eyed amazement. It was a twenty-dollar gold-piece. He replied as soon as he could close his mouth.

"Sure enough, Miss. Harper! I'll do it!"

Quickly, since he didn't wish to chance that the ladies might suffer a change of heart, he jumped back into his wagon and drove straight away, eager to complete his task.

"So... Do you think that Watkins person will come?" Rosalee asked in their native tongue, watching the wagon recede up the dirt road.

They only conversed in this fashion when they were alone, speaking an ancient dialect no human ear, Greek or otherwise, had heard for several thousand years.

"Oh, he will come, I promise you," Merrilee replied with a mirthless smile. "I took pains to saturate that note with a compulsion the likes no one has seen since the fall of Delos!"

"Ah, those were the days, weren't they?" Rosalee sighed.

CHAPTER TWO

Los Angeles. Present Day

THE DAMNED FELINE WAS giving me an accusatory stare as I poured a couple more fingers of Cuervo into my coffee cup.

"What?" I barked but got no reply. However, her inscrutable stare spoke volumes. "Okay, so I'm drinking too much."

Admittedly, it was a bit of an understatement as it was only 9:30 in the morning. I took another sip as she watched. Finally, I had enough.

"Can't you cut me some slack? I'm kinda working through my depression here!"

I guess Ruby didn't like my tone of voice, or perhaps she was just tired of sitting in judgment. In any event, she jumped from her perch on the office couch and trotted across the room to inspect her food and water bowls. Cats have a lot in common with genies—you can't expect any sympathy from either of them.

Yeah, I was feeling sorry for myself. Not that I had much to complain about, except for my love life, or actual lack of same. Delinda Djinn, the object of my desire, had stopped taking my calls shortly after our last conversation.

I had spent the last several weeks missing her in a way that opened up a pit in my stomach even the tequila couldn't quell. I suppose there was no one to blame other than myself.

Naturally, to the untrained eye, cat not included, it would seem everything in Mark Tonnick's life was a picture of perfection. My Private Investigator license was paid, and up to date, checks were coming in regularly—and I even drove a company car, courtesy of my client, Bruce Ashton and his mega-communications conglomerate, AC&C. Yeah, I had it all, except for the thing I wanted most.

You probably think I should move on, and really, if I could, I would. But it's complicated since Delinda Djinn and I are bound by magic. Before you decide I'm completely mental, let me explain. Delinda and I go back to my Marine Core days in Iraq. There, I only barely survived an IED attack that left me with some clay shards permanently embedded in my cheek. I didn't know it then, but when that clay vessel got blown apart, it literally let the genie out of the bottle. My narrow escape from death left me with a star-shaped scar on my face and an invisible one on my psyche. I didn't find out until much later that Delinda was responsible for me surviving the explosion that killed everyone else in my unit.

After my stint in the armed forces, I came back to LA and figured I'd get into the PI business. For a while, I was getting by, running skip traces on bail jumpers, tailing cheating spouses, exposing scammers, and all the rest. But then, the economy took a dive, taking my prospects with it. I ended up working on spec deals, got behind in my rent, and couldn't afford to renew my license or pay the phone bill. My entire world was turning to shit in front of me.

But everything changed when Delinda Djinn and Bruce Ashton unexpectedly entered my life. At first, I had no clue why they hired me at double my usual rate to track down and retrieve something extremely dangerous. It was only afterward I discovered the real reason for my change of fortune. It all came back to those pieces of pottery in my cheek.

Eventually, I learned those clay shards came from a vessel that once housed a genie. You know the type; the beautiful girl in the pointy shoes and gauzy dress who appears in a cloud of smoke to grant you three wishes—that kind. Except for the beautiful girl part, none of the rest happened to me.

At first, I didn't believe any of it. It was only later, after I was up to my neck in cursed objects, immortal beings, and every other type of supernatural crazy you can imagine, that I accepted the fact Delinda was the former occupant of the bottle or jar—or whatever it was.

Even after that first escapade, I wasn't entirely convinced about the existence of magic and everything else it implied. However, on my next job for AC&C, a few things happened that completely changed my outlook.

The case started out simple enough. Still, by the time it was over I was nearly killed by a resurrected Shaman and saved only by the intervention of a Native American deity. As a result, I'll just say I'm less skeptical now, and let it go at that. All of which brings me to my current dilemma.

Delinda has told me in no uncertain terms that she and I can never be together—Yeah, in that way. Evidently, genies, or ifrits or whichever term you prefer, have more in common with nuns than with say, the girl I took to prom. The last interaction Delinda and I had ended after I made a move on her. Ever since, it's been radio silence. She even disappeared from my dreams—which were admittedly a very guilty pleasure. A very petty move on her part, if I might say so. Did I mention I never even got three wishes?

Otherwise, I can't complain. My retainer, now that I'm on AC&C's payroll, has been very lucrative. Thanks to that, I'm up to date on both my office lease and the small apartment I rent above Mrs. Krenzman's store. I've got money in the bank and a newly remodeled office.

Regardless, lately I spend my days in a funk; pounding back shots when I'm not reviewing background checks on AC&C's potential personnel hires. Take my word for it, if there's anything worse than being depressed, it's being bored shitless. In both regards—I'm batting two for two.

My freeloading feline, Ruby, is about the only creature that can put up with me when I get this way. I've never owned a pet before, but the cat and I have arrived at an agreement. She listens to my drunken musings, and I keep food in her bowl. I'm fairly sure she has the better part of the deal.

I was about to refill my coffee mug again when my mobile rang. I intended to mute the ringer, but when I saw the display, my jaw dropped in amazement. Whoever said, "Thoughts are things" might have gotten it right. It was Delinda Djinn.

"Hey," I said tentatively. "How are you?"

"Are you busy?" she asked, ignoring my question.

I could tell she was trying to sound casual, but her voice was tight, and my intuition told me she was uncomfortable. By inference, I knew she was only calling because Ashton had asked her.

Maybe it was the tequila, or perhaps I was as nervous as she was. Whatever the reason, my reply was probably a little too flippant.

"Oh, yeah, I'm up to my ears with lots of exciting detective stuff… Like vetting prospective secretarial pool candidates."

"Glad you find the work so rewarding," she said without a trace of humor.

"Beats getting shot at," I replied.

"Got you a new office, didn't it?"

She had me there. A month ago, my place was shredded by gunfire, and me almost with it. If you saw what my office looked like before that happened, you might have considered it an improvement. After the fact, I used the insurance money and some of my bonus dough from AC&C to fix the place up. Nothing fancy, but at least now the castors on my office chair aren't prone to fly off in different directions anymore.

"Yeah, it did. I take it you're not calling me for a date?"

"Ashton wants to see you." Her icy reply spoke volumes.

"Okay… When?" I asked.

"Now."

"Now?"

"Have you been drinking?"

"Of course not!" I lied.

She hung up before I could say anything else. As I got my coat, I suddenly realized my head was clear.

"Cheap genie trick, not to mention a waste of good tequila," I grunted to the cat before I headed downstairs.

On the way out, I stopped in on Willy. He runs the pawnshop, the building's anchor store, seeing it's the only storefront in the building that's not currently empty.

"Hey, Willy," I yelled, sticking my head inside his door. "I'm going out for a while."

"Jesus, Mark… What am I… Your mother?" he yelled back.

"No… She was much better looking. Say, if I'm not back in a couple of hours, would you mind feeding Ruby?"

Willy walked out from behind the counter and over to where I was standing. Willy's a big guy, in every sense of the word, which makes him partial to oversized Hawaiian shirts and baggy jeans. I don't think I've ever seen him wear anything else.

"Shit, Tonnick. Sometimes I think if it wasn't for me, that cat would starve!"

"Come on, Willy. You're the one who convinced me to keep her."

"Good thing I did, too. Your feline early warning system was all that saved your bacon."

"You'll get no argument from me," I said, walking out to the street through the grimy double glass doors.

Willy was right on that account. Ruby's sudden screech was all that kept me from being perforated along with the rest of my office, which is what can happen when you're unlucky enough to make it to the top of a mob boss's hit-parade. As a result, my furry confidant has become a permanent part of our office building—cat box and all.

I keep my new car, thoughtfully provided by AC&C, parked down the block in a covered lot so it won't end up on blocks like my last one did. East Hollywood isn't a great neighborhood, although my building is technically on the world-famous Sunset Blvd. That being said, the glitzy, upscale section of the Sunset Strip is a couple miles west of here. Most of the buildings and storefronts in my area are relics from the late fifties and early sixties. Mere shells left behind from Hollywood's heyday.

All of my neighbors are small businesses struggling to keep their doors open, make a buck, and provide for their families. I've got a connection to more than a few of them because when I was down on my luck, they never hesitated to help me out. That's the main reason I resolved to stay put when my fortunes took a drastic turn for the better. I've arrived at the conclusion that you have to lose practically everything before you find out who your friends are. Having said that, it's a helluva way to have learned that lesson.

My newly acquired ride was waiting for me, a late model Toyota Prius, tastefully appointed with AC&C's logo prominently featured on both front doors. Bruce Ashton clearly isn't one to pass up an opportunity for free advertising. Hey, I'm not complaining—the magnetic signs come off so I can do surveillance work when called upon, and the car starts up every time, something I couldn't say about my previous set of wheels.

Ashton, my rich client, works out of his Bel-Air estate, which occupies an entire block in the middle of LA's wealthiest neighborhood. Surrounded by tall wrought-iron fencing, his mansion is a stately, three-story affair that would be equally at home in the English countryside—not that I would have a clue.

After security buzzed me through the big gates, I made the quarter-mile drive up the driveway to the circular courtyard. There, my buddy Al stood waiting for me. He was slight of frame and dressed in black slacks and a collared white short-sleeved shirt with no tie. It was considerably more formal attire than he usually wore, but as Ashton's main man in charge of household affairs he was expected to look the part.

"How goes it?" he greeted me loudly as I exited my car. His dark brown eyes glistened brightly in his bald head, and a warm smile spread across his Mediterranean features.

"It goes," I replied, mounting the broad steps up to the landing where he was standing. It was good to see his friendly face.

"How have you been, Al?"

"Real fine… Although it's been a bit boring lately."

I gave him a knowing smile. "Relative to our last adventure, I get it… Murder and mayhem notwithstanding. Don't tell me you miss the adrenaline rush?"

"I do, just a bit," Al admitted as he finished shaking my right hand with his left. "Even if taking care of this place is better for my health."

"That's not a bad thing," I said, thinking about our mutual brush with death. "Especially since, according to you, you're not immortal anymore."

"Yep," Al nodded. "That chariot has left the arena."

Along with my relative sanity, I thought. Originally from Greece, Al has always claimed he's more than a few thousand years old and might have lived practically forever until a crazy sociopath cut off his right hand. Until then, the mystic Circle of Solomon was embedded in the palm of that hand. Al swears that relic had kept him alive all this time. Now, he's just like the rest of us—riding on the train of mortality. And we all know where that's heading. In light of that, I don't understand how he hangs onto his sunny disposition, all things considered. Nevertheless, he swears he's good with it, and who am I to argue?

I followed Al into the house, through the vestibule, and down a long, wainscoted hall. From all my previous visits, I knew the hallway dead-ended at the tall oak doors to Ashton's private study.

Bruce Ashton is another of the nearly immortal, courtesy of his Circle of Solomon. Having amassed his fortunes over centuries, he was now the CEO of the telecommunications conglomerate AC&C. He came close to losing his circle to the same madman who took Al's—but fate and I intervened at the last minute, saving his life and according to some, civilization as we know it.

Al knocked before we entered the darkened room—its usual state per Ashton's aversion to strong light. Delinda Djinn was already seated and made it a point to ignore me as I walked in.

"Mr. Tonnick, please take a seat." Ashton intoned. His voice was firm, and as usual, it wasn't an invitation. "You too, Al," he added.

I sat in an overstuffed leather chair next to Delinda, and though I was looking straight at her, she still made no effort to even spare me a glance. She was dressed in a light green skirt that ended just above the knee, and a crisp, white blouse modestly buttoned up several inches beneath her neck. Her long, brown hair was pulled back into a neat ponytail that ended below her shoulder blades.

"Happy to see you too," I whispered.

"I'll get right to the point," Ashton continued. I assumed he heard and disregarded my aside. "Since you all did so well on the Palm Springs affair, I need the three of you to work together again."

Delinda looked like she was going to say something, but Ashton raised his hand, making it clear he wasn't through.

"And, this matter also has financial ramifications for AC&C. This time, however, the numbers are far more substantial."

Delinda cleared her throat. "I'm not sure I can work with Mark again."

Even in the dark, I knew Ashton was staring at the three of us.

A long moment later, she cleared her throat again and added, "It's… Personal."

"Fine with me," I snorted. "I don't need your help!"

Truthfully, I was surprised at myself. I'm sure I sounded more hurt than angry—which was how I felt, but nothing I wished to advertise.

There was more silence until Bruce Ashton spoke again. There was just enough anger in his reply to get everyone's attention.

"As long as you wish to remain in my employ, you'll do as I ask."

He waited for a moment for that to resonate before he began again in a more conciliatory tone. "You two will have to put your issues behind you for the time being. I need you both at the top of your game."

Was he looking at Delinda? It was impossible to tell.

"That will only happen if you work together," he added.

"Yes, but," Delinda interjected. "It's just…"

"It's my fault, Mr. Ashton," I interrupted.

Somehow, I mustered enough resolve to address her directly.

"I'm sorry for making you uncomfortable. I promise I'll be on my best behavior."

I tried my hardest to sound sincere—I didn't even cross my fingers. I had already arrived at the same conclusion Ashton had.

"That isn't saying much," she replied under her breath.

"Scout's Honor," I promised earnestly.

She shook her head. "What does that mean?"

From the tenor of her reply, I thought she might be softening.

"It means I'll remain professional at all times."

I glanced over to see how Ashton had reacted to our conversation. The guy was way too smart not to know what had been going on between us.

"Good," Ashton pronounced. "Now that's settled, we can get down to business." It wasn't a request.

"Al, you have the paperwork?"

"Yep, right here, sir," Al acknowledged, rummaging through a large manila envelope he had taken off a side table.

He handed Delinda and me several sheets of paper.

"Mr. Tonnick, what do you know about wine?" Ashton asked before I even glanced at the cover sheet.

"I'm a tequila guy," I answered. "When it comes to wine, I don't think my palate is refined enough to recognize the difference between good and bad… If that's what you're asking."

Ashton chuckled. "In a way. Everyone's palate is unique, but personal preferences aside, I'm sure you're aware the wine business generates astronomical revenues."

"Yeah, I guess so. But what does that have to do with anything?" I remarked, genuinely puzzled.

Delinda, while still avoiding eye contact with me, was intently studying the papers she was shuffling through. On the heels of my comment, she looked up at Ashton in surprise.

"You own a winery?" she said.

Ashton sighed loudly before he replied. "Yes, I'm afraid so. One of AC&C's investment brokers has made it part of our portfolio. As it turns out, our exposure is substantial. The property includes several hundred acres of vineyards and a large winemaking and hospitality facility."

"So, what's the problem?" I asked, peering at the folio's first page, which read "Taskert Vineyards."

"Unfortunately, a great number of things," Ashton said. "It's taken Phillip Taskert several years to get the operation ready to open, and according to him, they've done everything the right way... Despite all of that, the result is well below our expectations."

"So, in other words," Al offered, "the wine sucks."

Al's never one for mincing words, another reason why I like the guy.

I looked over at Delinda, who still hadn't lifted her eyes off the page.

"Bad choice in winemakers?" I ventured.

"No," she said, still staring down. "According to what I'm reading here, Derek George is one of the best vintners in Napa Valley."

"Well, maybe the grapes are bad," I ventured.

It was hard to see in the dim light, but I imagined Ashton was shaking his head as he replied. "No, the grapes are fine. The vineyard sold several tons of grapes to other local wineries to help with their cash flow. As far as we know, the wine all these other entities made from them is outstanding… Excellent, in fact. I should point out there is one other thing that's unusual. Another large investor, Richard Kaffee, has been buying out the other stakeholders in Taskert's winery. He has also made us an offer… As you can imagine, it's for far less than we've already invested. All things considered, it's likely there's more going here than meets the eye."

There's something baked into my DNA that always dredges up the worse case scenarios first.

"So, do you suspect someone is screwing up the wine on purpose to force investors to sell at a loss?" I ventured.

"That's why I'm sending you," Ashton answered without hesitation, "to investigate every aspect of this matter."

Despite the darkened room, I swear the old guy was looking directly at me when he added, "But, be aware... Both the vineyards and the castle Taskert has resurrected on the property have much history."

The small hairs on the back of my neck stood up. From experience, I knew precisely what Ashton was suggesting. My relatively short history with him and this crew have taught me to take his inferences seriously.

I said, "You're thinking there might be something..." The last word of my sentence—'supernatural,' caught in my throat, but I'm sure everyone caught my drift.

"Possibly..." Ashton replied softly.

"Great," I said, not bothering to conceal my sarcasm. "I wonder if haunts prefer white or red."

"When are we going?" Delinda asked, ignoring my lame attempt at humor.

"Tomorrow at ten," Ashton replied. "You'll be leaving in my corporate jet from Van Nuys Airport and flying to Oakland International. There will be a rental car waiting for you. Napa Valley is only an hour's drive from there."

Sure. The way Delinda drives, I had no doubt we'd arrive at our destination in less than twenty minutes after we deplaned.

I assumed the meeting was over, so I got out of the overstuffed chair and was about to leave the room when Ashton unexpectedly called after me.

"Mark, sit down," he said. "Al, Delinda, I would like a word with Mr. Tonnick... In private."

I sat back down and waited, expecting a well deserved dressing down. Ashton didn't speak until we were alone in the study.

"I'm aware of what's going on with you and Delinda..." he began.

"I really didn't mean to screw things up between us," I blurted. "But..."

Ashton finished my sentence for me. "You're in love, and now you've been told that's impossible."

I nodded weakly. The old guy's got eyes like a cat, so I'm sure he saw the expression on my face.

"In the short term, you'll just have to deal with it. Both of you need each other… As I told you some time ago, because of your complementary magic, Delinda is far more powerful when the two of you are together."

He paused to let that sink in.

"With all due respect, that can't be true," I objected. "I have no magic of my own."

"You're wrong about that."

"Really?" I replied, "Isn't that something I would be aware of?"

Ashton let loose with something that sounded like a cross between a cough and a laugh. "I would have thought by now you'd have seen for yourself. Why do you think you always find yourself embroiled in such strange events?"

"Truthfully, I've chalked that up to the company I've been keeping."

"You're deflecting," Ashton retorted. "But, in any event, you'll need to come to terms with it on your own. Of course, once you do, it will change everything…"

"What do you mean?"

In the darkness, it was hard to tell, but I thought he made a slight wave with his hand as he said, "If I told you, it would never happen. You'll have to just trust me on that account."

"So, what do I do in the meantime?"

"Be patient… And for god's sake, think before you shove your feet in your mouth!"

That made me smile. Frankly, I had never known Ashton to display any sense of humor.

"Anything else, sir?"

Was he smiling too? I couldn't be sure.

"Yes… Find out what's really going up there and protect our investment!"

The meeting was over.

CHAPTER THREE

LATE AFTERNOON TRAFFIC IN Los Angeles is soul-crushing. I could have made better time crawling on my hands and knees. As it was, I got back to my office about two hours after I left Bel-Air.

On my way upstairs, I stopped at Willy's to ask him to feed the cat during my absence. He complained just enough to make a show of it, but in truth, Willy's more fond of that animal than I am.

Regardless of Ashton's little pep talk, I was still in a funk from my very unsatisfying tête-à-tête with Delinda and thought it was a good time to call it a day. I garaged my ride and set about my usual walk home in the hopes it would improve my mood.

My upstairs studio apartment is inside Mrs. Krenzman's mini-market, which is only a block and a half away from my office. While these days I can afford better digs, I still feel it's my responsibility to look out for her.

Mrs. Krentzman is a lovely, white-haired, Russian woman in her late seventies who single-handedly runs the tiny store. It's a testimony to her strength that she keeps the business going, especially after her husband was shot to death by some punk looking to rob the place. If it hadn't been for her generosity, and the pre-packaged deli sandwiches in her store, I would have starved to death back when times were tough. Nowadays, I figure the least I can do is to be there for her. She would never tell me, but I know my rent money helps keep the place open.

As always, when I walked into the store, she greeted me loudly in her thick accent.

"You're home early. What no clients?"

Then she looked at me closely and shook her head. Mrs. Krenzman may have none of Delinda Djinn's magical powers, but that doesn't keep her from reading me like an open dime-store novel.

"You're sad… Still?"

"Yeah," I replied good-naturedly. "She still wants nothing to do with me."

"Then she no good," she proclaimed confidently. "You have to find someone else."

I laughed, and then suddenly, my attention was drawn to the front door. A guy was walking into the store. Both of his hands were buried deep inside the pockets of the dark gray hoodie that partially covered his face. When he raised his head, I saw he was Hispanic, about sixteen.

I tensed up—not at his ethnicity, but on account of his furtive appearance. It's a rough neighborhood, and this wouldn't be the first time somebody had walked in off the street with less than honest intentions. My hands balled into fists as he approached. I don't carry a weapon. My policy is based on a slew of personal reasons, but I was prepared nevertheless.

What I wasn't prepared for was when the kid came up to me and asked, "You Tonnick?"

He took his hands out of his pockets and stared at me with an expression that spoke volumes. He hadn't come to fight, he had come for help.

"Yeah," I replied, uncurling my fists. "That's me. What's up?"

"The people in the neighborhood say you're a good man… An' that you help people."

"Sometimes," I said warily.

The kid didn't look like he had any dough, and I don't need any Yelp reviews, so I was about to blow him off, but he spoke up before I told him so.

"I need to hire you… To find my sister."

Something in his eyes resonated with me. The sadness in them struck me as authentic. It's a sad fact that once you do enough of what

I do, you can spot the fakers. In my business, you run into every con you can possibly imagine. You especially have to beware of the worst of them—the stalkers who want you to help them by putting a bullseye on their victims. But when I see a kid in trouble, I'm the biggest sucker there is.

"Go on," I prompted.

He nodded and pulled a crumpled photo out of his jeans.

"This is her… Michalena, she's fifteen," he said, handing it to me.

The photo showed a smiling, dark-haired Hispanic girl. She had dark brown eyes and a flawless complexion. From her expression, it appeared she didn't have a care in the world.

"What's your name?" I asked.

"Juan… Juan Reynoso. Our mother owns the taqueria down the street."

"I know the place. Your mom makes a mean chile relleno."

Juan brightened at my reply. "So you'll help us?"

"If I can. When was the last time you saw your sister?"

"Yesterday. She left for school but never came home."

I didn't bother to ask him if his family called the police. Most immigrants in this town didn't trust the cops—especially given the current political climate.

"Did you check with her friends?" I asked. "Any chance they might have an idea what happened to her?"

"Sí…" He hung his head. "Her best friend is Anna Garcia." Juan hesitated before he added, "But her brother is in a gang. I'm afraid to go there."

"Do you have an address or a phone number for Anna?"

"No," he replied. "I only know she lives in the corner house on Formosa and Childress."

I had driven through that area occasionally, and I remembered it as a typical older, blue-collar neighborhood. Most of the homes were built during the thirties and forties in the old Spanish style. Out of necessity, the majority of the people living there had been doing so for a very long time. Ironically, many of the current residents couldn't afford to buy their own homes at today's prices—nor could they afford to move.

"Juan, I don't know of any gangs near that area, are you sure?"

"Yes, Michalena told me that Anna's brother, Carlos, is a very bad man."

"Your sister should pick her friends more carefully," I said. "Do you think Anna's brother has anything to do with your sister's disappearance?"

Juan shrugged. "No se… I'm not sure."

Mrs. Krentzman had come over during our conversation and was peering at the photo.

"She look like very nice girl," she said, smiling warmly at Juan before looking pointedly at me. "Mr. Tonnick find her, no problem!"

It was no use arguing—now I had a new client and a scheduling conflict.

"Okay, Juan… I'll see what I can do before I leave town tomorrow."

He nodded, though his face fell at the news. "We will be grateful for whatever you can do, Señor Tonnick. Thank you."

As he left the store, Mrs. Krentzman slapped me on the arm. "What you waiting for?"

She was right. With any missing persons case, the first few hours are the most critical. However, before I started knocking on Anna Garcia's door, I thought it best to know what kind of 'bad man' her brother was. Since time was of the essence, I decided to call in a favor.

Brent Todd answered his phone after the third ring. "What do you want, Tonnick?"

"Happy Wednesday to you, too," I said, pausing for a moment before adding, "As a matter of fact, I do need your help."

Todd exhaled, as though he was girding himself for something very unpleasant. But he did owe me. In the past few months after I cleared his name, Homicide had promoted him to lead detective—a textbook example of the 'Peter Principle' in practice.

"What kind of help?" he huffed.

I could picture him running a hand through his short black hair. He still had a headful, compared to what I still had left of mine.

"I need you to look up a guy named Carlos Garcia. I need to find out if he's connected to any gang or other illegal activity." The phone went suddenly silent. "Hey, Todd, are you still there?"

"Want the good news or the bad news," he finally said.

"Good news first,"

"Okay, the good news is I don't have to go through any files."

"What's the bad news?" I asked.

"Carlos Garcia *is* the bad news. What do you want with the guy?"

"I need to ask him a few questions. I thought I'd see what you had on him before I go over to pay him a visit."

"Are you out of your goddamn mind!"

"Is that a rhetorical question?"

"Jesus, Tonnick… You sure know how to pick 'em. Why do you need to talk to him?"

"I just want to have a short conversation about a missing fifteen-year-old girl… A friend of his sister's."

"Look, you can't just drop in… And believe me, he's nobody you want to piss off."

"Come on, Brent. If I bring a cop with me, he might hear me out instead of shooting me on the spot."

Another pause, followed by another exasperated exhale. "What? You want me to go over there with you?"

"Yes, I do," I persisted. "First, a young girl's life might be at stake, and secondly... You owe me!"

"Shit!" he muttered in resignation. "When?"

"How about right now?" I replied. I knew he realized I was smiling. "Pick me up at Mrs. Krenzman's."

An hour later, Brent Todd and I pulled up to the Garcia house. It didn't stand out from any others in the surrounding neighborhood. The lawn in front of the single-story stucco home was neatly kept. The flowerbeds lining the front of the house were overflowing with colorful pansies, and the knee-high white-picket fence surrounding the yard appeared freshly painted. I expected to see Mr. Rodgers standing on the porch.

Like the other houses on the street, the garage was set back from the front of the house. The driveway that led to it was unpaved, and the unkempt clumps of grass grew between two spaced rows of aged bricks that barely accommodated the wheels of the white, Cadillac SUV parked there. I also noted several other expensive cars that were parked out on the street nearby.

"I hope you know what you're doing," Todd said under his breath as we got out of his unmarked Crown Vic.

The two of us walked up the path to the front porch. I saw a hand briefly pull one of the window curtains aside. Good, I thought. In addition to the car's pedigree, if anybody looked like a cop, it was Brent Todd. Despite being impeccably dressed as he usually was, even a blind man would make him in two seconds flat. I only hoped his presence would be enough to guarantee some civility—and minimize the possibility of gunfire.

Mere seconds after I rang the doorbell, a beefy Hispanic man opened the door. He was definitely not what I expected. The guy looked like he had just arrived after a round of golf at a country club. His orange sport shirt bore a high-end brand insignia and was neatly tucked into the waist of his pressed, light tan slacks that fell over the tops of his unlaced black Nike sneakers. Other than the intricate sleeve tats that covered both his arms, he'd seem right at home on the first tee.

Todd had already pulled out his badge. "Mr. Garcia, I'm lieutenant Brent Todd, LAPD. Can we have a few minutes of your time?"

"I have my lawyer on speed dial," he said evenly. "Do you have a warrant?"

I spoke up. "Actually, we'd like to speak to your sister, Anna. We're hoping she could help us locate Michalena Reynoso. Anna was the last person to see her."

Carlos Garcia didn't reply. He just stood there looking through us, as though we weren't there.

"Her family is very concerned," I added.

Unexpectedly, he looked down at his feet for a moment. When he looked up again, he said, "Come in… Please."

Todd was as surprised at the invitation as I was, but we followed Carlos into the front room. Two other heavily tatted men, not nearly as well dressed as our host, were sitting on the couch eyeing us warily.

"Out," Carlos ordered softly.

Moments later, the three of us were alone.

"Anna's gone too," he said. "They've run off together."

"How do you know?" Todd asked.

"I found this," he replied.

He reached into an end table drawer and handed Todd a piece of blue-lined notebook paper. I looked over Todd's shoulder and saw the handwriting on it was distinctly the work of a young girl's. In a mixture of Spanish and English, it simply read: "Mi Hermano, please don't try to find us, we are fine. M and I are going to hunt down Momo and avenge Gia."

"What the hell does that mean?" I asked. "Who's Momo? And why avenge Gia?"

Carlos took the paper back from Todd and sat down on the couch.

"Momo is a crazy game on the internet. She makes kids kill themselves… Like Gia did." He took his phone off the side table and swiped the screen a few times. "Some say she's real… A bruja… A witch!"

He held up his phone, which displayed a distorted image of a woman with scraggly hair and eyes bulging out of her head. Bizarre and disturbing as it was, I was tempted to laugh, but even I have enough sensitivity to keep my mouth shut—especially if a bad-ass like Carlos Garcia takes it seriously. I also thought about what Ashton said earlier, about how these kinds of events seem to find me. Unconsciously I rubbed the scar on my cheek.

Todd asked, "Where do you think they went?"

"And where do you suppose they might search for somebody they've only seen on the internet?" I interjected.

Carlos shook his head, still staring at his phone. "I don't know. But Anna took some money… Enough to get just about anywhere."

"What?" I pressed. "Enough for an Uber? Bus?"

Garcia coughed up a humorless laugh. "A thousand dollars. Enough for whatever."

"Okay," Todd said. "Do you want to file a missing person report?"

Garcia looked past Todd and settled his gaze on me.

"You're not a cop, right?"

"No, I'm a Private Investigator, working on behalf of Michalena's family."

"Okay, Mister..."

"Tonnick. Mark Tonnick."

"All right, Tonnick, now you're working for me too." He turned to Todd. "Cops don't do shit. Especially for guys like me."

"This isn't about you; it's about your sister," Todd shot back. "I'm going to file it anyway."

He used his phone to capture a photograph of Anna that rested on the fireplace mantle. I held out Michalena's picture for him to do the same.

"We'll do our best to find them regardless of what you might think," said Todd.

Carlos watched us silently for a long moment before he spoke again.

"This is my fault. She sees how I take care of my own. When someone hurts me or my crew, I strike back twice as hard. After this girl, Gia, Anna's friend at school, began texting Momo, she went missing. A few days later, they found her body somewhere in Griffith Park. She killed herself… My Anna took it really hard. She said she'd make it her business to see that Momo didn't get away with it."

I tried to sound reassuring. "From what you're telling us, it doesn't seem like either Anna or Michalena are suicidal… And since there's no Momo in real life, maybe the girls will give up after a day or so and return home."

When Carlos replied, I realized why he wanted his men to leave. He sounded genuinely afraid.

"Listen, I've heard things from people who say Momo, and her magic is real... And very, very powerful."

He took a deep breath and looked me directly. Now I didn't see fear, only murderous resolve.

"You find Anna. I don't care how or what it costs, but you find her... Alive..."

Carlos didn't have to add the words "or else"—it was implicit in his expression and voice. Before I could respond, he stood up from the couch, stepped over to the door and threw it open. A clear invitation to leave.

"We'll contact you the minute we know anything," Todd said.

I followed Todd out, but not before Carlos stuck something in my hand. I looked at it as the door slammed shut behind us. It was a hundred-dollar bill with a phone number on it.

"My retainer," I said, holding it up so Todd could see it.

As we were driving away, he said, "I have to tell you, it might be wise to walk away from this one."

"Really? Things are just starting to get interesting. Besides, I'm not certain that I can."

Todd grimaced and shook his head. "Why would I ever think you'd do the smart thing?" We'd barely gone a block before he added, "I think you should give Santiago Luna a call... He's special division."

"Special division? What the hell is that?" I asked. "Never heard of it."

"Yeah, it's something we don't advertise. Luna is the guy who gets stuck with all the crazy shit."

"You mean like Momo?"

"Yeah. Like that and more. He might be able to give you a hint where to start. I'll get a BOLO out for the kids, but Garcia's right... It probably won't amount to shit."

He didn't have to explain. Every year about twenty-thousand folks go missing—half of them kids. Many of those stories don't have happy endings.

I had Todd drop me off at Mama Reynoso's taqueria. I intended to update the family with what I had learned—but not all of it, since the Momo angle was the kind of thing that might send Juan's mom, Maria, over the edge. Instead, I only told them Michalena and Anna had gone away together for reasons as yet unknown. I explained I was leaving town the following morning and that LAPD missing persons had been notified. Under the circumstances, it was the best I could do.

As I walked back to my apartment, I called Hollywood Division, where Todd said Santiago Luna was stationed. After being transferred to nearly every desk in the West Bureau and hung up on twice, I finally got through to Luna's voice mail and left a message to call me back.

I put my mobile back into my pocket hoping whatever awaited me tomorrow in Napa Valley would resolve itself quickly. Little did I know.

CHAPTER FOUR

Napa Valley, California. 1865

HENRY WALKER WATKINS WAS pruning his vines when he saw William Grayson's wagon plowing up clouds of dust on the dirt road leading to his farmhouse. The boy seemed to be in a greater hurry than usual, and so Henry rose from his work and headed down the hill to meet him.

"What's the rush?" Henry called out as William brought his wagon to a halt.

His roan's neck was covered in a foam of sweat.

"No need to put your horse though that, it's just a sack of beans!"

"Oh, he'll be right as rain," William replied, stepping down from the wagon. "I'll walk him real slow back to town."

He handed the folded note to Watkins. "But, Mr. Watkins, I was asked to get this to you… It's from them Harper sisters. You know, from up the road."

William sounded breathless as if he had run the whole distance instead of his horse.

"I know who they are," Henry said, pulling off his hat to run a hand through his thinning brown hair.

"Never met 'em though," Henry added, ignoring the funny tingle that traveled up his arm to his spine as he took the note and broke the wax seal. "Wonder what they want?"

William, pleased that he had dispatched his task so handily, had turned to fetch the bag of beans out of the wagon bed.

"Seemed pretty important," he said, lifting the sack up over his shoulder. "Usual place?"

"Go on," Henry replied as he read. "You can put it in the kitchen."

Henry was a tall man with a strong and compact physique that had been hardened over his years of tilling the soil. More at home in the field with his grapes than he was with any social setting, his first reaction was to decline the invitation to meet with the Harper sisters. Despite that inclination, he felt he must see them—and even more inexplicably, the sooner, the better.

The subject of the meeting, according to the note, would be wine. Recently, Henry had shifted his focus from growing grapes to producing wine and had nearly one hundred acres of various varietals with which he was experimenting.

Without waiting for William to leave, Henry Watkins went directly to his stables. With his usual efficiency, he hitched one of the horses to his surrey and set off to the Harper sister's farmstead. Oddly, it was as if he had no choice in the matter, although that thought never occurred to him. His only focus was on getting to the Harper's as quickly as possible. Twenty-five minutes later, he had arrived.

"Why, Mr. Watkins," greeted Merrilee as she answered his knock at the door. "How good of you to come."

She rolled her wheelchair back from the doorway, making it easier for him to enter.

"Good day, Miss Harper," Henry said in a formal voice. "I came as soon as I could. What about wine did you wish to discuss?"

"Please have a seat," Rosalee said as she entered the front room, bringing her wheelchair to a stop beside her sister's.

Henry sat down on a chair with carved wooden armrests and elaborate needlework upholstery. He was so intent on the purpose that brought him that he didn't take any notice of the pattern. If he had, he might have recognized it depicted many of the ancient Greek Gods.

"We'd like to discuss a business venture with you," continued Rosalee.

"To make wine," added Merrilee.

Although he was inclined to demure, Henry found himself saying, "That's a splendid idea. When would you like to start?"

"Right away," Merrilee replied. "We'd like you to help us with our vineyard here. And, in return, we have something to offer you."

"Something we're sure you'd like," gushed Rosalee.

Henry acted like a man in a trance; nevertheless, he summoned enough presence of mind to ask, "What would that be?"

"Money," answered Rosalee.

"Yes, money," echoed Merrilee. "Lots and lots of it."

CHAPTER FIVE

Napa County. Present Day

THE FLIGHT FROM VAN Nuys to Oakland was entirely uneventful—meaning Delinda made it a point to ignore me as much as possible. After a few feeble attempts to make conversation, I had given up in frustration. Al, doing his best to be impartial, was forced to have separate dialogs with each of us. To describe the situation as awkward would have been doing a disservice to the very word.

What made it doubly difficult was how good Delinda looked. Her brown hair fell perfectly onto the shoulders of her dark green, short-sleeved blouse, accenting her deep jade-green eyes. Her black slacks were expertly fitted, revealing her athletic build and her long, shapely legs. On the fifty-minute plane ride, I found it nearly impossible to keep my eyes off of her—a fact I'm sure she couldn't help but notice.

As if that wasn't torture enough—Delinda knowing full well how nervous her driving makes me—spared no pains in redoubling her efforts in that regard. On the drive to Napa Valley, she seemed determined to set a new land speed record between the two points. With an epic disregard for caution, Delinda undertook the narrow two-lane highway with unfettered gusto. Blithely weaving our rental car around slower traffic while miraculously avoiding oncoming vehicles. It was evident she was relishing my obvious discomfort the entire time.

The front seat of our rental, a late model Lexus sedan, was fortuitously equipped with a passenger-side door grip, which I clutched for dear life.

"Delinda, can we at least talk to each other?" I asked, hoping to distract her enough so she'd slow down.

"There's nothing to talk about, Mark."

"Yes, there is… I know I was too… Forward. It's just…"

"Don't say it," she snapped.

She whipped the rental around a stake-bed truck carrying a load of onions, coming within inches from sideswiping the recreational vehicle heading in the opposite direction.

A few seconds later, I mustered enough courage to open my eyes again. "Listen! I'm sorry I tried to kiss you… Let's forget the entire incident ever happened."

"Sure," she scoffed. "As if you could ever do that!"

"Hey! It's not as if…"

"Enough!" Al interjected before I could argue the point. "Knock it off, both of you! I'm not happy about being in the middle of this… But as long as I am, I insist that both of you behave."

Al is somebody you don't want to piss off. Take my word for it. A couple of past lives ago, he kicked a lot of asses. From where he was sitting in the back seat, he made sure Delinda and I could see his stern reflection in the rearview mirror as he continued to admonish us.

"Bruce is relying on us to protect his interests, and the only way that will happen is if we can act as a team."

"I can if she can," I mumbled.

"Agreed," Delinda said quietly.

"Good," nodded Al. "Then let's concentrate on the matter at hand. We're almost there."

The stretch of road Delinda had been burning up runs the length of wine country, from Napa to Calistoga. Cradled in the center of two mountain ranges, the Valley's landscape is checkerboarded with numerous vineyards and wineries that line both sides of the highway. Thanks to our high rate of speed, it had all been a blur until we passed a town called Yountville. Here, Delinda slowed and turned left, off onto a black asphalt side road where a sign announced our destination:

"Taskert Vineyards." A smaller sign hanging underneath it read: "Winery Closed Today."

We continued down the road, past countless rows of grapevines that continued on up the rolling hillside ahead of us. Dominating the view near the base of the rise sat a gleaming stone castle. The structure appeared to be brand new, giving it the appearance of something one would see at an amusement park rather than on a European countryside.

The newly paved road ended at a large gravel parking lot where we pulled into one of the many unoccupied spaces. There were only three other cars in the lot, and Delinda parked next to them.

"We're here," Delinda pronounced unnecessarily, shutting off the engine.

"Very impressive," I said, stepping out into the sunshine.

It was a warm, cloudless day, and I could see even more rows of grapevines stretching off into the distance on the hillside behind the imposing stone structure.

"The castle is an interesting touch, but it looks a little out of place," I noted.

"Yup," Al agreed. "Phillip Taskert modeled it after the ruins of an ancient Irish castle. Or so he claims. You did read the brief, didn't you?"

"Sure," I lied.

"Then you know he was looking for a marketing story," Al replied. "So, a few of the foundation stones are genuine... Salvaged and brought over from Ireland, they have just enough authenticity to make for good advertising."

"I don't like the feeling I'm getting from this place," said Delinda. "There's something about it…"

She looked puzzled and preoccupied, although, at the moment, I was too relieved to have survived the car ride to fully appreciate her reaction.

"Why isn't the winery open?" I asked. "The place looks like it's ready to do business."

A well-dressed man who had just walked up the flagstone path leading to the parking lot answered my question.

"Our first release isn't ready yet," he said as he joined us.

His tone was friendly and unapologetic. Al was about to speak up, but there was no need.

"You must be the folks Ashton said were coming. I'm Phil Taskert, the proprietor. I sure hope you can help us get this show on the road."

"We hope so too," Al replied. "I'm Al Kleptos… This is Delinda Djinn and Mark Tonnick."

"How come you aren't open for business?" I asked. "Even without wine, this place should be swarming with tourists, regardless."

Phillip Taskert didn't return my smile. I took him to be in his early fifties. His ruddy complexion had seen plenty of sun, and unlike many at his age, the years hadn't touched his headful of thick, silver hair. He was what some might consider portly, but at a little over six-feet, he carried his weight well.

"It doesn't work that way, Mark," he explained, trying hard not to sound condescending. "Folks come to the Valley expecting to taste and buy wine. Frankly, that's where the money is. We'd quickly destroy our reputation by offering an inferior product... Which, I don't have to tell you, would be financially disastrous. This is a very competitive business."

Al cut straight to the chase. "I sampled the bottle you sent Ashton."

Taskert nodded and frowned. "It was terrible, wasn't it… We're already three and a half years into this venture, and other than the facility, we've got nothing to show for it."

"Why so long?" I inquired. "Did you have to wait for the grapes to grow?"

Our host slowly shook his head. It was plain that he regarded me as someone who knew nothing about this business—an accurate assessment on his part.

"No, the vineyard was here and already producing when we purchased it. Otherwise, we'd be waiting a lot longer before we could even start the winemaking process. Depending on the varietal, once you press the fruit, it takes a minimum of one to two years before the wine can be ready for release."

"Mr. Ashton mentioned there's nothing wrong with the grapes," Delinda said. "So why is the wine bad?"

"That's the million-dollar question," Taskert replied, motioning for us to follow him.

"Have you isolated the problem?" I asked, eager to reclaim at least a shred of credibility.

"In a way," Taskert demurred as he led us up the path to the castle. "We know what it is…"

"We just canna fix it!" interjected a stunning redhead in an unmistakable Irish lilt.

She had emerged from the outer gate of the courtyard to join us as we walked in her direction. Her blue skirt and her strategically unbuttoned tight white blouse did a magnificent job of displaying her shapely body.

Taskert said, "This is Lissette O'Hannon, our hospitality services manager."

Ms. O'Hannon gave everyone a warm smile as we introduced ourselves and shook hands. I was more than a little surprised when she locked her bright blue eyes on mine and held on to my hand with a grip that was equally soft and firm.

"Pleased t' meet you, Mr. Tonnick." Her eyes wandered to the star-shaped scar on my cheek, and neither of us spoke for a long, awkward moment.

"A pleasure," I finally replied.

"Mr. Ashton has told us quite a bit about you," she said, still holding onto my hand.

Taskert chuckled. "True enough. He said you knew nothing about wine."

I gave him a polite smile, not knowing where this was going.

He hastily added, "But he also mentioned you and your team were excellent at what you do…"

He sounded as though he wasn't exactly sure what that was.

"I hope we can live up to that," I replied. "We'll leave the winemaking to you."

"We're depending on you t' make it right," Lissette said, still smiling. "I'd hate t' see my castle go t' waste."

"Well, now it's our castle," corrected Taskert good-naturedly. "Iris and I met Lissette when we were vacationing in Ireland. We secured the castle from her family's estate in return for an interest in the winery."

Lissette's eyes were still fixed on my scar. "There's a lot a' stake here… For all o' us, Mr. Tonnick."

"Please, call me Mark," I said.

I had no idea what Lissette found so interesting about my scar. But, to be honest, I was too busy enjoying her attention to care.

Delinda cleared her throat louder than she probably needed. "Perhaps you can be more specific about what you expect us to find."

Was she upset at the reception Lissette was giving me? I certainly wasn't. With me, flattery will get you everywhere. Especially when it's coming from a lovely young woman whose interest in me seemed to be more than merely professional. With great reluctance, I dismissed the vast number of impure thoughts running through my mind so I could focus on the conversation.

"You can see," Taskert said, gesturing to the exquisite flowering plants and the lush landscaping that framed the stone castle walls. "This place has the potential to be a goldmine… But first, we need to solve our TCA problem."

I hadn't the slightest clue what TCA was, but I wasn't about to let a little thing like ignorance stop me from opening my mouth.

"Mr. Ashton intimated the possibility someone might be sabotaging your operation."

"Sadly, that's one conclusion," Taskert acknowledged with a neutral expression.

"What about your winemaker?" Al pressed. "Is there any chance he might have a hand in contaminating the wine?"

I didn't know what TCA was, but clearly, it wasn't something you wanted to drink.

"Unthinkable," Taskert frowned. "I've been working with Derek throughout the entire winemaking process, and I can tell you he's just as concerned about this as we are. Since he also makes wine for several other major wineries here in the Valley, his reputation is suffering too."

I nodded appropriately. "So, is it usual for a winemaker to work for more than one winery?"

"In wine country, it's quite the norm. The talented ones, like Derek, are in high demand."

"Where else does he work?" Al asked.

"Aside from several smaller wineries, like ours, Kaff Cellars is his biggest client… I'm sure you've heard of them."

In fact, I had, although I've never tried their wine. Mostly because their offerings start at around thirty-five bucks a bottle.

"Could be they're not crazy about having you as a competitor," I said.

"Hardly. Richard Kaffee is not only a friend, but he's also one of our investors."

I recalled that Ashton had told us Kaffee was buying out other investors in Taskert's winery. Curious that Kaffee saw potential here while others had lost faith. I wondered what he knew—and how he stood to profit from it.

Taskert and his comely hospitality manager led us through the elaborately landscaped courtyard by way of a rustic flagstone path until we arrived at an enormous set of ironbound wooden doors. Each of them was adorned with an ornately carved, giant "T." At our approach, the massive portals opened automatically, revealing a huge hall.

The castle's interior was as impressive as the exterior. Rough, fieldstone floors reflected the light from several immense chandeliers that hung high overhead from the arched ceiling. The stone walls were festooned with garlands of colorful fabrics and covered with tapestries that depicted medieval tableaus of hunting parties and half-naked ladies. In contrast, rows of computer monitors were lined up behind each of the three, granite-topped tasting bars that paralleled the far walls of the room. Above the counters, hundreds of glistening wine-glasses were threaded on wooden slats suspended from the ceiling by gleaming brass wires.

Everywhere you looked were tables and shelves full of branded merchandise; hats, T-shirts, wine-openers, coffee-table books, and other wine-related items. Everything about the place bespoke high-end retail. Aside from the tall empty bottle racks behind each of the counters, they were ready for business. The winery was like me on date night—ready, willing, and waiting.

"Beautiful, isn't it?" Lissette declared brightly. "We're good t' go… All we need is the wine."

"Why can't you buy wine elsewhere and label it as your own?" queried Al.

"We tried that," Taskert replied. "It didn't matter. Every bottle we opened in here was corked."

If Al had any eyebrows, they would have been arched in surprise. "How is that possible?"

"We thought it might be something in the air," Taskert said with a sigh of resignation that plainly signaled he had been over this before a hundred times. "But, we've had the heating and cooling system inspected by a dozen different companies, and none of them could find anything wrong."

I wasn't sure about what he was talking about, and I was hesitant to show my ignorance by asking what 'corked' meant. It didn't matter, for Taskert quickly decoded the confusion on my face.

"Out of all the wine a vintner bottles, a relatively small number of them become what we refer to as 'corked.'" Taskert pointed to the back of the room. "But one taste is worth a thousand words. Come with me."

A section of the tasting room's rear wall was formed from a tall glass partition. Behind the partition, stood several rows of large, stainless steel vats. In this area, there was no aspect of the medieval theme.

Instead, the immaculate space was a modern manufacturing facility in every regard.

Taskert led us through a set of glass double doors into the winemaking area and grabbed a wine bottle off a nearby table. He extracted a corkscrew from his pocket and deftly removed the cork. Immediately, he held the open container in front of our faces, one at a time. It had a markedly unpleasant smell reminiscent of dirty socks.

Taskert watched our reactions. "Smell that? The wine is corked. What you're smelling is a chemical contaminant, TCA. I'd pour you some, but I'm guessing that's not necessary."

"Not if it tastes like it smells," I remarked.

"Worse," Taskert said. "Every bottle is like this. As I mentioned, TCA is a problem that is only supposed to happen occasionally… Most wineries allow for about 5 to 7 percent of their bottling run to develop it. Mostly it occurs when wine is bottled with natural cork. In our case, the problem persists…"

He looked directly at me, adding, "Regardless of every precaution we've taken."

Delinda seemed genuinely puzzled. "And you've ruled out anything in the ventilation system?"

"As I told you, we've had everything completely checked out," Taskert replied impatiently.

I thought Al was joking when he asked, "Have you tried screw tops?"

Taskert took a deep breath before he answered. "We've tried screw tops, we've tried conglomerate corks… Everything you can think of… Nothing works!"

"I'm assuming you clean everything thoroughly… like with bleach?" I ventured.

Taskert's laugh had no humor in it. "Bleach? That will never happen… TCA is produced when the natural organic material in cork comes in contact with certain chlorides… Like those in bleach… Which is why we never use any chlorine cleaning products."

I nodded, again, acutely aware of my ignorance.

Taskert saw my reaction and did his best not to humiliate me further. "Naturally, we have other cleaning compounds, but they made no difference... Whatever we try, the results are the same. All the wine we bottle or open here ends up corked!"

"That's crazy," Al commented.

"Yes, it is," Taskert agreed wearily. "Every single damn bottle..."

"All o' em," Lissette echoed. She smiled weakly in my direction. "All ruined! It's horrible... We've hada throw away gallons o' product."

"And the barrels they were stored in!" Taskert added. "We've lost hundreds of thousands of dollars so far."

"Those are huge losses," Delinda said sympathetically. "Especially with no cash flow."

"That's an understatement," Taskert said bleakly. He paused to look around the room. "Derek!" he yelled. "Where are you?"

"Back here, with Clement!" a voice yelled back.

"Because of this issue, we've no reason to keep on a large staff other than our cellar master and a few vineyard laborers," Taskert explained. "We've also kept Derek George, our winemaker... He's on contract and has been around the clock to figure all of this out. I don't know what we'd do without him."

He took us through aisles of tall steel shelving stacked high with wooden barrels. "New French Oak," he said. "About nine hundred bucks each... All empty, but we dare not even open them for fear of contamination!"

I hadn't read much of the brief Al handed me yesterday, but I did recall the first paragraph. It stated, in all caps no less, that the wine business has an annual worth of about fifty-billion dollars. It was understandable why going after even a small piece of that pie would be tempting to Ashton and AC&C. Now, what started out as a wise investment with a promising return, might end up as a one-way ticket to massive losses.

We reached the rear of the building, an empty area flanked by several wide roll-up steel doors that occupied most of the back wall.

The two men who were standing there appeared to be arguing vociferously about something, but abruptly ended their conversation the moment they saw us approach.

Taskert introduced us to Derek George, the winemaker, and Clement Wagner, the cellar master. Derek, a slender, tall man in his late twenties, came forward to shake our hands. He was clean-shaven and kept his sandy blonde hair short. He was dressed for work in faded blue jeans, and a matching short-sleeved denim shirt with his name embroidered on the pocket.

Clement was much shorter than Derek and far more casually dressed. A John Deere branded baseball cap covered his head, allowing a few wisps of graying brown hair to peek out in several places. Both his camo shorts and lettered T-shirt were far too snug for his potbelly. The Grateful Dead logo on his stained shirt was partially obscured by his long, unkempt gray and white speckled beard.

As soon as we were done exchanging pleasantries, Delinda wasted no time in getting right to the point.

She asked, "So, do either of you have any clue as to where the contamination is coming from?"

Derek, clearly taken with her, replied warmly. "Not really. We have no idea how the trichloranisole, the TSA, is finding its way into every bottle. We've checked and double-checked everything we can think of and still can't figure it out. I'm sure Phil has told you that in normal practice, you would expect a small percentage of any bottling to become corked, but we're way beyond that."

"How could it get into everything?" Al asked, looking around at the gleaming stainless steel tanks.

"Oh, it don't take much," Clement chimed. He had a deep voice with a slight Southern drawl. "Couple of parts per trillion is 'nough... An' once it gets into the rubber hoses and gaskets, it's game over, dude! That's what happened to our Chardonnay tanks. Couldn't salvage any of it."

"What about the barrels?" I questioned. "How is it possible for those to become tainted?"

"Don't know," Derek responded. "We had several ideas, but so far, no one's found any reasonable explanation."

"Yeah, it's real strange, ain't it?" Clement added. "Almost like magic."

I was sensing another rabbit hole moment, but I wasn't quite ready to make the leap despite Delinda's sideways glance. Instead, I was wondering how far Taskert's competitors might go to keep his winery out of commission.

"So, are you thinking it's sabotage?" I began. "Could that be a real possibility? If so, who? And more importantly… How?"

Derek and Clement gave me blank looks, probably out of fear of offending their employer, but Taskert spoke up impatiently.

"We've been over all of this a hundred times. There's no good reason why this should be happening!"

"Unless somebody wanted you to go out of business," I said, pointing out what I thought was the elephant in the room.

Taskert dismissed that with a wave, "That's highly unlikely. While a few folks think every new winery that opens in the Valley will siphon off business from the rest, I can't imagine anyone resorting to product tampering."

"But, there's the issue with the land…" Clement added before a hard glare from Taskert silenced him.

"What issue is that?" pressed Al, sensing that another bit of dirt was being shoved under the rug.

"Nothing to do with us," answered Taskert. "There's a movement in the valley to expand the kind of crops we grow here, but that's beside the point."

I had a feeling that was a subject Taskert was reluctant to discuss. But before I could press him further, Delinda had moved on to another, more relevant matter.

"How good is your security?" she asked.

Taskert sighed. "Our security is more than adequate." He pointed up to a small camera mounted onto the ceiling. "We have those everywhere."

"Yes, but they don't work all the time," interrupted a new female voice. "We've had to get the company out here on several occasions to fix them."

We all turned to see the woman who had spoken. An attractive brunette in her late forties was walking towards us. She was fastidiously groomed with only enough artfully applied make-up to flatter her light complexion and large, brown eyes. Dressed in conservative business attire and displaying an expression as severe as her appearance, the difference between her and the smiling, casually clothed hospitality manager couldn't have been greater.

"This is my wife, Iris," Taskert announced. "She is our Chief Financial Officer. Iris, these are the people Bruce Ashton sent to help."

Eyeing us suspiciously, Iris returned our perfunctory handshakes as introductions were made.

"I'm not sure you'll be of much help," she remarked in a crisp and disdainful contralto voice. "We've nearly run out of time to turn the business around… If that's even possible."

"We'll do our best to help," I replied. "Obviously, there's a considerable amount of money at stake."

Iris gave me a reproving look as if my comment was beneath her reply.

"Obviously…" she shot back, glancing at her husband.

Behind her stylish glasses, Iris's eyes flashed arrogantly. I thought her expression implied she held him solely responsible for the winery's troubles. That was intriguing, I thought. I couldn't help but wonder what she thought of the young and attractive Lissette working beside him.

Taskert gave no sign he had noted his wife's unspoken inference as he picked up the conversation.

"Besides our investors, Iris and I have put every dime we have into this. And we're continuing to do so, even though we're on the brink of bankruptcy."

"How much time do you think you have left?" Delinda asked.

Taskert hesitated and looked over to his wife.

"Weeks… Maybe less," he replied.

Delinda nodded as she added her pessimistic assessment.

"So, even if we solve the problem, there may not be enough time to save the winery."

Iris seemed to have lost patience with the conversation. She huffed audibly and turned to her husband.

"Phil, why are we even bothering?"

"You know we're obligated," he answered wearily.

"Contractually, AC&C, as your majority investor, has the right to exercise oversight," Delinda reminded her pointedly.

"Fine," Iris snapped and turned to walk out the same way she had entered.

I got the distinct impression that Delinda liked Iris only a little more than she liked Lissette—meaning not very much at all.

Taskert gave us a thin smile. "Please excuse her. She's upset and frustrated… I'm sure you can understand why. Like I've already told you, we've had experts go over the place inch by inch."

The way he said it implied he had little hope we would do any better.

CHAPTER SIX

"WHAT'S AT THE BOTTOM of those stairs?" I asked, pointing to what looked like a stairwell near the back wall. "A basement?"

"Not exactly," answered Lissette. "That leads down to our wine caves. Would you like t' take a look?"

"Of course we would," Al said before I could.

Derick and Clement remained behind, watching as Taskert and Lissette led us over to the stairwell.

As we descended the steps, Taskert said, "We didn't dig the caves ourselves. We found them while we were excavating the foundation for the building."

"You mean they were here already?" I asked.

"Yes," Lissette volunteered. "An entire network of 'em dug into the mountainside."

At the foot of the stairs, earthen walls softly illuminated by several sconces surrounded us. Taskert continued his explanation as he reached for a switch box.

"In the late 1800s, they brought in Chinese laborers to dig tunnels all throughout the wine country. No doubt, this was one of them."

He snapped on more lights, which revealed a wide chain-link barrier several feet ahead of us. There, he paused briefly to unlock the padlock and remove the chain that secured the barrier. The gate was hinged at both ends and opened in the middle. Wheels under each of the ten-foot sections allowed him to easily push them aside.

Taskert motioned to the rows of widely spaced light fixtures overhead.

"Naturally, we added the lighting and a few more improvements." He continued to speak as we followed him farther inside the shaft.

"The tunnel goes straight into the mountainside behind the winery. We were told when we bought the acreage that there were several other wineries here at one time or another. Supposedly, there are sections of the vineyards that are over a hundred years old. So, when we stumbled onto these caves, it was like winning the lottery. So far, it's about the only good luck we've had."

The tunnel beyond the barrier looked old; the overhead lights revealed black lichen dripping from the earthen ceiling shrouded with dusty spiderwebs. As one would expect, the stale air was cool and reeked of raw earth. As we walked, we passed several places where the cave walls were mosaics of bare rock and gravel—all seemingly held in place by countless strings of white tendrils that weaved in and around them.

"Those are roots from the vineyard above us," Taskert explained. "Right now, we're about thirty-five feet below the surface.

"The constant temperature underground is perfect for aging and storage… At first, we began keeping our barrels down here. But when our wines began showing signs of contamination, we halted that practice to eliminate the possibility that the TCA was being introduced by something down here. Unfortunately, that didn't fix the problem either. Even after we started fresh above ground with new French oak, the stink was still in the wine… Maddening!"

About fifty yards farther, we walked by a narrower intersecting tunnel with another locked chain-link barrier that spanned the opening. Attached to the front of it, a large, white metal sign with tall red letters read: "Danger - Do Not Enter."

I stopped in front of the barricade and peered into the darkness, but it was impossible to see what lay beyond. Taskert noticed my interest.

"That tunnel's unstable," he volunteered. "Our engineers warned us it could collapse at any time… And with everything else going on around here, you can understand that fixing it is pretty low on the totem pole."

The group kept moving while I remained standing there—maybe because the scar on my cheek started to itch—a sure sign something crazy was about to happen. I looked around to see if Delinda was conjuring up some of her genie mojo, but she was yards ahead.

"Save them," a child's voice said.

It sounded like it came from directly behind me. I whirled around as the itching sensation grew more intense. Standing not five feet away was a young girl, clutching a crudely made rag-doll.

"You must save them," she insisted.

"How did you get down here," I asked.

"You must," the girl repeated as if she hadn't heard my question.

I moved towards her, and as I did, she faded away, vanishing entirely. I blinked several times as if that might offer some clarity, but it didn't. Instead, I was left standing there, wondering who she was—and whatever the hell it was she was talking about. In times past, I would have expended a great deal of mental energy questioning my sanity—sadly, however, that genie has already left the bottle.

Shaking off my disquiet, I caught back up with the group minutes later. Taskert had stopped to point out several rows of barrels lined up against the wall.

"See these? Every single one of them is tainted. About twenty grand worth of French oak, not counting the lost profits from the wine we had to throw away. They're useless now... Except, maybe for firewood." He stared at the pile darkly for a moment before he muttered, "Fucking unbelievable."

Delinda's voice snapped Taskert away from where his thoughts had taken him.

"Where does this tunnel end up?"

"I'll show you," Taskert replied.

He led us another fifty yards ahead to where the tunnel dead-ended, a short way after it intersected with a concrete driveway.

"We built a ramp and a doorway here," Taskert said, pointing to the long, steep incline. "So we could forklift our barrels in and out."

"Is it possible that someone could get inside the winery through here without being seen?" I asked.

Taskert shook his head. "Hardly. You can't see the entrance from here, but it's a long way up to the top of the ramp. If you keep on walking, you'll see there's a pair of steel roll-up doors, locked from the inside with double padlocks. After we scrapped the barrels, those doors have remained locked and haven't been opened since… And, we keep the stairwell entrance gate locked at all times for safety."

I walked further up the ramp until I could make out the roll-up doors. The entrance looked secure enough—only tiny beams of daylight peeked through around the steel frames. I turned to Taskert, who had followed me.

"Your wife said you were having problems with the video surveillance system. Any chance it might have been disabled on purpose?"

Taskert wiped his brow. "Honestly, I don't know…"

"In any event," I said, "I'd like to go over whatever security video files you have."

"I'll get you those," Taskert promised as we walked back down to the base of the ramp.

The end of the tunnel seemed different from the side walls, so I ventured over and used the flashlight app on my phone to get a closer look.

"Solid rock?" I asked.

Taskert was standing behind me. "Yes, it is. We think the cave would have extended deeper into the hillside if whoever dug it hadn't run into that. It's a huge chunk of granite."

While the caves were intriguing, I found myself remembering a portion of our earlier conversation.

Snapping off the flashlight on my phone, I asked, "What were you referring to earlier when you mentioned that some folks wanted to grow different crops?"

Taskert gave a short grunt before he answered. "It's a tempest in a teapot, really."

Delinda had walked over to join us in time to hear my question.

"Really? About what?" she prodded, arching an eyebrow.

"Land use," said Taskert. "Some farmers in the Valley want to tear out their grapevines to grow Marijuana. I'm telling you now, that won't ever happen. It would change the entire culture of the Valley, and not for the better."

"Why would anybody want to do that?" I asked.

"Money, pure and simple," Taskert replied. "One acre of cabernet grapes might fetch about five-hundred thousand dollars, but the same acre of Cannabis would be worth twice that."

Lisette and Al had caught up to the three of us.

"Napa County isn't ever going t' let that happen," added Lissette. "Not ever!"

Call me a skeptic, but in my experience, nothing ever remains the same over time. The word "never" is simply an article of faith, especially when there's money involved. Admittedly it struck me as a thin motive, but one worth exploring. Taskert must have read my mind.

"There's no way in hell, I'll ever tear out my vines to plant dope! I'd sooner salt the ground first!" he exclaimed.

"Provided you still own the property," I countered.

"This is my legacy," Taskert insisted. "Even if the winery goes bankrupt, I'll buy up the debt myself!"

He saw our negative expressions.

"This winery is my baby," Taskert went on bluntly, "and I have no intention of letting anyone… Or anything take it away from me!"

It could have been the lighting in the cave, but I thought I saw Lissette's features tighten.

"Any… Thing?" I asked.

"Nothing," Taskert snapped. "Just a figure of speech."

I wasn't ready to leap to any conclusion, specifically any supernatural ones, but Taskert's and Lissette's reaction was telling. It suggested there might be more to the story than either of them had offered us. That got me wondering if anyone else had crossed paths with my little miss ghostly.

Whether it was the aftermath of my paranormal experience or simply the oppressive atmospherics underground, the hairs on the nape of my neck began to stand up. With some effort, I shook it off. I had enough supernatural overtones for the time being, although, my intuition said that the specter I encountered had nothing to do with the wine contamination. I sensed an innocence to it, which left me with the conviction that someone far more corporeal was dumping crap into Taskert's vino.

Before I could press Taskert for more details about what he referred to when he said, "anything," he had already begun to walk away.

"Perhaps we should continue our conversation upstairs," Lissette suggested.

Strangely silent, Taskert led us back to the entrance, stopping only to close and lock the chain-link barrier behind us. While he did so, Lissette drew alongside me, making sure her words only reached my ear.

"I donna like it down here. Never have... It's creepy."

I contrived to hang back as we all mounted the steps, using the opportunity to touch Delinda lightly on the arm to get her attention. Initially, she scowled before she realized I only wanted to whisper a question. It was one I dreaded to ask.

"Did you sense anything strange down there?"

Typically, when it comes to unexplainable events, she's the first one out of the gate. This time, she only gave me a slight shake of the head. "I'm not sure," she whispered back.

"Well, I did," I said softly. "I'll tell you about it later."

She only nodded, and her expression remained unreadable.

When we emerged from the stairs, Lissette said, "I think we could all use a bit o' fresh air. This way," she smiled, staring straight at me.

I caught a brief glimpse of Delinda's expression. If she was upset at the attention I was getting from Lissette, she was hiding it well—much to my disappointment.

We followed Lissette and Taskert outside to the courtyard gardens, where we all took seats at a round, wrought-iron table that was shaded by a large umbrella. At any other time, it would have been a beautiful place for a picnic.

Taskert looked around the table and asked, "So, where do we go from here? Do you even have a plan?"

Delinda jumped right in without waiting for either Al or me to reply.

She said, "Yes, we do, as a matter of fact. We'll start by reviewing your security video before we take another, closer look around the facility."

Taskert's expression revealed his disappointment with Delinda's straightforward and mundane approach.

"I'll have Iris make whatever we have available to you," he said flatly. "And it goes without saying, you're free to wander where ever you want."

Lissette appeared equally unenthusiastic.

She said, "I donna see what good it will do. We've been over every square inch o' the property, and…"

Taskert raised his hand to interrupt. "Perhaps a fresh perspective would be helpful… In any case, we have to let them try."

"Can you tell me more about the castle?" Delinda asked.

It was clear her question caught them by surprise.

"What about it?" Lissette stammered.

"Any unusual history?" Delinda probed. She was smiling in a way that let them know she was aware that the subject she broached was one they'd rather not discuss.

Lissette looked like she was going to answer before Taskert's brief glance halted her reply.

"Not much to tell, really," Taskert deflected. "Most of what you see is new construction. We only used a few of the original foundation stones so we could lay claim to the castle's authenticity for publicity purposes."

I interrupted him with my question. "So, it didn't have a reputation for being haunted or anything like that?"

Taskert laughed mirthlessly. "Are you really asking me if I believe in ghosts… Or curses?"

I didn't answer him. There was no need; after all—I never said anything about a curse or a ghost for that matter.

Al had been studying our hosts carefully, and I was eager to get his take on the situation. Even if you don't believe how old he claims to be, there's a lot of wisdom lurking behind those watery brown eyes. After I got his attention, he made a point of looking at his watch.

"It's getting late," Al noted. "And, we have another stop to make this afternoon. We'll be back in the morning… That will give you time to round up the surveillance footage for us."

"Very good," replied Taskert, appearing relieved at the change in the conversation. "We'll have those video files ready for you then."

I glanced at Lissette, who noticed my wandering eyes and returned my smile. Perhaps it was my imagination, but she seemed to be flirting with me—not that I minded—on the contrary, I hoped I wasn't mistaken.

After exchanging a few more pleasantries, we found our way back to our rental car. Delinda spoke up the moment we were inside.

"What were you going to tell me about, Mark?"

"I saw a ghost down there, in the caves. It was a little Asian girl, around five years old, holding a scrappy looking rag-doll. She had long, jet black hair, and wore a plain brown dress."

"And?" Delinda prodded.

"And, she said I needed to help them. Who, exactly, she didn't say."

Al nodded knowingly. "As Taskert said, Chinese laborers dug most of the wine caves and planted nearly all of early Napa's vineyards. Without a doubt, your spirit sighting is connected to some event in the distant past."

"Great…" I said with no little sarcasm. "Why me? Why not haunt Delinda? She's the magical one in the group."

"Maybe you have more magic in you than you think," Delinda replied.

Al rubbed his chin thoughtfully. "So, do you suppose it has something to do with the TCA issue?"

I shook my head. "No, I don't think the spirit has anything to do with that. I can't tell you why, but I'm sure that something else is going on in those caves apart from Taskert's problem with the wine."

"Yep. Very possibly," Al agreed. "There's a lot of history here, considering the age of both the castle and the caves."

"Maybe the castle is haunted, and wine caves lead straight to Hell," I joked.

Al chuckled dryly. "Make fun if you like, but after everything we've been through, I thought you'd have a more open mind."

"Seriously? Isn't believing in magic, genies, juvenile haunts, and undead shamans enough? What could I possibly add to that list?" I punctuated my quip with the most innocent smile I could muster.

"Well, let's see," Al replied, just as Delinda brought the engine to life and hauled ass out of the parking lot. "I'm sure there's something you've missed," he assured me as I grabbed for my seatbelt.

Due to the sudden acceleration of the car, I frantically seized the passenger side handgrip, forgetting all about the snappy come back I was about to deliver. At the same moment, I turned my head slightly to the side in time to catch Delinda's smiling face reflected in the rearview mirror. She appeared to be enjoying my discomfort even more than usual. Maybe she was just a little jealous after all.

One can hope.

CHAPTER SEVEN

Napa Valley, California. 1866

THE HARPER SISTERS' VINEYARDS had become Henry Walker Watkins's sole obsession. Every morning at sunrise, he left his own vineyards and rode his horse-drawn surrey over to Merrilee and Rosalee's farmstead. Skipping breakfast, he was in a rush to undertake the work awaiting him. His routine was always the same. He began by spending several hours overseeing the Chinese field hands who were tending to the vines. Once he was satisfied with their efforts, he made his rounds in the grafting sheds. There, he ensured the workers were performing all the procedures in the exact manner he had taught them.

The preparation of the fruit-bearing scions of the Zinfandel and the other varietals to be top grafted onto the table-grape rootstock demanded skill and precision, as did the grafting procedure itself. When the grafts took, it would only take one season, two at the most, until the spliced vines produced useable fruit.

Until he had partnered with the Harper sisters, this technique was Henry's best-kept secret, a method he developed after much experimentation in his own fields. He had begun the work in the hopes the resulting hybrid would produce a plant resistant to the wine blight sweeping across Europe. There was no doubt in his mind that the destructive aphids would find their way to Napa. It was only a matter of time.

There was a time that Henry swore he'd never share this procedure with anyone—now, however, that vow held no meaning. This surprising change of heart was among the many other inexplicable changes in his personality—all of which he was seemingly unaware.

His strange behavior did not go unnoticed by those in his personal orbit. The foreman of Henry's vineyards had pointedly asked why, for the first time in memory, his employer had missed the harvest and the press. Incredibly, Henry couldn't or wouldn't offer an answer. He only stared at his puzzled foreman in silence for a long moment before he answered.

Then, in a voice, both flat and indifferent, he replied, "That is none of your affair. Your concern is only to make sure that all remains in order during my absence."

The foreman nodded and watched as Henry took leave of the property, convinced his boss had lost his mind.

Henry seemed oblivious that he had lost interest in all matters except for his endeavors on the Harper sister's behalf. On this morning, his focus was again entirely confined to his careful inspections of the new graftings, making sure none were less than perfect.

His diligence was rewarded six weeks later. Miraculously, the splices were completely healed, and the vine tops were already sprouting new leaves. He was amazed at the prodigious growth—it was almost magical.

Merrilee interrupted his inspection, calling to him as she rolled her wheelchair adroitly between the rows of vines.

"Henry,... How fare you today?"

"Fine, Ma'am," he replied. "The plants are coming along far faster than I thought possible."

"Wonderful," she beamed. "When will we start work on the caves?"

"I expect we'll begin very soon, Ma'am. Wing Ho is bringing a dozen men who are experienced excavators. They'll arrive later today, along with their families."

"Splendid. Splendid," Merrilee gushed.

Henry nodded, a broad grin splitting his grizzled features. Above all else, he considered it paramount that the sisters were pleased with his efforts. Their approval filled him with more gratification and joy than he could ever remember.

CHAPTER EIGHT

Napa County. Present Day.

"OKAY, AL," I SAID once we were back on the highway. "What now? Do we really have another stop?"

"Yep. We're going to another winery. It's only a few miles up the road, but before we get there, I want to share what Ashton told me before we left."

Neither Delinda nor myself said anything, so Al continued.

"It seems there's another aspect to all of this."

I couldn't help myself. "What? Ghosts? Curses?"

"No, it's about Taskert," Al replied, ignoring my jibe. "Even though he says he's losing money hand over fist, he still manages to live a lavish lifestyle."

"That's interesting," I commented, "considering he was complaining about losing every penny he has in the place."

"Exactly," Al agreed. "And, while you would think he's heavily leveraged…"

"You mean to the banks?" I interrupted.

Delinda's eyes left the road longer than seemed prudent to gift me with her disapproving glare.

"Why don't you let Al finish his thought instead of hijacking the conversation like you always do!" she snapped while speeding around a convoy of flatbed trucks as if they were standing still.

"Go on, Al. I'm sorry I cut you off," I quickly apologized.

The tone of Delinda's harsh rebuke took me by surprise, but I wisely let it go so she could return her attention to the road. To reward myself for such sound judgment, I allowed my thoughts to drift toward

Lissette's big blue eyes, her soft, smiling lips, and her other obvious assets.

"No worries," Al assured me.

I wondered if he also noted Delinda's edginess, as with some reluctance, I abandoned my lusty daydream and allowed myself to be drawn back into the conversation.

"As I was saying," Al continued. "Despite his failing venture, Taskert is still keeping current with all of his bank loans. Ashton thinks Richard Kaffee, the owner of Kaff Cellars, might be lending him the money. That's where we're headed next."

Even if you don't drink wine, it would be very hard not to have at least a passing familiarity with the Kaff Cellars brand. Their wine is pretty much everywhere—Although the bottle in Mrs. Krenzman's little corner market has remained unsold as long as I've rented the room above her store. Most of her customer's tastes run about twenty bucks cheaper.

"So, why would Kaffee, whose already as heavily invested as Ashton, be willing to throw good money after bad?" Delinda asked.

She shot a look at Al, who was sitting in the backseat, via her rearview mirror. Her gaze lingered there longer than I thought wise, considering our rate of speed.

"That's why we need to have a conversation with him," Al replied.

I was thinking about what Taskert said when we were down in the caves.

"Maybe Taskert and Kaffee have other plans for the property, despite what he told us," I ventured. "Or, maybe another entity holds the title on the land… Separately from the winery corporation."

"You mean he can bankrupt the winery, screw his investors, and still hold on to the real estate? That would be pretty crafty," Al reasoned. "But Ashton would never agree to a deal like that."

"Just a thought," I said.

"It still doesn't explain why Kaffee is buying out Taskert's other investors," countered Al.

"No, it doesn't," Delinda commented sharply.

Al pointed to a large sign at an intersection a hundred yards ahead. "Let's see what Kaffee has to say… His is the next winery on the road… Otherwise, we can speculate all day long."

"Good idea," I said. "He has to know what's going on… After all, Taskert's winemaker, Derek, works for him too."

"That leads me to wonder if Derek, Taskert, or anyone else has seen the ghostly child Mark saw in the caves," Delinda mused under her breath as she turned the Lexus onto a side-road paved with crushed gravel.

"She wasn't old enough to drink," I joked.

Al didn't seem to get it.

"Anyway, what kind of spirit would go around ruining wine?" he asked.

I couldn't resist. "A ninety proof one?"

"I should have seen that one coming," Al laughed.

Delinda made a point of disregarding my humor as she added, "The spirit might have nothing to do with the wine, but whatever she wants is no laughing matter. That I can promise you."

"You're right," Al agreed. "There could be other elements in play…"

I saw from his reflection in the rearview he was addressing me when he added, "We need to keep an open mind… Don't we?"

"My mind is completely open... As always," I said, knowing they would regard my statement as sarcasm.

The road to Kaff Cellars meandered through acres of grapevines for a half-mile or more. Rounding a bend, we drove into a covered parking area that sat across from a sizable building. Behind it lay a large, man-made lake surrounded by meticulously manicured verdant lawns and shaded by groves of tall trees.

Unlike Taskert's stone castle, the architecture of Kaff Cellars was a combination of rustic and modern elements, all of which combined to create an unmistakable upscale vibe. No wonder their wine was so damn expensive.

The building was framed in rough-hewn wooden beams trimmed with hammered brass accents. Spanning the length of it was a long line of darkly tinted, tall glass windows; designed both to attenuate the sun and conceal the interior.

The same classy wooden beam and brass design was carried over onto the cantilevered structure that shaded the parking area. I couldn't tell from my vantage point, but I'd take double or nothing the overhangs were roofed with solar panels.

Delinda pulled the rental into a spot alongside a late-model Bentley.

"Wow, we've got the least expensive car in the lot," I noted as we got out of the Lexus.

We left the shade of the overhang into the bright, late afternoon sunshine and approached the front entrance. Before we got there, we were greeted by a young woman. She was smartly dressed in high heels and formal business attire, attentively standing at a small outdoor podium under a frilly green umbrella. At first, I assumed she was a parking attendant until she began to speak.

"Do you have reservations for a tasting today?" she asked, looking down a large pad of paper lying on the top of the podium.

"No, we don't," replied Delinda in a far friendlier tone than she had taken earlier with me.

Not deterred in the least by Delinda's reply, the greeter jumped right in.

"No problem," she proclaimed in a perky, over-the-top happy tone of voice. "I'm sure we can fit you in! Would you like to learn about our tasting packages?" Without giving us any time to respond to her question, she added, "They start at fifty dollars per person."

I noted she was careful to emphasize "start."

"Thank you very much," I answered. "Actually, we're not here to taste, we were hoping to have a word with Mr. Kaffee."

"Do you have an appointment?" the woman asked, her smile fading.

Her enthusiasm had waned appreciably, which led me to think she got a piece of the up-sale—in any case, it appeared to me as if she was deciding we were worth her time or not.

While our conversation had been going on, Al had been scribbling something on a piece of paper. He folded it in half and handed it to the woman.

"If you would kindly give him this, I'm positive he'll want to see us."

She gave us a doubtful expression. "I can't do that. I'm not allowed to leave my spot."

Delinda spoke up. "That's all right, I'm sure we can find him."

The woman began to object, but Delinda touched her lightly on the wrist, and her expression changed midstream.

"Sure, go right ahead," she offered with a faraway look in her eyes.

Delinda's self-satisfied smile caused me to glance back at the greeter as we approached the entrance. I had the distinct impression she was utterly confused by what had just happened.

"Jedi mind trick?" I whispered.

Delinda ignored my question. I didn't even get a weak smile.

Damn, you'd think a genie would know how to let go of things.

Once inside the building, we were met by another woman with an arm full of leather-upholstered menus. Al repeated that we were there to see Mr. Kaffee, but before the menu lady could respond, a man came forward.

His flat-top buzz cut, erect posture, and muscular build all screamed ex-military. He wore a dark suit that was just a tad too tight around the armpits. More importantly, his ill-fitting jacket revealed the bulge of a holstered weapon.

"How can I help you?" he asked with no trace of warmth. His mannerism only reinforced my first impression—the guy wasn't here to sell wine.

I wondered why a snazzy place like this needed an armed bouncer. I looked around the room at the seated clientele before concluding no one in this crowd was going to beat up on anything—except their wallets.

"We'd like to speak with Mr. Kaffee," Al reiterated.

Plainly, getting an audience with the boss was no easy feat. This time Al didn't bother with the folded paper.

"You can tell him that Bruce Ashton sent us," he said forcefully.

"Wait here," the man said flatly before he walked away.

About five minutes later, the bouncer came back, followed by two men who were having an animated discussion. The taller of the two was in his early fifties, and the other appeared to be in his mid-thirties.

"You'll bring the Richebourg '49 with you?" asked the younger man.

He wore his lightweight gray suit jacket unbuttoned. The tie, loosened at the collar of his navy blue shirt fluttered over the bulge of his belly as he walked.

"Of course," replied the older man. "And the '52 Bordeaux as well. Can you fill all the seats?"

"Still working on it. I'll call you later," said the man in the suit as he continued towards the entrance.

The older man, who I presumed was Kaffee, nodded and paused for a brief exchange of words with the bouncer before he approached us. Richard Kaffee was dressed in elegant sports clothes and wore an expensive Rolex on one wrist and a braided gold bracelet on the other. His broad smile and healthy tan befitted his trim, athletic build.

The strong scent of his musky cologne assailed my nose as he approached. While I'm not fond of strong fragrances, that wasn't all that made a poor first impression on me. Despite Kaffee's fit appearance, there was a quality to his demeanor that I disliked right away. Admittedly, that conclusion was self-serving, although based on several observations.

First, he looked past Al and me as if we weren't there. Instead, his attention was fixed entirely on Delinda. Also, he seemed to project an air of arrogance that reminded me of Tommy "the shark" Rosselli. Rosselli was a big-time crime boss who was now serving a deservedly long sentence in a Supermax Federal Prison—thanks to the three of us.

Kaffee immediately took Delinda by the hand to introduce himself.

"Hi, I'm Richard, so nice to meet you… Miss?"

"Delinda Djinn. Please call me Delinda," she replied in a voice so sweet I thought I'd need an insulin shot. "This is Al Kleptos and Mark Tonnick."

The way she said my name brought sucking on a lemon to mind.

Kaffee gave the two of us a perfunctory nod, but plainly his focus was firmly fixed on Delinda.

"So, why did Bruce Ashton send you?" he intoned unctuously. "It's been a while since Bruce and I have spoken."

I replied before Delinda could answer. "He sent us to look into Phil Taskert's operation. We were hoping you could fill us in about your business relationship with him and his winery."

Kaffee tore his eyes away from Delinda long enough to give me a sour look. "Oh?"

I said, "Specifically, we'd like to know what's keeping him afloat financially."

"You would have to ask him," he replied with a smirk. "I only hope I'll be able to recoup my investment…"

"Well, then you might be interested in this," Al said, handing Kaffee the folded paper he had initially offered the woman who had greeted us.

Kaffee unfolded the note and studied it for a moment.

"This is interesting. Ashton wants to buy me out? Why would he do that?"

It was a struggle for me not to show any surprise. Under the circumstances, I couldn't imagine Ashton doing such a thing. It was entirely out of character—even if the man had more money than God. Regardless, I expected Kaffee to jump at the offer.

Instead, he neatly folded the paper and handed it back to Al.

"Tell him I'll have to think it over."

Delinda had remained quiet through this whole interaction, studying Kaffee carefully.

As Al pocketed the note, she flashed Kaffee a smile and said, "While you decide whether to sell your shares to Bruce, tell me more about your operation and what you do here."

Genie magic wasn't necessary to charm Kaffee; the guy was spellbound from the moment he set eyes on her. He returned her smile with a mouthful of perfect teeth.

"I would be devastated if you left before I could show you... Everything," Kaffee replied in a melodious baritone.

"That would be very kind," purred Delinda. She turned to Al and I, "Would you two mind?"

Mind? I felt like the top of my head was about to explode.

Kaffee said, "While I show Miss Djinn around, please allow me to arrange a complimentary tasting for you."

I was about to say something snide, but Al gave me a swift and surreptitious elbow in the ribs.

"That would be great," he said. "You two, take your time."

"Yeah," I echoed. "Have fun."

It took a herculean effort to keep from sneering. I'm not sure I succeeded, but Kaffee wasn't paying the slightest attention to either Al or me—his interest was clearly elsewhere. Delinda took his offered arm, and they strode off together with the concealed carry guy trailing behind him.

"Okay... What was that all about?" I said to Al.

"She knows what she's doing," he said, cracking a smile.

"That wasn't all I was referring to... Has Ashton lost his mind?"

"Glad to hear there's more than just woman trouble occupying your thoughts," Al said.

"Well, that doesn't make me feel any better. I don't get good vibes from that guy... Or this place. I'd bet dollars to donuts this entire operation is a money laundromat."

"Yep, I wouldn't doubt that for a moment," Al said in a way that suggested he didn't care one way or another.

"Let's get back to Ashton's absurd offer to Kaffee."

Before Al could answer, the woman with the armful of upholstered menus walked up to us.

"Would you gentleman please follow me," she said graciously.

We took a seat at a nearby table next to a large window that offered a perfect view of the lake and the lush grounds. Moments later, another lovely young woman, dressed entirely in black, lined up four stemmed wine glasses in front of each of us.

"This isn't such a bad way to spend the afternoon," Al said.

"Come on, Al," I replied impatiently. "Since when does Ashton want to buy Kaffee's shares?"

"He doesn't. In fact, Bruce never made that offer," Al grinned. "I wrote that note myself just to see Kaffee's reaction."

I looked at Al with a new appreciation. "That was sneaky... And clever. He should have snapped up the offer right away."

"Yep, he should have. Plainly, he knows something we don't."

"I'm curious, though. What would you have done if he had taken it?"

Al shrugged. "I would have thought of something, but I had a hunch he wouldn't."

"Why?" I asked.

"Just a feeling. I also had a thought Taskert and Kaffee might have some other business connection apart from the winery."

I took another look around the crowded tasting room. "You think he and Taskert are making money with some other venture?"

Al started to reply when he was interrupted by an attractive young woman who presented herself at our table side. She was dressed in tight black yoga pants with a long white shirt that reached down to the middle of her slender thighs. A fresh-faced strawberry blonde, she looked barely old enough to drink herself.

"I'm Allison, your server," she chirped with a big smile. "We'll start you off with our award-winning Chardonnay. It's from our upper vineyard, where the chalky soil and ideal microclimate produce a more intensely flavored press."

I nodded like I knew what she was talking about. Al looked more interested than I would have expected.

"It's ninety-five dollars a bottle, but club members get twenty percent off all purchases," she said as she poured two fingers worth into our wine glasses. "I'll be back in a few minutes," she added, leaving us to repeat the exact same spiel at another table nearby.

"At that price," I said, attempting to keep my voice down despite my incredulity. "This better be the most spectacular wine on earth!"

"It's not," commented Al after he took a sip. "But you're missing the point."

I took a swallow and coughed. Smooth it wasn't.

"So, what point is that?"

"Wine's value and attraction are subjective," he said, looking at me with an amused expression. "And, it's only natural that when one spends big money on a bottle of wine, the pride of ownership becomes just as important as the taste."

I took a second sip. It wasn't any better.

"Jesus… Is it supposed to burn on the way down?"

"Well, there's a reason for that…" Al paused and took another sip. "This Chard isn't very well balanced. Too much acid made worse by the lack of secondary malolactic fermentation."

"English, please…"

Al chuckled and said, "Are you getting some bitterness on the back of your tongue a moment after you swallow?"

"Yeah, now that you mention it, I do."

"That's what I was talking about."

I shook my head. "I still don't get it. How do you know all this?"

As soon as the words left my lips, I remembered I was speaking to someone who swore he was thousands of years old.

Al grinned as he poured the rest of his glass into the stainless steel vase at the far edge of the table. I did the same.

"People have been making wine as long as I can remember," he answered. "And, though you might find it hard to believe, it hasn't really changed much over the last few thousand years… Hell, you should have seen what they were serving back in Caesar's time! Then, as today, a wine's value lies purely in the tastebuds of the guy holding the glass, or in that case, the goblet."

Before I could reply, the server returned with a different bottle and poured a small amount of pinkish looking liquid into a second set of glasses.

"This is our Grenache Rose. A perfect wine for those Saturday afternoon barbecues, or just sitting outdoors on a summer day. This is forty-five dollars a bottle and ready to drink now."

I nodded politely as she spoke and tried to appear appreciative as she picked up our used glassware and trotted off to the next table. I tried a small sip—it was sweeter than the last offering, but truthfully, if I were going to drink anything on a hot summer day, it would be Don Julio with a beer back. The remaining contents of my glass joined the Chardonnay in the stainless steel vase.

We tasted three other white wines, and after replacing our stemware once more, our server poured five different reds. I quickly lost track of which were which, noting only the prices our server quoted grew more and more expensive with every wine she presented. I realized even if I were to cultivate a taste for this stuff, I could never afford it, even with Ashton's generous retainer.

While I was dumping my last glass, I observed the other tables in the room. People were sipping wine with a reverence that wouldn't have been out of place in my mother's synagogue. Come to think of it, the wine wasn't much better there, either.

At the table next to ours, I overheard a couple signing up for the "Kaff Klub," to save the twenty percent on the case of the reserve something-or-other they had ordered. Similar scenarios were occurring at other tables. The servers were processing credit cards on portable, handheld units, ensuring all transactions were done without delay—or any second thoughts before the buzz could wear off.

I was so engrossed with the action around the room I didn't even notice our waitress returning to the table and laying down the fancy leather folio. Al opened it and held up the receipt. 'Complementary' was stamped on the front in big red letters.

"I sincerely hope you enjoyed it," Al remarked. "Believe it or not, that was the two hundred dollar tasting."

CHAPTER NINE

Napa Valley, California. 1867

"THESE ARE FOR YOU, Auntie," said Wing Ho's young daughter as she brought a plate of her mother's bread into the kitchen. Her soft eyes glistened with excitement, as she handed the warm loaves to Merrilee, as though the plate held something far more precious than coarse, brown bread.

"It's your favorite," the little girl added breathlessly.

Merrilee had formed an unlikely attachment to five-year-old Mei-Ling, despite her natural reluctance to form bonds with any child of man. The youngster's unreserved trust and innocence touched her heart in ways she never thought possible.

"Thank you, dear," Merrilee replied warmly, taking the offering from the smiling child's hands. "They are my very favorites!"

Mei-Ling clasped her tiny hands together with joy and leaned forward so that her long, black hair fell over her ears and around her rosy cheeks.

"I love you, Auntie," she said guilelessly, before kissing Merrilee affectionately on the cheek and receiving a hug in return.

Those were the words she always spoke to Merrilee before she took her leave to return where she and all the Coolies lived—safely out of sight in the underground caves. While Merrilee regretted that Mei needed to spend her childhood in such a dark and damp place, she appreciated the necessity.

Precautions were warranted, for the seeds of anti-Chinese sentiment sown throughout the whole of California had already taken root. Of late, the blood-red blooms of hate were ripening, and eager hands were impatient to pluck them.

Later that same evening, she realized why that particular metaphor had come to mind, as the vineyard's first harvest was to begin shortly after midnight. Henry had assured her and Rosalee that was the time when the sugar in the fruit would be at its highest level.

Under his watchful eyes, the grapes were carefully handpicked by lantern light. Nearly every laborer in the sister's employ set to the task, including those who were digging in the caves throughout the day. Although there was still more work to be done, Henry had determined the excavations were complete enough to accommodate the anticipated barrels of newly made wine.

Over the past ten months, Henry's physical appearance had continually and steadily declined. Although he had become hollow-eyed and oddly mechanical in his mannerisms, he still obsessively supervised each of the vineyard's many operations. He barely ate, and his lean body had grown emaciated—and yet—he never seemed hungry. Rest also evaded him. When he attempted to sleep, slumber could only find him for a few fitful hours.

On this night, the night of the harvest, there would be no sleep at all, for the crush had to begin at first light. He knew the natural fermentation process would have already started from the moment the fruit was plucked from the vines. Time was of the essence.

Henry watched as Coolies unloaded basket after basket of fruit into the press. He arranged for the apparatus to be brought from his own winery, which over the last several months suffered from his neglect. Indeed, Henry hadn't even bothered to return home in the evenings for many weeks. The sisters provided him a room in which to stay and fed him on those few occasions when he felt like eating.

A month before, the foreman of Watkins's vineyard quit in disgust, frustrated with Henry's strange behavior. Not long afterward, the rest of his employees also left as he had fallen behind on their wages. Regardless, Henry appeared untroubled by these events. Nor was he concerned that his own vineyards lay abandoned and in disrepair—his grapes were left unharvested, to shrivel and rot on the untended vines.

Utterly unaware he was being driven by a force beyond his control, Henry's unnatural compulsion consumed him. During the rare moments in which his mind would begin to stray, his head began to ache until, like a barn-sour mare, his concentration returned to the work at hand.

Watching as the juice flowed out from between the wooden slats in the winepress, Henry's brain could only contemplate how best to complete the barreling process. He was so engaged, he didn't hear Merrilee roll up behind him in her wheelchair.

"Good morning, Henry. From the look of it, you've done very well."

"Thank you, Ma'am," he replied without allowing his gaze to stray away from the streams of dark, red juice. "We're going to fill forty or fifty barrels before we're done... After ten or twelve days of fermentation, we'll let it sit for another few weeks before we bottle it."

"The sooner, the better," she replied.

"You can't rush wine," Henry said mechanically, after a long pause.

His eyes never left the trickles of juice escaping the press, so he was unaware that Merrilee hadn't heard, having rolled away. On her return to the farmhouse, she navigated the ramp up to the porch and into the kitchen. There, Rosalee was waiting for her.

"Are we there yet?" Rosalee asked as her sister joined her.

"Close," replied Merrilee. "Although, I'm afraid we're close to losing our Henry. The spell is quite strong, you know."

"There's nothing to be done about that. We can't release him. It would kill him for sure, and the Chardonnay crop is almost ready to harvest."

"He'll not last much longer than that," said Rosalee. "But there is one more thing we'll need from him."

Merrilee's thin, bird-like features lit up with her sly grin. "Yes... There certainly is."

CHAPTER TEN

Napa County. Present Day

A HALF-HOUR AFTER we finished our tasting, Delinda found us. Al and I were sitting by the lake, entertaining ourselves by watching the ducks and birds while listening to couples arguing over which varietal was best suited to their tastes.

"So, how was the wine?" Delinda asked as she walked over.

"Some were better than others," Al answered.

"I plan to stick with tequila," I said. "How did it go with Kaffee? Did you find out anything new?"

"Actually, I did," she confided, smiling like the proverbial Cheshire Cat.

She took another nearby lawn chair and positioned it so she was facing us, which, in my opinion, improved the view considerably. I signaled my impatience with a deep sigh.

"So… Are you going to tell us, or do we have to guess?"

She waited for an instant for dramatic effect before she answered.

"First, Richard considers himself quite the charmer…"

"Imagine that," I muttered under my breath, though I suspected she heard me.

"But I did find out more about his connection with Taskert," she continued.

"And…?" prompted Al.

"Well, for one thing, much of Taskert's cash flow comes from auctioning off his library of investment wines. It turns out the wine auction business generates huge amounts of cash. Taskert and his wife acquire the wine, either from their own collection or on consignment from other brokers."

"So, what's Kaffee's role?" I asked.

"He also sells bottles from his own wine collection. Aside from that, Kaffee uses his reputation in the business to bring in the buyers. He and the auctioneer, the man we saw leaving earlier, take a cut for that, and for coordinating the sales."

"That explains how Taskert has kept himself afloat," I remarked. "But why isn't Kaffee interested in cashing out of Taskert's operation?"

"Yep, that is curious," agreed Al. "He's certainly aware of the problems there, but it seems he has no intention to sell his shares."

Delinda nodded. "Kaffee only told me he has faith that Taskert can turn the winery around. My suspicion is, however, he's got something else in mind."

"Like what?" I asked.

"I don't know exactly, but hopefully, I'll find out more tonight. He's taking me out to dinner."

If her accompanying smirk was calculated to make me jealous, or at the very least uneasy, she had it one-hundred percent right. Again, I wondered if Lissette flirting with me earlier had something to do with it.

"Wonderful," I said with no enthusiasm. "I'm sure you'll have a great time."

Delinda smiled slyly. "I'm sure we will."

It took an effort to put aside my growing dislike of Kaffee, but I succeeded in keeping my tone of voice level.

I asked, "Any ideas what Kaffee's got up his sleeve?"

"Only that he plans to profit somehow," she replied.

"I'm wondering if he's behind the TAB contamination," I mused. "It certainly scared off most of the other investors."

"That's TCA," Al corrected. "But, if you're right, it could explain why Kaffee didn't jump at my bogus offer to buy him out."

"Sure," I agreed. "And, after he gets his hands on all the shares… Magically, the problem goes away!"

Delinda nodded. "Well, if that's the case, he'll never admit it." She gave us an impish smile, adding, "At least not on purpose."

"So, even if he 'accidentally' cops to it," I said using air quotes, "there's another question… Why does he need 'Mr. Muscle?'"

"I asked him that… Casually, of course," she assured us. "Richard says Gustave is there to provide extra security."

"Probably because he overcharges for his wine," I snarked.

Delinda shot me a reproving glance. "Really, Mark, don't you take anything seriously?"

She paused to let me respond, but I only shrugged and let her continue.

"Apparently, some of the wines he's auctioning are very valuable, and Richard feels the extra precaution is necessary."

"Okay, but then why doesn't Taskert have more security, too?" I asked, "Especially if the wine is coming from his collection."

"You're right," she agreed.

"Yeah," I said. "Unless Kaffee's got something else to be afraid of."

"Oh, he'll tell me," Delinda said confidently. "You know how persuasive I can be."

"Yeah, but using genie magic is cheating," I grinned.

"You have your investigative technique," she shot back. "I have mine."

Despite the apparent momentary thaw between Delinda and I, Al looked pensive.

"You know, now I think we should have another quick conversation with Taskert about this before we check into our accommodations." Al proposed, rising from his chair.

Delinda also got to her feet. "Why not? Hopefully, he's still at the winery."

I was just getting comfortable, and besides, all the short pours of wine had made me drowsy. With an effort, I abandoned my chair and followed them back to the car.

Minutes later, we were on highway 29, driving back to Taskert's winery at unthinkable speed. Suddenly, I heard a loud snap and followed by a sharp jerk as the front of the car abruptly nosed down.

"We lost the front tire!" I yelled. Adrenalin had replaced whatever alcohol remained in my system.

"Brilliant deduction," Delinda scoffed as she skillfully turned the wheel into the direction the car had begun to spin.

A huge truck was coming at us in the opposite direction, and I braced for the inevitable head-on impact. I felt the scar on my cheek itch in the same instant the truck driver stood on the horn.

Unexpectedly, the front of the Lexus rose as if the tire had re-inflated. A fraction of a second later, we swerved back onto our own lane—scarcely avoiding being sideswiped by the passing tractor-trailer. I glanced at Delinda, who returned my look with an arched eyebrow and a knowing smile.

"Do you also consider that cheating?" she said.

I was too busy trying to catch my breath to answer as she guided the Lexus off the pavement and onto the dirt shoulder. As soon as we stopped, I stumbled out of the car to examine the passenger side front tire. Despite the shredded sidewall, it appeared to be fully inflated. Then, as I watched, the tire sagged and flattened. Frankly, I didn't care if it was crazy genie magic or not, I was just glad to be alive.

"Miracles don't count as cheating," I muttered out-loud to myself.

"Thanks, anyway," Delinda retorted dryly.

She was standing right behind me. I hadn't seen her exit the car, but that was par for the course. Al was already fishing around in the trunk for the tire iron and the jack. I helped him lift out the spare—it was narrower than a standard tire. Plainly, it was intended for temporary use only, but it would get us back on the road.

It didn't take long for the two of us to swap out the tires, however, as we lifted the damaged tire into the trunk, something fell out of it.

"What's this?" Al said as he held up the small piece of metal.

He handed it to me, and I recognized what it was at once.

"Shit! That's a bullet. Somebody shot out our tire!"

The round had flattened on impact with the metal wheel rim, but enough of the slug remained for me to determine it came from a high-caliber rifle.

Al shut the trunk and turned to Delinda and I. "So much for rolling out the welcome mat."

"And we only just got here," I said. "I wonder, did they want to just scare us off, or kill us?"

"Oh, I'm sure they'd be pleased with either result," Al remarked. "Unless, of course, the gun went off accidentally."

At that moment, I was proud my sarcasm was rubbing off on him.

"Hardly," I snorted. "Somebody doesn't want us poking around Taskert's winery."

I glanced over at Delinda for her reaction, but she seemed to be looking off in the distance. I was familiar with that faraway gaze of hers. It was a sure sign of trouble—as if getting shot at wasn't bad enough.

"A glass of bad wine for your thoughts," I prompted, waving a hand in front of her eyes.

She swatted it away as she made a dash for the driver's side door.

"We need to get over to Taskert's winery right away," she said as she slid back behind the wheel. "Something's going on there. Something terrible!"

Al and I quickly got into the Lexus without commenting. One should never argue with a genie. Especially one with Delinda's track record.

We quickly reached the road leading to Taskert's property. As we turned off the highway, we immediately saw the sea of blinking red and blue lights looming ahead. Thankfully, Delinda braked and slowed before we plowed headlong into the cluster of police and emergency vehicles that filled the parking lot.

"What the hell happened here!" Al exclaimed, reacting to the sight of a black, zippered body bag being rolled over to a waiting ambulance on a gurney.

"Just as Delinda said, something terrible," I said as I left the car.

I approached an officer who was watching as several EMTs loaded the gurney and its unknown occupant into the ambulance.

"Excuse me, officer, I represent one of the winery owners… Can you tell me what's going on?"

The cop seemed unsure of how much he could reveal, but relented when he decided I wasn't going leave without an explanation.

"Looks like a possible suicide. That's all I can say. If you want more info, you'll have to talk to the detectives."

Without waiting for Al and Delinda, I walked over to the two men the cop pointed out. They were conferring with one another and making notes as they spoke. Both were dressed in the standard investigative attire—light sports jackets, white shirts, and loosened ties.

I pulled my PI creds and held them out in front of me as I approached them.

"Detectives, I'm Mark Tonnick. My associates and I are working on behalf of the winery."

"Is that so?" remarked one of them, clearly unimpressed. He was the taller of the two and appeared to be older than his colleague. His craggy features were tanned from years in the Napa Valley sun and shaded by the long bill of the white baseball cap he wore. While his sunglasses concealed the color of his eyes, they weren't as successful in diminishing his look of disdain. His tone of voice made it very clear he considered me out of his league.

"What's happened?" I asked, ignoring his implied slight. Clearly, someone had died, and I needed to know who it was. "Accident?"

"Maybe," answered the younger detective. He was a bit thicker in the middle than detective number one and seemed to be sweating profusely in the late afternoon sun. Hatless, his thick head of unkempt brown hair was tousled even further by the occasional breeze. He stood almost six or eight inches below my six-foot frame, and his goatee made him look more like a college professor than a homicide investigator.

"Is it Phillip Taskert?" I prodded.

"No..." The perspiring detective said, wiping his brow. He took a moment, deciding what to tell me. Finally, sounding only slightly more friendly than his partner, he added, "It was Derek George... Know him?"

"By the Gods!" exclaimed Al, who had overheard as he and Delinda came up to join me. "We just saw him not two hours ago."

Now, the first detective who had spoken eyed us with far more interest.

"Then, we'll need to take your statements... Starting with why you're here in the first place."

"No problem," Delinda offered. "We'll tell you everything we know."

"Where's everybody else?" I asked.

"No one else was here when it happened," stated the tall detective in sunglasses.

"Just the dead guy," added the other.

"We notified Mr. Taskert right after we secured the area," the tall detective continued without looking up from his notes.

I suppose when he realized we weren't going to go away, he decided introductions were in order.

"I'm Detective Reeves," he said, pushing his sunglasses up higher onto the bridge of his nose before motioning toward the detective with the goatee. "And this is Detective Feinstein."

"These are my associates, Al Klepios, and Delinda Djinn," I said. "We're here at Taskert's request to investigate some irregularities at the winery. We only just arrived this afternoon, around 2:30. Shortly afterward, we took a brief tour of the facilities with the Taskerts and their hospitality manager. It lasted for roughly a half-hour... Forty-five minutes tops... During which we met Derek George for the first time. Right afterward, we drove to Kaff Cellars... We've been there for the past couple of hours before we came back."

"What brought you back," Reeves asked.

"We hoped to find Taskert here," I replied. "We wanted to talk to him."

"So do we," said Reeves. "He said he was on his way." He jotted something in his notebook. "So, Derek George was alive when you left?"

I gave the detective my best, 'You've got to be shitting me' expression before I said, "Very much so… Otherwise, you'd have heard about it. Speaking of which, who called it in?"

Detective Reeves took a deep, exasperated breath. "It was a 911… From a couple who had probably been tasting a little too much fruit of the vine… They said they wanted to see the castle up close and drove in, ignoring the 'winery closed' signs. According to them, the doors were open, so they wandered inside… Where they got the shock of their lives."

"Yeah, nothing brings on instant sobriety like stumbling onto a corpse," added Feinstein dryly.

"Literally?" I asked.

"No," Feinstein said reluctantly. "He was hanging from a chandelier."

"So, you're figuring it for a suicide?" I asked.

The two detectives looked at each other for a moment.

"We're looking into that possibility," Reeves confirmed, glancing down at his notebook, avoiding eye contact.

I saw through his dodge at once.

So did Al, who said, "And, I take it you have doubts about that?"

Reeves's expression darkened, but he remained silent—which in itself answered the question. We all turned at the same time at the sound of a woman's voice. It was Lissette, running towards us.

"O' Lord!" she wailed. "Is it true?"

She had left her car, a Honda Accord, askew in the driveway without bothering either to close the door or turn off the engine.

"I jus' canna believe it! Phil called an' told me Derek died! I cam'a quick as I could!"

Reeves nodded. "And you are?"

"Lissette O'Hannon, the winery hospitality manager. How did it happen? Everything was fine when I left!"

"When was that, Ma'am?" Detective Reeves interjected.

"'Bout two hours or so. I left a while after these folks," Lissette answered, motioning in our direction.

Reeves jotted in his notepad before he asked, "Who else was here?"

Lissette wiped her reddened eyes with a tissue, streaking her mascara. She took several deep breaths before she spoke.

"Clement, Phil, and Iris, an' o' course, Derek." She paused and motioned to us again. "Then, Phil and Iris went up t' Saint Helena, and I went t' run an errand… Clement left right before I did. I was already home when Phil called an' told me what happened."

"What kind of errand?" inquired Feinstein.

"I drove t' the bank… T' deposit a check. Phil wanted it in his account as fast as I could get it there."

"Where was Derek at the time you left?" asked Reeves.

"I'm not sure, I didn't bother t' look… My concern was t' get o'er t' the bank before it closed for the day."

Reeves jotted in his notebook. Without looking up, he asked, "Can you give us the name of the bank?"

"O' course," Lissette replied.

As she gave the detectives the details, I took advantage of their distraction to slip away. As casually as I could, I made my way over to the courtyard with Al and Delinda following close behind me.

"Shouldn't we mention to the cops we were shot at?" Al asked.

I shook my head warily. "What good would that do? Whoever did it is long gone, and there's no obvious connection to what happened here…"

When we reached the far end of the courtyard, I was shocked into silence. Contrary to my expectations, no uniforms were stationed at the winery entrance, nor was the area cordoned off. The unsecured crime scene suggested that homicide investigations might be rare in wine country. Still, that was a poor excuse for not deploying someone to prevent contamination of the scene. I got another surprise as we drew closer.

The big, iron-bound oak doors leading to the tasting hall were wide open as Reeves had described. There was no need to go inside as we could see everything we needed to from where we stood. Aside from the length of chain dangling from one of the massive chandeliers, I took note of the sizable pool of congealing blood directly underneath it. To the side of that stood a tall, orange A-frame ladder stenciled with "Napa FD."

"A chain?" I remarked. That seemed like a strange choice for someone who intended to commit suicide. "I've never seen that before. And, judging from the amount of blood on the floor, it appears to have sliced his neck wide open."

"Maybe he couldn't find a rope," Al ventured.

"Or a ladder?" Delinda asked rhetorically. "It looks as if the fire department needed to use their own ladder to get him down.... Which could only mean..."

Al finished her sentence. "Murder."

I nodded. "From the way Reeves reacted when Al asked him, he thinks so too... And, whoever did the deed didn't bother to hide the fact."

We all took another look around the room. Al said what we were all thinking.

"Without a ladder, I'd like to know how he got up there in the first place."

"I can think of a few," Delinda said in a way that plainly stated her implication.

I shook my head. "Obviously, whoever hoisted him up there carried it away. Or, do you think a supernatural something-or-another flew him up there, put a chain around his neck, and gave him the old heave-ho?"

Delinda's eyebrows narrowed in disdain. "Really, Mark. Do you have to be so rude..."

"Rude?" I snapped.

I admit to being a little touchy. Okay, a lot. In any event, I wasn't having much success keeping my feelings to myself.

"And, so Juvenile!" she countered. "Why are you resistant to my suggestion that other forces could be at play here! You're the one who saw the spirit."

"True… But I think there's a connection to our incident on the highway… Ghosts don't go around shooting at folks. And it goes without saying, a bullet from a long gun doesn't qualify as a supernatural event!"

"I didn't say it was!" she said sharply.

"I'm glad to hear you admit that," I retorted.

"Stop being a dick!" Delinda barked.

She was right. I was acting out like I was still in high school. It was time to de-escalate.

"Sorry," I said in a much softer tone. "I guess I'm a little burned out when it comes to things that aren't easily explained."

Delinda shook her head. "I hadn't noticed." Despite her sarcastic reply, she paused long enough to give me the arched brow before she coyly added, "So, you have another theory?"

"Yes, I do," I said. "I think Derek was dead before somebody hauled him up there on a ladder and hung him with the chain."

"That could work," she conceded. "So, where's the ladder?"

"Plainly, it's not here," I observed, looking around the room. "The killer probably hid it somewhere… Or, could be he took it with him."

"Hoisting Derek up there would have also taken considerable strength," Al added.

"True," I agreed. "That's why I can't imagine someone dragging him kicking and screaming up the ladder."

"What are you doing here!" boomed a voice behind us.

We turned to find a red-faced, uniformed officer angrily waving a roll of yellow crime tape.

"Nothing," Al said politely. "We didn't go inside… We only wanted to take a look so we could have a better idea of what happened."

"I don't give a shit what you wanted!" the cop hollered. "Leave, or I'll arrest your asses!"

"A true professional at work," I complained under my breath as we walked away.

CHAPTER ELEVEN

WE EMERGED FROM THE courtyard gardens just as Taskert and his wife drove up in their shiny, top of the line, Mercedes. The car had barely come to a halt when Phil Taskert jumped out of the passenger seat, heaving the door closed behind him.

"Derek is dead? How?" he yelled, racing over to where Lissette and the two detectives were standing.

"Murdered," I volunteered as we walked up and joined the group.

Iris had exited her car in time to hear me say the "M" word.

"Murdered?" she repeated, looking around warily.

My uttered conclusion drew reproving looks from both detectives.

"We're not sure," said Reeves quickly. "We're looking into it."

Normally I wouldn't have blurted out my point of view. But perhaps the combination of drinking Kaffee's wine on an empty stomach and feeling pissy about Delinda's dinner date had screwed with my sensibilities.

I turned to the Taskerts and asked, "Do you have a tall ladder on the premises?"

Feinstein and Reeves might have arrested me at that moment, except they were just as interested in Taskert's answer as I was.

"I'm sure we do, why?" Phil Taskert replied.

Reeves exhaled loudly. The cat was out of the bag, so he said, "Because we found him hanging from one of the chandeliers."

A static burst from a nearby officer's belt radio interrupted him. The detective motioned for the uniform to move farther away from us to reply to the call.

"We've looked around, but we haven't found the ladder... Yet," added Reeves pointedly.

"What?" exclaimed Taskert, looking genuinely surprised. "Is that why you think he was murdered?"

"Where might you keep a ladder tall enough to reach those chandeliers?" pressed Feinstein, disregarding Taskert's question.

"In the back, behind the fermentation tanks," Taskert answered. "We have a few A-frame types and extension ladders."

It had taken the Napa Fire Department's sixteen-foot A-frame ladder to reach where the chain was wrapped around the fixture, a fact that wasn't lost on Feinstein either.

"Mr. Taskert, when was the last time you saw Derek alive?" Reeves asked.

"When we left," Taskert replied, his eyes narrowing. He didn't try hiding his resentment at being considered a suspect. "Derek said he was going to inspect some of the equipment before he locked up and went home."

He paused for a moment before adding, "This morning, when I was showing these folks around the winery, we heard Derek and Clement arguing about something."

"Do you know what the argument was about?" Reeves pressed.

"No, they stopped the moment they saw us approach," Taskert answered.

"Wait here," Reeves ordered before he and Feinstein walked over to confer with the uniform who had been talking on his belt radio.

I took advantage of the detective's absence to ask the obvious question.

"What about the chain Derek used to hang himself? Is that something you have lying around the winery?"

The color drained from Taskert's face. "Chain?"

I glanced over at Iris and Lissette. They both looked as if they had seen a ghost.

"Dear God!" Lissette whispered before covering her mouth with her hand, but the words had already escaped her lips.

Iris shot her husband a dirty look that insinuated that this was somehow his fault.

Noting their odd reactions, Delinda asked, "What is it about the chain?"

Lissette looked questioningly over to the Taskerts.

Iris put up her hand in warning. "I'm not sure what you mean," she said sternly as she turned towards Lissette.

"It won't do you any good to keep things from us," Delinda declared, locking eyes with Phillip Taskert.

"We've had a few accidents," he reluctantly admitted. Now Iris was glaring at him, but he waved her off with a small motion of his hand. "They happened during construction..."

"It's the castle's curse," Lissette mumbled under her breath.

"Nonsense!" barked Iris. "Don't we have enough troubles without spreading rumors and lies?"

"A curse? What kind of curse?" I asked, glancing at Delinda.

Frankly, after my experience in the cave, I expected to hear corroboration about the winery being haunted, not cursed. Although it occurred to me they might not know the difference.

"Don't be foolish!" Iris snapped, glaring at Lissette. "There is no curse! It's all just coincidence!"

Lissette's face grew dark with anger. Before she could reply, Taskert raised both his hands in an attempt to de-escalate the situation.

"Stop it! Please!" he implored forcefully. "A man has died, our business is at stake, and all you can do is argue?"

Taskert saw the look on our faces and quickly added, "Seeing the winery fail is the last thing Derek would have wanted."

Lissette nodded solemnly, her features growing more relaxed, but Iris's stern expression remained unchanged. I've chased enough unhappy couples to know there was more going on with this group than they were willing to share.

I decided the direct approach was the best and asked, "Have there been any other strange events you'd like to tell us about?"

In reply, everyone shook their heads. It was all rather unconvincing as far as I was concerned. Then, what Taskert said next only reinforced my suspicions.

"Perhaps, in light of this terrible tragedy, we should postpone your inquiries," he proposed, addressing the three of us.

How convenient.

"That's not going to happen," I replied flatly.

I glanced over to Al and Delinda. It didn't take a mind reader—or a genie, to know they were thinking the same thing I was.

"I'm sure that despite this horrible event, Mr. Ashton would want our investigation to continue," said Al.

"After all, this incident could be related to the contamination," I added, drawing dark looks from Iris and Lissette.

I was toying with the idea Derek might have played a role in sabotaging Taskert's operation. That was an angle worth contemplating. At the very least, it could offer a motive for his murder —all talk of curses and hauntings aside.

"That's a ridiculous assumption," Taskert protested. His voice had grown softer when he saw Reeves heading back in our direction.

If the detective was aware we were having a moment of disagreement, he kept it to himself. He returned to tell us they had found Clement Wagner, the cellar master at the Yountville dog park.

A few minutes later, a patrol car drove into the lot. Clement was sitting in the back seat with a brown and white Corgi cradled beside him. He kept his eyes straight ahead, pointedly ignoring us as the car slowed to a stop.

Instead of resuming our discussion, all of us stood silently watching as Clement and his dog got out of the police cruiser. A moment later, Reeves pulled him aside to question him alone. During their short interview, Clement angrily motioned in our direction several times.

That was telling.

Soon afterward, Reeves closed his notebook and waved Clement off. I wondered what the cellar master had said that led the detective to end his interrogation so abruptly. I got my answer when Clement stomped over to where the rest of us were standing. He looked pissed, but it was hard for me not to laugh since his Corgi was struggling comically on its short legs to keep up with him.

"Goddamn it, Phil… If you're trying to pin this on me, it won't work! I've been at the dog park for the last two hours, with dozens of witnesses to prove it!" Clement shouted.

"What are you talking about?" Taskert sputtered. "I never accused you of anything!"

"Bullshit! The cop said as much!"

"Hell, no!" Taskert yelled back. "I never pointed the finger at you. I only said you were one of the last people to see him alive."

"If anybody killed Derek, it was you!"

"How could I have killed him? Are you out of your fucking mind?" Taskert retorted at the top of his lungs.

Both he and Clement were growing more and more red-faced as their confrontation continued.

"Everybody in the Valley knows you hated him!" roared Clement.

"Stop it!" Lissette screamed, pushing the two men apart. "Just stop it!"

Her intervention took their confrontation down a couple of notches, although their anger was unabated.

"Yeah, we had our differences," Taskert admitted. "But he was crucial to our winery's survival! I was counting on him to solve the contamination problem!"

"But he couldn't, could he?" Clement retorted. "He found out you were tainting your own cellar… And so you killed him!"

"Fuck you, Wagner! You're finished here," Taskert exploded. "Fired!"

"Fuck you back! That's fine with me!" Clement yelled as he furiously hurried away at a pace that again outstripped his dog's ability to keep up. "I quit!" he bellowed, turning back and stretching his pet's retractable leash to the limit.

Taskert curled his hands into fists and was on the verge of charging after Clement.

"Phil, mind your temper," Iris chided. "You'll give yourself another aneurism." She reached out and touched his shoulder. "The last thing we need is more trouble."

Taskert wiped his brow. He was sweating profusely, despite the cool afternoon breeze rippling through the valley. Shaking with anger, he pulled a silver pill case from his front pocket and retrieved a small yellow tab from inside it.

"I can't believe he thinks I had anything to do with this!" he croaked, nearly choking on the pill.

"He donna mean it," Lissette said. "Clement's jus' upset. He and Derek were close friends."

Iris scowled at Lissette's reply. "Don't make excuses for that man! He doesn't deserve it."

The loud argument had drawn the attention of the two detectives. Feinstein and Reeves caught up with Clement as he stomped away. After a brief conversation, Feinstein helped the angry cellar master and his small dog back into the squad car as Reeves returned to where we were standing.

"Mr. Taskert," Reeves began in a soft, even voice, "Mr. Wagner blames you for Derek's death." He paused for a moment, watching for any reaction. No one said anything before he added, "Would you mind explaining why?"

"Derek and I disagreed on how and where the contamination was getting into the wine," replied Taskert. "He felt it was a result of environmental factors, and I was beginning to suspect it was being introduced intentionally."

"Anything else?" asked Reeves.

"No. That's all. Certainly, nothing to have killed him over," Taskert asserted. "I don't think Clement's thinking clearly. We're all shocked, but as Lissette said, he and Derek have worked together for a long time."

Reeves nodded. "Do you know of anyone who might have wanted Derek dead?"

"No, of course not," Taskert answered quickly, looking down at his shoes.

I took Taskert diverting his eyes as a classic tell. He might be lying or just nervous at being put on the spot. If Reeves were even half as good a detective as he should have been, he would have seen it too. I wondered if Taskert knew more than he was saying.

Reeves made more notes in his pad. "Thank you, Mr. Taskert." Then, addressing the rest of us, he said, "You are all free to go for now. We'll be in touch if we have any more questions."

Phil and Iris quickly got back into their car and drove off.

"I should go too," Lissette said, watching as the Taskert's sky blue Mercedes made its way back towards the highway.

I followed her back to her car. One of the uniforms had parked it on the far side of the lot.

"I'm very sorry about Derek," I said. "But, if you're up to it, I'd like to know a little more about why you think the castle is cursed."

She didn't meet my eye. "Right now, I jus' wanna go home."

Before she closed the car door and drove away, she added, "Besides, you donna believe in curses, do ya?"

She didn't give me a chance to answer—but that was just as well.

"Nice of you escort her to her car," said Delinda disingenuously when I rejoined her and Al.

"It's getting late," intervened Al.

While Al's blatant intent was to prevent another argument, he was right. The sun was beginning to set, and we had yet to check into our accommodations.

"Yeah," I agreed. "It's been a busy first day on the job… And aside from getting shot at and nearly killed, we're now embroiled in a murder investigation. And we're still at square one as to why we came here in the first place."

Al nodded. "Yep, but our being here is sure making somebody nervous."

"Let's just hope the body count doesn't get any higher," I said.

"I'm with you on that one," Al replied. "But what about the castle being cursed? They sure didn't want to discuss that."

I looked over at Delinda and said, "I can vouch for the fact the caves are haunted... But cursed? What's all that about?"

She answered without even a trace of condescension. "It's something to consider. Curses are very different from a simple haunting. They can be powerful… And tricky. They are also difficult to detect since, by their very nature, they're designed to strike without warning."

"That's hardly comforting," I frowned. "So, what you're saying is you wouldn't necessarily sense anything was amiss?"

"Possibly. Curses, especially dark ones, are in a class by itself. Which is why they can be so dangerous…"

"Even for you?" I asked.

"For anyone," she replied, looking away as her voice trailed off.

Al and I shared a brief glance. It was hard to say if he was as surprised as I. Frankly, that Delinda had any weakness at all was troubling. And the thought that even she could be in danger was doubly disconcerting. I resisted the urge to assure her I'd never let anything happen to her.

What the hell could I do, anyway?

Wordlessly, we piled back into our rental. Delinda rolled down her window as Detective Feinstein approached the car.

He stuck his head halfway through it and said, "All of you…. Just a friendly word of advice. This is our case… Let us handle it."

"It's all yours," I replied politely. "But, we will still be investigating other issues here at the winery."

"Before you do, you'll have to wait until we release the crime scene," Feinstein pushed back. "Until then, this place is off-limits. Understood?"

"We do," Al nodded. "Any idea when you'll be finished?"

"We'll call you," Feinstein said tersely.

Sure you will, I thought.

"We're staying at the Hideaway Resort," Delinda said sweetly.

The detective softened at her smile while she pretended not to notice.

"You will let us know as soon as you can, won't you?" she added.

Unless I missed my bet, Detective Feinstein would do precisely that, thanks to genie magic.

CHAPTER TWELVE

Napa Valley, California. 1867

"WE KNOW YOU'RE HIDIN' 'em!" yelled Miles Russell from the saddle as he and ten other mounted men approached the Harper sisters' farmhouse.

Russell and his self-appointed posse had come down from Sonoma, seeking any Chinese laborers they could find. They fancied themselves as part of the "Sandlotters" movement, a faction of the California Working Man's Party that wanted to push cheap immigrant labor out of the state. The disappointment on Russell's face was evident as he looked around. The vineyards were deserted.

He realized his mistake. As he and his men had drawn closer to the farmstead, they had urged their mounts into a gallop. The gouts of dust raised by their advance had warned the Coolies working in the vineyards. The Chinamen were smart enough to know what a large group of riders might portend. Now he could only watch warily as Henry Walker Watkins emerged from the farmhouse to confront them.

"We are not hiding anyone," Henry insisted. "You have no right to be here!"

Russell was a big, coarse featured man, with a voice as outsized as his belly.

"You lie! We already chased them Chinamen out of Sonoma. Heard you hired 'em down here to work on your vineyard. Give 'em up, ya hear! Fuckin' Coolies are stealing jobs from every white American in the Valley... We're gonna put a stop to that right here an' now!"

"Truly?" Retorted Henry leaning on his cane. "Are any of you willing to get up at dawn to prune the vines? Or perhaps you're eager to dig from morning to night, fifty feet underground?" Anger had cleared his mind, if only for the moment.

None of the mounted men replied.

"I didn't think so," Henry scoffed. "Get the hell outta here!"

One of the men drew a pistol and made to aim it at Henry, but at that moment, Rosalee rolled down the ramp in her wheelchair from the front porch. She motioned with her hand, and simultaneously the horse the gunman was riding reared up, bucking the man out of his saddle and onto the ground.

Closely behind her came Merrilee, cradling a double-barrel shotgun.

"Get out!" she commanded. "And don't come back."

"You'll be sorry!" Russell spat back.

His blotchy, sun-reddened face twisted in a fury that was equally directed both at the old woman and his own man who was clumsily remounting his horse.

"Not as sorry as you'll be if you don't git!" Merrilee said, with a wave of her gun.

"We'll see about that, won't we!" Miles Russell ranted as he wheeled his mount around and rode off, followed by the rest of his men.

Henry limped closer to the sisters as they watched the column of horsemen ride away. "They're a cowardly bunch, but I don't reckon they'll be gone for long," he said.

His ire had diminished, mostly because his brain had become cloudy again.

Merrilee waved her gun. "We'll be waiting for 'em."

Henry shook his head. "Don't underestimate men like that. Wing Ho told me many of his countrymen and their families were hounded out of Sebastopol by brigands like those. It's a dangerous time in California to be Chinese... Or Mexican. No wonder those folks are afraid to show their faces anywhere."

Rosalee nodded. "Yes, I can see why our workers prefer to live in the quarters they've made for themselves down in our wine caves."

Merrilee added, "They're safer that way. The last time the Grayson boy came and delivered our supplies, he heard tell of a rumor. He said that up in Sonoma, all the Coolies there have gone to ground. Some say they've dug secret tunnels beneath the whole of downtown!"

"I wouldn't doubt it," agreed Rosalee. "Not for one minute."

"We'll need to keep an eye out for those brigands!" Henry said before he left to reassure the workers that they were safe. After he was out of earshot, the sisters continued their conversation in the old tongue.

Merrilee sighed. "The nature of man hasn't changed much since we've left the old country."

Rosalee had a faraway look in her eyes as she said, "Nor in the centuries afterward. But then, we've seen our own share of persecution, haven't we?"

"Yes, we have, sister… Without a doubt, we have."

CHAPTER THIRTEEN

Napa Valley. Present Day

TRUE TO FORM, ASHTON had booked us at one of the swankiest resorts in Napa Valley. The Napa Hideaway was a charming collection of individual villas scattered over an acre and a half of exquisitely landscaped grounds. In every direction one looked were fountains and sculptures; even a small creek of rushing water meandered through the property.

The sumptuous surroundings made it difficult for me to keep in mind this wasn't a vacation. If anything, the situation here had become deadly serious. From my perspective, Derek's bizarre murder might have been set in motion by our arrival at the winery. Was it intended to be a warning, like our incident on the highway? Or, perhaps someone was afraid Derek might say or do something that could implode whatever scheme was in play. Plainly, it was in our best interest to unravel this mess before someone decided to take a shot at something other than our tires.

It was half-past seven o'clock before I finally found my assigned lodging—mainly due to the challenge of deciphering the map they had given me at the check-in desk. Just as I began fumbling with the key to the cottage door, my mobile rang. I fished the phone from my pocket at the same time I pushed open the door and entered the room. Surprised and distracted by the spacious and well-appointed accommodations, I didn't answer until the fourth ring.

"This is Mark," I said, tossing my overnight bag onto the day couch.

"Santiago Luna here. I got your message… I also spoke to Detective Todd."

I refocused and quickly replied, "I take it he told you I wanted to find out more about this Momo thing."

"He did, but I suppose you already know what started as a meme evolved into a crazy game. One that was killing kids all over the world."

I didn't want to admit he lost me right around the word, meme, but the last part got my attention.

"Actually, I had no idea it was that bad."

"Yeah, it was. But thankfully, like the Slenderman thing, it's mostly yesterday's news."

"So, it's over?" I asked.

"Yeah, mostly, but the meme still pops up every once in a while. On the internet, nothing ever really goes away."

"Does anybody know who's behind it?"

Luna chuckled. "Are you kidding? It's not just one person… Like everything else that goes viral, it passes through hundreds or even thousands of hands… Then it turns up in everything from YouTube videos to text messages."

"Yeah, I get it," I replied, thinking I should have known that. "But, how does a thing like that become dangerous?"

"In this case, it was deliberate," he answered. "When the craze started, pictures of Momo would pop up in random webpages as a relatively harmless scare. Then, suddenly, contact numbers began circulating along with an invitation to play the Momo game… Kids would text the number, and Momo would challenge them to do certain things… Bad shit, really, since a lot of kids ended up killing themselves."

"How was that possible?"

"Believe me, it was… Especially since children were specifically targeted. The game would start out innocently enough… Momo begins directing the player to do harmless tasks… But soon, the challenges escalate into more dangerous actions. Like daring the kid to hold a knife to their own throat, or jump off the roof of a tall building."

"You're kidding? Why would they do that?"

"Because Momo threatens their family or friends. Plus, these are impressionable children we're talking about," Luna explained. "I can't begin to tell you what they can be coerced into doing."

"How did this get started? Is there a real Momo?"

Luna coughed a weak laugh into the phone. "You haven't googled the image yet, have you?"

"I only had time for a quick peek at it yesterday," I admitted. "I'm on another case right now."

"When we hang up, take another look. There's a bunch of bullshit miss-information out there... but the image of Momo was originally created as a sculpture by some Japanese artist who called it 'Mother Bird.' Claims it came to him in a nightmare... That, I can believe! Besides the crazy-ass face, the statue has no body below the boobs... Just two scaly chicken-legs; however, the face is all you ever see online, and that's scary as hell. As I mentioned, the craze is over for the most part, and not a moment too soon if you ask me."

Not for some, I thought. "So, from what you know, if anyone were to go searching for Momo in real life, where would they go?"

"Now, you're kidding, right?"

"I wish I were," I said grimly. "I've got a couple of missing girls looking for her."

"To do what?"

"Kill her... To revenge the death of a friend," I answered. "Todd's got LAPD's Missing Persons Unit on it, so with a little luck, they'll turn up soon. Do you have any ideas where the MPU should be searching?"

There was a long pause on the other end before Luna answered. "Can't help you there. The Momo meme was all over the map, pretty much world-wide. A group of crazy hackers probably started it with no agenda other than to fuck with people's heads."

"What kind of asshole thinks getting kids to hurt themselves qualifies as a recreational activity?" I fumed. "You don't need to answer that, I was thinking out loud."

Luna sighed. "No problem, I've asked myself the same question. If I can come up with anything else that might help, I'll call you back."

I thanked him again and rang off. As Luna suggested, I googled the Momo image again. The longer I stared at it, the more I realized how profoundly unsettling the image was. It creeped me out—and I'd like to think I'm not nearly as impressionable as a kid, although I'm sure Delinda would disagree.

Now, as a practical matter, finding the missing girls was entirely out of my court. As well-intentioned as I was in agreeing to take the case, my commitment to Ashton came first. I wasn't happy about that, but there was no way I'd be able to spend any meaningful time trying to locate them. Once again, my pelican mouth had overloaded my hummingbird ass.

While I was here in Napa, there was nothing I could do except hope that either the LAPD MPU would find Anna and Michalena—or that the girls would give up their wild goose chase and return home. In any event, it was an unsatisfying feeling—to say the least.

I put my phone down and stared out the picture window of my cottage onto the resort's lawns and gardens. With nightfall, the grounds were tastefully illuminated by well-placed landscape lighting. I took it all in and tried a few deep breaths hoping it would help me relax. It didn't. I was still wound up tighter than a musical snow globe at Christmas time.

I absentmindedly rubbed the scar on my cheek, reflecting on what Ashton had told me. I don't need any more convincing that Delinda and I are bound together, especially considering my experiences over the last few months. And I knew better than to dismiss his claim that I had some kind of magical power. As far as I'm aware, however, the only magic trick I know is how to make money disappear.

My prior brushes with the supernatural have made me far less skeptical than I would have been otherwise. But if I had any real magical talent, I certainly didn't know what it was. Just for the hell of it, I tried directing my will at my overnight bag, commanding it to rise off the day couch, but it didn't budge. Big surprise.

Suddenly, my phone started buzzing, startling me out of my unsavory reverie. Saved by the bell. It was Al.

"How 'bout something to eat?" he asked.

"Sounds good," I replied, both thankful for the distraction and the reminder I hadn't eaten since breakfast. "I'll meet you out in front in ten minutes."

In the hopes that things might be clearer after I had some food in me, I grabbed a windbreaker and stepped outside into the fresh nighttime air. We wouldn't have to venture very far to eat. Earlier, when we had driven through town, I had seen restaurant after restaurant lining the main thoroughfare next to our resort.

It was a pleasant stroll to the edge of the property, where I waited out on the sidewalk until I saw Al emerge from the grounds. I called out to him as he approached.

"Let me guess... Delinda isn't coming. Probably said she's not hungry."

Al shook his head. "She's out to dinner with Kaffee, remember?"

"Oh yeah," I replied. "Forgot all about her date with 'Charming Richard.'"

For a scant second, Al looked like he was going to say something about my comment. Instead, he held off, probably because he decided I didn't want to hear anything more on the subject—a good call on his part. Wisely, he chose to steer our conversation directly to the matter at hand, which was getting us fed. After a short discussion, we settled on the nearest restaurant, Cafe Moderne, directly across the street.

The place appeared small, but if the menu prices posted out front were any indication, it was very upscale. Even so, when you're on someone else's expense account, details like those are of little import. As we entered, I saw that most of the tables were occupied. Nevertheless, they seated us after only a few minutes in another area farther inside the restaurant I hadn't noticed.

"This place is bigger than it looks from the outside," I commented as we settled in.

"What are you having?" asked Al, perusing the menu.

The menu was only a single page and printed daily, according to the pronouncement at the top.

"I think I'll go for a rack of lamb," I replied. "Seeing it's the only thing on here I can pronounce without embarrassing myself."

"I'll have the coq au vin," Al announced. "Chicken cooked with wine, just in case you were wondering."

"I wasn't. I'm not entirely without class," I said.

Al was polite enough not to argue the point. I waited until after the waiter left with our order before I asked Al if he had ever heard of 'Momo.' He gave me a puzzled look and asked if it was something on the menu.

I lapsed into a brief explanation, hitting all the main points. Al didn't laugh or dismiss any of what I told him.

He said, "Half bird, half-woman? We had a few of those back in the day… The Harpies."

"Yeah," I nodded. "I've heard about those… From Greek mythology."

Al chuckled. "They weren't just a made-up myth… Take my word on it. Those creatures were real enough, with enough magic in 'em to live as long as I have. Could be one of 'em figured out how to get on the internet. Once they set their sights on something, they never let go of it. They weren't referred to as the 'Hounds of Zeus' for nothing."

I looked closely at Al, trying to see if he was joking or not. His expression gave nothing away.

I had to ask, "Come on… Are you serious?"

He sighed impatiently. "Of course, I am. With all the crap that happens in this modern world, why would that surprise you?"

Al was right. I already knew that cursed objects could be repurposed as EMT generators, so more unthinkable possibilities might be just as likely.

"I guess I shouldn't be," I conceded. "Anyway, it's an academic question at this point. It's not my case anymore."

Al nodded thoughtfully. "Well, then let's return to the problem at hand. Got any ideas why Derek was murdered?"

"Maybe Momo did it," I joked.

"I was hoping for more than that," he replied good-naturedly.

"Well, I can come up with a few reasons," I said. "But it's all conjecture... However, let's start with the possibility that Taskert is looking to tank his own winery on purpose. Perhaps Derek found out about it and was blackmailing him. Or what if Derek was fooling around with somebody's wife or girlfriend? Either would be enough motive for murder. But, none of those ring true, for a very simple reason."

Al considered for a moment. "Because of the manner of his death?"

"Exactly," I said, tearing apart a dinner roll. "Why not just shoot the guy? Or make him disappear?"

"Certainly a lot easier," Al agreed. "So why the elaborate staging?"

"It was to send a message," I ventured. "Or a warning."

"To who?"

"To us. I mean, what other explanation is there?"

"Dark forces?" said Al, reaching for a small baguette.

I knew he was yanking my chain, but I still passed him the butter. At the moment, our only danger was running out of dinner rolls. The food was taking a long time coming.

"Ha, ha," I jibed. "Let's leave the supernatural explanations behind for the moment. Consider what the cops are making out of all this. Their most likely suspects are Taskert, his wife, Lissette, and Clement... Not including us."

"So, if you think one of them killed Derek, how did they manage it? Everyone seems to have an alibi."

I shrugged and laughed. "So they say. Which leaves what? Dark forces?"

"I see you're not ruling anything out."

"It was a joke, Al."

He cracked a smile. "And here I thought you were keeping an open mind. Also, by the way, I spoke with Ashton before I called you about dinner. As you might have expected, he wants us to keep poking around—regardless of the current circumstances. Also, the fake offer I made to Kaffee yielded some surprising results... Ashton got a call from Kaffee's attorney late this afternoon."

"Uh-oh," I interjected. "About taking up your bogus offer?"

Al's smile got bigger. "Not quite… Kaffee still wants to buy Ashton out."

"What? Are you joking?"

Still smiling, Al nodded. "No, I'm serious. Ashton said they raised the amount they initially offered him."

"I suppose that makes as much sense as anything else so far. So, what did Ashton say? Did he agree to sell, or did he turn the offer down?"

"Neither," replied Al. "He only told them he'd take it under consideration. So, in light of that, shouldn't we add Kaffee's name to our suspect list?"

I thought about it before I answered. "He was never off mine. Although, I'm not sure how Derek's death would have helped him take control of Taskert's winery."

"Make's it more complicated if you want my opinion," Al replied. "Besides, we know Kaffee was showing Delinda around at his winery around the time Derek was killed."

"Yeah, but where was Mr. Muscle? For all we know, he could have been the one who shot out our tires… After he offed Derek."

"Fair point," Al said just as our dinner arrived. "And he looked strong enough to hoist Derek up a tall ladder."

"Especially if you agree with what I said earlier… That Derek was dead before he was strung up on the chandelier."

"Yep," said Al. "I don't see it any other way."

The waiter appeared to ignore our morbid discussion as he set the plates down, but I reminded myself this was a small town, and I needed to exercise more care as to who might overhear us.

Now, we directed our attention to our food. In between mouthfuls, our conversation turned to the quality of the fare. I was famished, which might have colored my judgment, but the food was excellent and well worth the extravagant prices. Especially since I wasn't paying for it. It's worth mentioning that as a guy who lives off Mrs.

Krenzman's day-old deli sandwiches, anything warm and easy to chew qualifies as a gourmet experience.

After we polished off dessert, Al paid the check with an AC&C company credit card. I was a tad disappointed since that meant I couldn't put it on my expense account and bill it with a markup. Next time, I thought.

The waiter had just returned with the receipt when my phone rang. There was no contact information displayed on the mobile's screen, but I answered it anyway. You never know, maybe I won a free Las Vegas vacation. I'm used to disappointment, so it wasn't unsettling to find it was Carlos Garcia, Anna's dad, and criminal badass.

"Hey, Tonnick, you're fired," Carlos said the moment I picked up. There was no trace of anger in his voice, which, if you're talking to a big-time gang honcho, is a good sign.

"Did the cops find Anna and Michalena?" I ventured, jumping to what I hoped was the obvious conclusion.

"Sí... They found them in Oakland. They had Anna call me to say they're okay. The social worker said they're sending her and Michalena home tomorrow."

I was struck by the coincidence of their nearby location, but I was so glad to be off the hook I didn't give it a second thought.

"Great news," I replied. "I'm relieved to hear they're safe." Getting fired from this job was the best thing that had happened to me all day.

"Yeah, so thanks for nothing... But you can keep the C-note."

"I'm happy to return it," I said. "I'm just glad it worked out."

"Muy bueno," he said before breaking off the call.

Al, who had been watching me during the phone conversation, asked, "Working another case?"

"Not anymore. The Momo thing worked itself out on its own. I agreed to take it on only because I figured things here would sort themselves out quickly. Boy, was I wrong."

"Wouldn't be the first time," Al quipped.

"And probably not the last," I retorted, smiling at the truth.

We left the restaurant and walked back to the resort. There, both of us went in separate directions as our cottages were on opposite ends of the grounds. I had just entered my room when my phone rang again. I hoped it was Delinda, but it wasn't—the number was one I didn't recognize. Still holding out hope for that free Vegas getaway, I answered anyway.

"This is Mark."

"Mark," said a female voice in an accent I recognized immediately. "This is Lissette…"

That was a surprise.

I asked, "Are you all right?"

"As well as can be expected under the circumstances. Do you have time to talk?"

"What about?" I asked.

"I think it's best I tell you in person…"

"Do you want to meet tomorrow at the winery?"

There was a pause before she replied. "If y' donna mind, I'd prefer to come t' you… Alone. Where are you stayin'?"

"The Napa Hideaway," I glanced at the envelope with my keycard. "I'm in 'Chalet Primativo.'"

"I'll be there in twenty minutes."

CHAPTER FOURTEEN

A HALF-HOUR LATER, there was a soft knock on my door. When I opened it, Lissette O'Hannon was standing there. She had changed into blue jeans and a thin white blouse, which, although not quite see-through, pointedly revealed she wasn't wearing a bra. Pun intended.

"Can I come in?"

"Please," I smiled, closing the door behind her.

I motioned to the two linen accent chairs facing the fireplace.

"Have a seat."

"Today was horrible," She groaned, slipping off her sandals.

She sat down in the chair with her legs folded underneath her. Her soft, red hair moved gently as she shook her head to emphasize her words.

"I don't know what I'm goin' t' do… 'Cause with Derek's death, it doesn't look like the winery is ere going t' open, and my shares 'll be worthless."

I didn't reply. Call me cynical, but I wondered what her angle was—don't get me wrong, I liked what I was looking at—and, it's not every day a beautiful woman insists on dropping by my hotel room. Plus, I was sensing from the way she was dressed and her general demeanor that she had something else on her mind besides merely complaining. So, while a little voice inside my head was saying, "Don't look a gift horse in the mouth," something was disquieting about the way she was staring at me.

"That's an interesting scar," she said, clearly aware of my notice. "Duya mind if I ask how ya got it?"

My voice tightened despite my attempt at a casual reply. "It's a souvenir from my tour in Iraq. I have other scars from those days, but only that one's visible."

"I'm sorry," she said, "I didna mean t' pry."

"That's okay," I replied, "I didn't mean to be so touchy."

She looked away and wrapped her arms around her chest, pushing up her ample cleavage, emphasized by her minimally buttoned blouse.

"I'm sure Phil and Iris wouldn't approve of what I'm about t' tell you…"

"What's that?" I asked, although admittedly, my mind wasn't purely on what she was going to say.

"It's about the castle. Y' see, the ruins o' Tenhelm Castle has been part of my family's estate for several generations."

"Yes," I remarked, "Taskert mentioned he acquired the castle from you."

She nodded. "I met Phil and Iris accidentally when they got lost driving 'round the Irish countryside. They ended up at my farm during a downpour. Long story short, while they were waiting out the rain, we got t' talking. That's when Phil learned there were a few stones left from a medieval castle on my property. He thought a castle theme would be a grand thing for the winery he and Iris were planning t' build in here in the States.

"I warned him about the awful reputation the ruins had, but he dismissed it completely." She paused for a moment before she added, "The only reason I considered selling was 'cause I needed the money… And, Phil offered me a small interest in the winery, plus a visa an' the position of hospitality manager. In truth, I had na choice. 'Fore the Taskerts walked into my life, I was about t' lose the whole estate t' back taxes."

I nodded to convey my understanding. "So, earlier today, when you said there was a curse on the castle, were you were serious?"

Lissette's expression darkened, and her eyes drilled into mine.

"Truly. My grandfather acquired the lands, including what was left o' the castle right after the war. He ran several upscale hotels and restaurants in England 'fore he came t' Ireland, an' had done well for himself. O' course he knew very little about the history o' the area and t'was only after he bought the place that he heard the rumors…"

Her voice grew softer as she continued. "Stories 'bout mysterious deaths over the years, which, according t' local legend, all had one thing in common… Strangulation… Or decapitation. All involving chains o' one sort or another"

"You mean, like Derek's death," I noted. "But what about the construction accidents Taskert spoke of this afternoon? Do you believe they were related?"

She drew a deep breath. "Aye, them too. There was an accident on the first day o' construction. They were placing the castle cornerstones Phil had shipped o'er from Ireland. The crane was lowering one of 'em into place when the chain holdin' it snapped. A long piece o' the broken chain flew off and killed the worker puttin' it into place. It hit 'em so hard it almost took his head off. T'was horrible!"

"Were there other accidents?" I prodded.

"Aye," she said hesitantly. "A worker driving a forklift loaded with construction materials wasn't watching where he was going. The man drove right into one of the excavation barriers." She paused before adding, "A chain barrier."

"Could be a coincidence," I ventured. "Accidents happen all the time during construction."

Lissette stiffened. "Nah, for sure, it's much more than coincidence!" she said forcefully. "Back in Ireland, when I was growin' up, my parents had strict rules 'bout never going near the old ruins. But, 'round the time I was ten, there was a boy my age, name o' Brendan. One afternoon, he dared me t' follow him there. I was terrified, but I still snuck off with him up into the meadows… O'er t' the place where the old castle used t' stand. I was afraid t' get close to it, but Brendan laughed, an' threw rocks at the ruins, making fun o' me for bein' afraid."

She shuddered visibly at the memory. "But I got more frightened with every passin' minute and ran away, leaving him up there alone.

The very next morning, I heard somethin' terrible had happened. Brendon was dead… Killed inna freak accident… Or so they said."

She paused to make sure she had my full attention before she got to the punchline. "They found him caught up an' strangled in the chain o' his bicycle."

"Is that even possible?" I asked, trying to imagine such a thing.

"That's what folks said," Lissette confirmed. "After that, I never dared t' go there again. Weeks later, Brandon's mother ventured out t' the ruins… She fancied herself t' be a druid-witch, an' brought sage to burn, an' holy water t' sprinkle o'er the castle stones t' rest her son's spirit. On her way back home, she got tangled up in a bunch 'a wire fencing. Supposedly she tried t' struggle free of it, an' it cut right through her neck."

I said nothing as I was busy arguing with myself about adding cursed castle stones to the list of stuff I'd rather not think about. That list was already long enough.

Lissette sighed in frustration. "Ya donna believe me, do ya?"

I kept my expression neutral as I answered. "Did Taskert? I assume you told him about the curse."

"T' be sure, I did… But he dinna believe me. Joked 'bout the legend would be good for business, an' that the tourists would lap it up. But that was before the accidents."

I nodded while my brain was busy multitasking, weighing equal parts of lust and curses.

There was a bit of satisfaction in her voice as she added, "I'm not sure what he thinks now that it's all come home t' roost."

Why is it that women always like it when they're right?

I said, "So, you're convinced the curse had something to do with Derek's death?"

"And the construction accidents!" she insisted, getting to her feet. "All came along with the stones o' the castle! And, I wouldn't wonder that's the reason all the wine gets spoilt too."

"What about other strange events?" I asked. "You know, like unexplained sightings…"

"Like ghosts an' such?" she replied, eyeing me askance. "Naw, I haven't seen nothin' like that, although we had some staff early on that weren't comfortable staying there after dark."

She swept a wisp of red hair from her forehead and sat back down.

"There I go, riling myself up," she smiled apologetically. "I really need t' calm down… I could use a glass o' the wine I brought. Would you like t' join me?"

She reached inside her bag on the floor beside her and pulled out a bottle. She got out of her chair and brought it over to me so I could examine it—and her—more closely.

"It's really very nice," she murmured.

Before I could reply, Lissette produced a small wine opener and used it to expertly peel away the foil and extract the cork.

"This is a Romberg Reserve Merlot," she announced, pointing at the two stemmed wine glasses the resort thoughtfully provided on the fireplace mantle behind me.

I took one and handed her the other.

"I promise that you'll enjoy this," she said, pouring a generous portion into each of our glasses.

After we clinked them together in a wordless toast, I took a sip. She was right about the wine. I thought it tasted much better than anything I had sampled this afternoon at Kaff Cellars.

Lissette gave me another warm smile. "I guess you'll be goin' home now?"

"No," I replied. "My client still wants us to look into what's going on with the winery."

I waited for a reaction, but there was none.

"I hope you're not disappointed," I said, returning her smile.

"O' course not," Lissette said as she topped off my glass.

Somehow, I wasn't convinced.

"Especially if ya tell me whatever ya find out," she said, moving closer. Then, more seductively, she added, "Canna see your gun?"

Hoping it was a metaphor, I answered, "Those things are dangerous."

"I know," she murmured.

The next thing I knew, she was sitting on my lap, crushing my erection —but I didn't complain. As her face drew nearer to mine, the scar on my cheek began to itch and then burn—as though someone had pressed a hot match to it. Lissette's eyes were closed as her lips sought mine. Choosing to ignore the pain in both my crotch and my face, I did the same. Suddenly, at the moment our lips met, her wine glass exploded with a loud crack.

"Jesus!" she screamed, leaping back, still holding the intact stem in her hand.

We were both covered in wine and pieces of glass.

"Are you hurt?" I asked, even though I could see she wasn't. The burning sensation in my cheek had stopped and unhappily, along with the glass, the mood had also shattered.

"No, I donna think so," she replied, as she put the stem on the mantle and glanced from her undamaged hand to her wine splattered clothes.

"I don't know what happened," I said lamely. Oddly, most of the wine had ended up on Lissette's white blouse, which now clung tightly to her ample bosom.

"Canna use your restroom to clean up?"

"Please do," I insisted, still harboring hope for the original outcome I had anticipated.

I was almost finished cleaning up the glass when she emerged from the bathroom. Sadly, she was fully clothed.

"I should be goin'," she announced as she snatched up her sandals and bag.

Without another word, she tore out the door almost forgetting to shut it behind her.

All I could do was sit there, wondering about the strange train of events that had derailed what could have been a gloriously lustful encounter—even if it amounted to revenge sex. Anyway, there was no question the entire incident was connected to the sudden pain from my scar. I couldn't help but wonder if Delinda might have had something to do with that after all.

As I stood there, pondering the unsettling ramifications of that supposition, there came several loud knocks at my cottage door. Ever the optimist, I thought Lissette might have decided to return.

No such luck. When I swung the door open, it wasn't Lissette standing there—it was Al. I knew immediately something was wrong.

"Delinda just called me," he began breathlessly. "She's at the hospital. Someone just tried to kill Richard Kaffee."

CHAPTER FIFTEEN

Napa Valley, California. 1867

HENRY WALKER WATKINS WOKE up with a start to discover he was covered with sweat. He tried to sit up in bed, but he was so weak it was almost impossible. Finally, with a tremendous amount of effort, he levered himself up on his elbows. His dream had been remarkably intense. And although he could remember only parts and pieces of it, portions remained vividly etched in his memory. It was ironic that those were the bits he wished to forget.

Even during those few snatches of dream state that coursed through his consciousness, Henry was fitfully aware that for the first time since adolescence, he experienced a wet dream. The pictures in his mind remained hazy, but he vaguely recalled having sex with two women who reminded him of the Harper sisters—except they couldn't have been.

In his nightmare, they were beautiful and young as they writhed and undulated against his body, awakening his desire. Their lips and soft breasts caressed every inch of him until he became aroused beyond his wildest imaginings. First one, then the other slid up and down over his erect manhood until he climaxed inside each of them.

More indistinct was his blurry realization that below both of his paramour's perfectly formed genitalia, any resemblance to the human form vanished. Their scaly legs were thin and birdlike with avian talons where their feet should have been. And strikingly, besides the arms that held him fast during the act of procreation, soft, leathery wings had encircled his body.

The memories were all too much for him to process, exhausted as he was. Henry fell back onto the bed, and despite the warm night air, he shuddered involuntarily before his fatigue dragged him back into an exhausted slumber.

Just before dawn, Henry awakened to shouting and gunfire. Struggling out of bed and over to the bedroom window, he peered outside. Miles Russell and his men had returned with a vengeance. He saw the sisters, fuming with anger in their wheelchairs, on one side of the front porch. Although helpless, they were guarded by a gunman who kept his pistol pointed in their direction. While he couldn't see the rest of the marauders, he assumed from the muffled screams and faraway gunfire they were chasing the workers out of the fields and into the wine caves.

Henry grabbed his cane and stumbled outside, snatching up the sister's double-barreled shotgun on the way. He made it as far as the front porch before the man watching over the sisters shot him three times. The shooter expected the sisters to scream in fear, but instead, they began muttering in a tongue the man never heard before.

Henry's killer, barely in his seventeenth year, fell to his knees as though a heavy weight had been dropped onto his shoulders. Then, without even realizing what he was doing, the assassin raised his pistol up under his chin and pulled the trigger.

The sisters ignored the explosion of the bullet and the ensuing rain of gore and bits of splintered skull as they hurriedly rolled their wheelchairs to Henry's side.

Even as he clung to life—teetering on the thin divide between this world and the next, Henry remained utterly obsessed with the welfare of the winery.

"They're killing our workers," he began in a voice little more than a thin wheeze. "Who will harvest the grapes?" His collapsing lung made it challenging to speak, but he was still able to complete his thought before he died. "Who will make the wine?"

"He's right," Rosalee said as Henry drew his last breath. "There'll be no one left."

"First things, first," hissed Merrilee, her eyes glittering with hate. "First things, first."

CHAPTER SIXTEEN

Napa Valley. Present Day

SINCE DELINDA STILL HAD the keys to our rental, Al and I called for a ride-share to take us to the hospital in Yountville. While we were waiting for the driver to show up, I pressed Al for more answers.

"Do you have any details?" I began. "Was Kaffee shot?"

Al slowly shook his head. "Don't know. She called to say she was following the ambulance from Kaffee's house to the hospital... And for us to meet her there."

"She went to Kaffee's house after dinner?" It took an effort to keep my voice from pitching up with every word. "What happened? Were they making out on the couch at the time?"

Al shot me an angry look. "Come on, Mark. Don't be a child."

"Sorry, Al," I said. "You're right. That was totally out of line."

Was my guilty conscience rearing its ugly head?

My phone vibrated, announcing the car's arrival. Twenty minutes later, the driver dropped us off in front of the hospital. Delinda was waiting for us in the main lobby. As we walked in, she rose from her chair to greet us. As usual, her expression didn't reveal much.

"He's in surgery now, but I'm sure he'll be all right," she announced as we rushed up.

"Are you okay?" I asked.

"Why wouldn't I be?" she countered.

Typical.

"How did it happen?" said Al right away.

I was sure he jumped into the conversation quickly so I wouldn't have the opportunity to start another argument with Delinda.

"After we left the restaurant, Kaffee's driver took us directly over to his place," she began. "He said he needed to get some wine from his house for the auction and asked me in. His intentions were obvious, so I politely said I'd wait in the car. He insisted, and I refused again. Since he wouldn't take no for an answer, I made sure he had a sudden urge to drive me home."

"Shocking," I interjected, although her statement made me reflect that she never resorted to magic to thwart any of my advances—or did she?

Ignoring my interruption, she continued. "Then, he ran into the house and came back out with a wine-carrier. He asked me to step out of the car for a moment so he could put the wine into the back seat. The moment I stepped out, there was a gunshot, and he fell to the ground."

"Any ideas why Kaffee was shot?" Al asked.

Delinda paused before she replied. "He wasn't the target… I was."

That got my full attention. "What! Are you saying the shooter missed?"

"He didn't," she replied flatly. "Kaffee was standing behind me."

Her inference was clear.

"Did you see who took the shot?" I asked, making a point not to acknowledge her unspoken assertion that the slug had passed harmlessly through her and into Kaffee.

"No. Whoever it was fired from behind a shed on the property. I didn't have a chance to even catch a glimpse... Besides, I was busy staunching Kaffee's wound. I had to move fast, or he might have bled out."

That surprised me, as I assumed she could have used her magic to heal him. She must have read my expression.

"You are the only one I can heal… Within limits," she said quietly, looking me straight in the eye before she added sadly, "No one else."

Perhaps it was the twinge of regret I heard in her voice that led me to conclude that was only the result of the pottery shards in my cheek rather than any special concern for me on her part. Although it occurred to me she wasn't referring to Kaffee. If so, that was a question for another time.

Al picked up where I left off. "Delinda, are you confident that bullet was meant for you?"

"One hundred percent," she confirmed.

"That clinches it," I said, snapping out of my momentary funk. "Somebody really doesn't want us here, which leads me to wonder if the shooter was the same guy who took out our tire on the road."

Delinda nodded. "That would be my assumption, too."

"Then, chances are they might come back for another try," I said slowly.

In a visceral reaction, my entire body had tensed up with anger, and my jaw was clenched as tightly as my fists were. Some asshole had tried to murder a person I cared about. Even if killing a genie was impossible, I wasn't about to let that go unanswered.

Not surprisingly, Delinda sensed my growing rage.

"Let it go, Mark. They can't hurt me... But they *can* hurt you and Al."

She was right, of course, but I was still pissed off.

I asked, "What about the cops? Where are they on this?"

"The police were already here. I told them everything I could, but naturally, they assumed Kaffee was the intended victim. They'll be back to question him as soon as he's out of recovery."

It was a struggle for me to process everything Delinda had said without letting my emotions distract me. I closed my eyes and took a deep breath. When I opened them, Delinda was regarding me strangely.

"I'm fine," I volunteered. "Just centering myself enough to ask the right questions.

"Like what?" she replied.

"Like, while you were at dinner with Kaffee, did he seem worried? Upset? Afraid?"

She shook her head slightly. "Actually, I would say he seemed to be in a good mood… which looking back on it, strikes me as odd, seeing his winemaker was just murdered."

"That *is* weird," I agreed. "You'd think he'd be upset about that."

"Yep," concurred Al. "At the very least, he might have mentioned it."

"No, he never did," said Delinda. "But he probably didn't want undercut the romantic mood he was trying to set," she added with a wry smile.

I dismissed her last remark as the detective part of my brain was entirely focused on drawing conclusions from her factual account.

"I'm beginning to think," I began, "that someone is afraid we're going to find more than just crappy wine."

"Yep, it sure looks that way," agreed Al. "But what's worth killing over?"

"Money," I replied. "It's always about money. But at least we can eliminate Lissette. She couldn't have been the shooter, she was with me."

"What?" Delinda said, frowning.

Only rarely had I ever seen such a surprised expression on her face.

I nodded. "She left my room only minutes before Al came to tell me Kaffee had been shot."

Delinda was still staring at me. "She came to your room?"

"She did," I replied cooly. "And she brought wine."

Of course, I didn't volunteer that she left wearing most of it.

I saw Al was suppressing a smile. "Sounds like a good time was had by all."

"Not really," I blurted.

"I'm sure she didn't stay long," stated Delinda with a great deal of certainty.

Now it was my turn to be surprised. Then it hit me. "Hey, did you have something to do with that?"

"No, how would I?" she protested.

"Well, first my scar began itching, you know… As it always does when you do your thing… And then it started to burn!"

"Your scar was burning? Are you sure?"

"Positive, it hurt like hell… It never did that before."

Delinda's expression grew more serious. "It was a warning. What took place next?"

If there's one thing I know, it's never lie to a genie, but I neglected to explain all of the circumstances leading up to the wine glass exploding in Lissette's hand.

Suddenly, it occured to me. "Was that your doing?"

It looked to me like she was stifling a laugh when she answered, "I had nothing to do with that. If it was anyone's magic, it was yours."

"Mine?" I said incredulously. "You've got to be kidding."

"I'm not. Obviously, it was warning you… Protecting you," she insisted. "You should take that seriously."

"Are you jealous?" I asked, trying not to smirk.

"No, merely concerned for your safety," she demurred, successfully sounding disinterested.

I was about to dispute that, but the look in her eyes discouraged me from pressing her further.

Instead, I only asked, "Then, what kind of danger do you think she poses to me?"

"I don't know, but what you've described is very troubling," she replied ominously.

"Could have just been crappy glassware," I said half-jokingly.

Al wagged a finger at me and said, "Remember Palm Springs?"

I did. It was a night I'd never forget.

"Come on, Al. You're not suggesting that Lissette might be possessed?"

Al shrugged. "It's one possibility."

I reflected on her come hither expressions, ample breasts, and promising lips. If she was possessed, it was one hell of a friendly ghost.

"I don't think so," I said confidently.

Delinda cheerfully demolished my reverie. "So before she ran away screaming from you... Did you learn anything useful?"

"She didn't run away screaming," I countered. "But I did find out a couple of interesting facts. According to her, she met Phil and Iris when they were vacationing in Ireland. The castle ruins were on her family estate, and the Taskerts ended up buying them from her, despite her warning that the ruins had a reputation for unexplained deaths. Lissette also mentioned she has a small interest in the winery."

"Okay. That's interesting," Delinda said. "Anything else?"

I cocked my head and said, "Other than she wanted to seduce me?"

Delinda gave me the eyebrow arch. "Don't be stupid. She probably wanted you to tell her what we were up to."

"That crossed my mind, but I had no intention of stopping her," I grinned.

Delinda didn't reply. Al glanced at her and then at me, wondering when the fireworks would start. A few visitors traversed the lobby during the next few minutes as we all sat silently. I'm sure Al appreciated the momentary lull.

Finally, I spoke up. "Okay. Where are we so far? Other than curses, spirit appearances, and rumors of mysterious deaths, do we have anything more... Ordinary?"

"Yes," Delinda replied. "After a few glasses of wine at dinner, Kaffee mentioned more about the wine auction business he and Taskert are involved in. He alluded that the auctions generate sizable amounts of cash on a regular basis."

"And you were going to mention this, when?" I said contentiously.

"I was about to when you started blabbing about your romantic escapades," she retorted.

"Hey, knock it off, you two," Al admonished. "Let's stick to business, shall we?"

Thankful for Al's intervention, I took a breath and calmly asked, "How much money are we talking about?"

Delinda also took it down a notch. "Kaffee bragged about the value of the wine they planned to auction this week. He and Taskert intended to present several bottles that would sell for nearly half a million dollars apiece."

"People have been murdered for a lot less than that," I said. "Is it possible you're mistaken about being targeted? Maybe it was about heisting the wine."

"It wasn't about the wine," Delinda said sharply. "After the shot was fired, no one ran over to snatch it."

I cleared my throat, hesitant to bring up the obvious question. "But if you were the target, why didn't they take another shot?"

She replied with a slight shrug with her shoulders. "I suspect they were surprised when Kaffee went down instead of me. That's the only reason I can think of. Believe me, if they had shown themselves…" Her voice trailed off.

She didn't need to finish her thought. I squelched a smile trying to decide whether she'd turn the shooter into a toad or a pig.

"Makes sense," I agreed. "But I have to ask… Do you suspect Kaffee set you up?"

"I'm not sure," replied Delinda. "It's possible. He did insist on having me leave the car."

"Hardly a coincidence," I remarked. "So, what type of exposure does he risk if we continue our investigation of Taskert's winery?"

"If you take into account all of his financial interests, the possibilities are nearly endless," Al said thoughtfully.

He was right.

"There's an obvious way Kaffee might benefit from our absence," I offered. "The contamination problem would remain unsolved…"

Delinda interrupted, completing my sentence. "And, Taskert's winery would be worth far less."

"Yup," Al agreed. "And in that case, it could make it that much easier to buy Ashton out… At an even lower price."

At that moment, something else occurred to me. "Al, did Ashton mention when Kaffee's attorney offered him the buyout?"

"No, he didn't…. Why?"

"Because it confuses the issue even further," I said.

"How so?" Delinda asked.

I replied, "If, according to Al, Ashton was in the midst of taking Kaffee's offer under consideration, why use such a heavy hand?"

"You mean, like putting a bullet into me," said Delinda.

I nodded, "Exactly. You would think he'd wait until Ashton came to a decision… One way or another before acting."

"So, if that's the case, it might rule out Kaffee altogether," Al stated.

"Which brings us right back to where we started," I said. "No obvious suspects and no obvious motive."

"So, where do we go from here?" asked Delinda.

"Not sure," I replied. "But before we leap to any more conclusions, we should re-examine our list of suspects."

"Like darling Lissette?" Delinda pointedly prodded.

Before I could respond, she stood and walked over to the lobby desk. After a brief word with the woman on duty, she returned to her seat.

"Like I thought. He's in recovery. The injury wasn't that serious after all," she said.

"I'm surprised they told you that… HIPPA rules and all," I observed.

Delinda smiled brightly. "Why would you be surprised?"

Before I could think of a suitable comeback, Mr. Muscle, the bouncer we had seen at Kaff Cellars earlier in the day, burst into the hospital lobby through the double glass doors.

"What happened!" he roared as he walked up to us. The attendant at the lobby desk scowled intensely at his loud and abrupt entrance.

"He was shot," I replied. "Weren't you supposed to be protecting him?"

"He didn't want me around for his hot date," he said, lowering his voice and frowning at Delinda. "Sounds like it almost got him killed!"

Delinda didn't react to his thinly veiled accusation.

Addressing him more politely than he deserved, she said, "He'll be okay… And, even if you were there, there was nothing you could have done. It was an ambush."

"If you were with him," the guy scowled. "How is it you don't have a scratch on you?"

"Plainly, they weren't aiming at me," she replied emphatically.

Mr. Muscle didn't respond, but I could see the involuntary twitch beneath his left eye. A moment later, he stormed past us to the information desk.

"Interesting reaction," Delinda observed.

"It was," I agreed. "What now?"

"Let's go," Al suggested. "It's late, and I think we've had more than enough excitement for one day."

"You won't hear me argue," I said. "Tomorrow, we need to ask Taskert for more detail about his business relationship with Kaffee."

Al nodded. "Is it just me, or don't you find it interesting that neither one of the Taskerts made an appearance tonight to see how Kaffee's doing?"

"They might have called," Delinda ventured. "We'll find out in the morning. And, speaking of conversations, I'd like to have one with Ms. O'Hannon as well."

I couldn't wait to see what that would be like.

"After a late breakfast, right?" I asked hopefully.

Nobody replied.

CHAPTER SEVENTEEN

THE HOLDING ROOM IN the Oakland Children's Services Building was kept intentionally sparse. Resembling a prison cell more than a detention area, the grimy, institutional green walls were absent of any decoration. The stainless steel sink and toilet were behind a flimsy privacy panel, and the only furnishings were the cots the two girls had spent the night on.

Anna got up from her bunk and kicked at it in disgust.

"We've got to get out of here! I'm not going to let anything stop us!" she insisted. "We're too close."

The CS Building in Oakland was never designed to be anything more than a temporary holding facility. It was built initially to accommodate young children, but over time it had been hardened to prevent damage or vandalism from those who were older than their years and prone to violence. Still, the mission remained to house children safely for a minimum amount of time until they could be reunited with family or placed with foster parents.

The reality was a much different story. So far, Michalena and Anna had spent nearly eighteen hours in the locked room after being brought in the night before.

"Last night, they said we'd be on a bus for home in an hour," Anna said. "That was total bullshit! If we don't get out soon, we might be stuck forever!"

Michalena sighed loudly. "How? The door is locked... And even if we get out, they'll just find us again!"

"Come on, we can't just do nothing... Remember what we promised Gia," Anna chided, giving her friend a stern look. "There's no way her death will go unpunished.... We're going to take the bruja down!"

"What if she's not there? What if we got it wrong?" fretted Michalena.

Anna's features grew hard. She had more of her brother in her than even Carlos realized.

"We didn't get it wrong," Anna objected firmly. "Momo's hiding in the Napa Mountains, and we're going find her and rip her a new one." With a wicked smile she added, "Two new ones!"

Both girls were thoroughly searched when they were processed, but Carlos had taught Anna well. The caseworkers found only what she allowed them to find. They had taken her phone and the few dollars she had left in her purse but hadn't discovered the five, one-hundred-dollar bills Anna had safely stashed in her butt-crack, nor several other items secreted on her body.

"I haven't forgotten our promise," Michalena said. "But how do we escape from this place?"

"This way," Anna declared, pulling two bobby pins from her thick, black hair. "My brother showed me this once."

She bent the first bobby pin in half, and then once again at a right angle before she pushed it into the key slot. Gently, she turned the lock slightly in the direction she expected a key would open it. She unbent the second bobby pin and curved one end of it up before inserting it on top of the one already in the lock.

Carefully, she fished around inside the cylinder, feeling for the first of what she knew would be four or five pins. Once she found it, she used the bobby pin underneath as a fulcrum and levered the pin up. Like the door and the building, the lock mechanism was old and worn. Anna patiently slid the rest of the pins up one at a time. Each success rewarded her with a soft click.

"There... Easy peasy," Anna whispered as the last pin went into place.

"Lemon squeezy," Michalena added softly.

With a muted giggle, Anna pushed open the door and peered outside into the hallway.

"It's clear," she whispered. "I saw a sign pointing to the stairs when they took us off the elevator. We'll go that way!"

Two hours later, when the overworked social worker came up to escort them on their bus ride back to LA, the room was empty. Weary after working a double shift, she could only shake her head in frustration. Now there would be a slew of paperwork she would need to file. Even that would have to wait until after she informed her supervisor—who wouldn't be in for another hour.

At a Seven-Eleven twelve blocks away, Anna purchased a prepaid cell phone for thirty dollars and logged into her brother's Uber account. A few minutes later, the driver arrived to pick up her and Michalena.

"All the way to Napa, ladies?" the driver said brightly as he opened the rear door for the two girls to get in. "You don't look old enough to go wine tasting," he joked.

"We hired you to drive, not to play twenty questions," snapped Anna.

"Okay, okay," said the driver.

The only good news, the driver thought, was that the fare had already been debited. He figured if he kept his mouth shut for the remainder of the trip he might end up with a five-star rating. He had already given up any hope for a tip.

As it turned out, for the entire ride neither he nor the girls engaged in conversation. When he dropped the girls off in Downtown Napa, he only received a terse, "Thanks" as they slammed the car door shut. When he checked his phone some time afterward, he saw the girls had left him no rating and no tip. "Entitled Bitches," he muttered to no one in particular.

CHAPTER EIGHTEEN

Napa Valley, California 1867

ONCE BILL TULLY HEARD the shots, he rushed over to the house and discovered a scene far different from what he imagined. He wasn't surprised to find the old man lying lifeless on the porch, but he was shocked to see that Ryan, the youngest member of the posse, was also dead. While it was unclear to him who shot who, Bill wasn't taking any chances. He kept his revolver trained on the two spinsters who sat next to the body of the old man, glaring at him from their wheelchairs.

He reckoned Miles Russell would want the old ladies dead too—no witnesses meant exactly that. All things considered though, he knew better than to second guess his boss. The smart move was to wait for orders than to incur the ire of Russell's infamous hair-trigger temper.

As the would-be killer pondered these issues, his eyes wandered away from his charges for only a single instant. Since he felt unthreatened by two old women in wheelchairs, he was utterly unprepared for what happened next.

The transformation was nearly instantaneous. Age dropped away from the women's narrow faces in the same moment their heads stretched and elongated, nightmarishly distorting their features. The shawls and blankets covering their shoulders and legs fell away, revealing naked, supple breasts and bird-like talons instead of feet on their thin, scaly legs. The broad, black, leathery wings that sprouted from their muscular shoulders began beating the air faster than the eye could follow.

Stunned by this impossible and unexpected event, Bill dropped his gun at the same time both creatures rose from their wheelchairs. The buffeting rush of air from their powerful wings drove him backward. Tully cowered and turned to run, only to find he couldn't—for his feet were no longer on the ground.

He screamed in horror and surprise at the astonishing swiftness by which he was snatched up in the monster's sharp talons—struggling vainly as they carried him straight up into the sky. Higher and higher, they flew, waiting until the vineyards below receded into tiny checkerboards before releasing their grip.

Bellowing in terror, Bill Tully spent his last moments shrieking and clawing at the air as if seeking an invisible handhold until his heart failed from pure shock. He was dead even before he crashed into the Earth, head first.

A short distance away, Miles Russell and his vigilantes had discovered the hillside entrance to the wine caves and the Coolie's underground hideaway. The opening wasn't large enough to accommodate their horses, so they dismounted and proceeded into the tunnel on foot. Neither dissuaded by this minor inconvenience nor worried about encountering any resistance, they rushed into the darkness. From their past experiences, they knew the Chinese were a passive people, especially in the face of superior numbers and weapons.

Russell and his gang viewed their mission as a holy crusade. They saw themselves as righteous Christian knights purging the land of unclean foreigners who had come to despoil and corrupt their way of life. None harbored any doubt about what had to be done to protect the white, working man's rightful place in California. The Chinese Coolies, and others like them, needed to be excised—akin to cutting the bruise out of an otherwise perfect apple.

The vigilantes made short work of rounding up the workers and their families. Some of the captives had to be beaten to their knees, but most followed the instructions and assumed the face-down position in the dirt. Even when they began hearing the gunfire, none dared to rise, although there was no question of what was happening. Within seconds, every one of their number—men, women, and children—suffered the same violent fate. If there was any consolation, it was only that their deaths were swift.

Russell and his posse left the caves and returned on horseback to the Harper sisters' farmhouse to find it deserted. One of the two men they left behind was gone; the other, young Ryan, lay dead nearby the body of the old man.

"What the fuck!" Russell cursed when he saw Ryan's bloody corpse. Enraged, he ordered his men to stay put as he circled the clapboard house on his horse.

"Bill! Bill! Where the hell are you?" he yelled repeatedly.

He broadened his search but found no sign of Bill Tully or the women. Finally, Russell galloped over to where the rest of his men were waiting impatiently.

"Shit!. Where the fuck did they get off to?" he shouted.

"We gotta find them sisters!" insisted Reg Putter, Russell's second in command.

Like Russell, Reg was an ex-state militiaman and recognized the importance of leaving no witnesses behind. They had done the same thing at Grouse Creek after their regiment massacred two hundred fifty members of the Pomo Tribe.

Reg's only comment at the time was, "A good start."

At Russell's urging, several of the men dismounted and went through the farmhouse—searching every inch before emerging empty-handed.

"Bill wouldn't have just left," said Russell. "Something musta…"

He was interrupted by one of his men yelling furiously. The horror in his voice was unmistakable, even from fifty yards away in the vineyard.

"Boss! Boss! Here quick!"

Russell and the others cantered over to where his man was staring down at the ground. It was Bill Tully, or more correctly, what was left of him. Impossibly, he appeared to have fallen from a tremendous height. There could be no other explanation for why his body had burst open like an overripe melon.

"Mother of God! What happened?" Putter demanded, but no one answered.

Unsurprisingly, none of the onlookers were much discomforted by this gory display. They had seen far worse—much of which they had themselves inflicted. Nevertheless, Russell's confusion was mirrored by the rest.

Several in the group began running their horses down row after row of grapevines, searching for any signs of the missing women. After a long while, they gave up and joined the others, who were busily at work covering up their crimes.

Along with the old man, they dragged Ryan and Tully's bodies inside the house, then set it ablaze. The group remained long enough to ensure the fire did its work. Watching as smoke from the conflagration pushed aside the morning sunlight, turning it as blood-red as the flames that eagerly devoured the clapboard building.

There was no need to deal with the corpses in the tunnels, for none would think to look there. Ignored and reviled in life, the Chinese were —and would remain—invisible, even in death.

While Russell and his men engaged in torching their homestead, the sisters hovered overhead. They flew high enough to stay out of sight from the horsemen below while they observed with eyes far sharper than any human's. Seething with anger, the sisters circled, waiting until the column of mounted men had galloped away. Only then did they alight and venture inside the caves.

"Agapité o Theós!" Rosalee exclaimed, lapsing into Greek as she saw the carnage.

The wanton murders were terrible enough—but when Merrilee found the body of Mei-Ling, she experienced a depth of rage and sadness far beyond any she had known in her unnaturally long life. The sight of the little girl, still holding her favorite doll, the one Merrilee had sewn for her, elicited the unfamiliar sensation of moisture filling her eyes.

Perhaps her extreme reaction was simply a result of remaining in human guise for so long, but as Merrilee kneeled next to Mei-Ling's body, stroking the child's bloody hair, she shed the first tears she could ever remember. Until that very moment, she never knew it was even possible for a harpy to weep.

Over the centuries, she and her sister had witnessed more than their share of death. But this was different—and tore at her heart in unimaginable ways.

"They died like dogs," Merrilee whispered as she stared up at her sister, reluctantly rising from the dead child's side.

"Worse," Rosalee added somberly. "They were slaughtered like cattle."

"The world of men will pay for this!" Merrilee hissed. "We shall make them pay!"

Rosalee nodded in agreement. "Yes, Sister, we will."

CHAPTER NINETEEN

Napa Valley. Present Day

MY PHONE WOKE ME. Usually, it would have interrupted my favorite recurring dream—about making love to Delinda. But, I hadn't dreamed of that since she and I had our parting of the ways. In any event, I supposed it was for the best since the dream always ended the same way—with Delinda dissolving away into wisps of smoke right before the climactic moment. Even so, it was difficult to decide which was the bigger disappointment.

"Yeah," I croaked into the phone. Although my eyes weren't able to focus yet, I recognized what the blurry letters spelled: Unknown number.

"Is this Mark Tonnick?"

I recognized the Southern drawl at once. "Yeah… What time is it?"

"Seven-thirty… It's Clement Wagner. I gotta see you and your team right away."

"Can't it wait?" I asked as I pushed away the down comforter and struggled to an upright sitting position.

"No. It's important… Really important."

I sighed and contemplated my pants, hanging just out of reach. "Okay. Where and when?"

"The winery. As soon as you can."

Clement hung up before I could object, or remind him that, A: He was fired, and B: The winery was a sealed crime scene.

Before I threw on my clothes, I called Al and told him to get dressed. That proved to be unnecessary since he was already up and back from the breakfast buffet in the resort's lobby. I was about to call Delinda when the door of my room flew open, and there she was.

"Hey, I thought it was locked," I said.

"I think you better put on your pants," she said. "The clock's ticking."

"How the hell would you know?" I said, fastening my belt.

"Why wouldn't I?" she said, conveying her low estimation of my cognitive abilities in a single glance.

I wasn't about to belabor the point with her. After all, what good is it being a genie if you can't impress your associates with a few magical entrances?

"If you know what's coming all the time, why didn't you stop the bullet that caught Kaffee?" I jabbed.

She wasn't amused. "I'm not a prophet," she snapped. "Otherwise, I would have."

It was way too early for a wry retort, at least for me. I didn't even get the chance to try, because at that moment, Al popped into the doorway, bright-eyed and impatient to get started.

"What are we waiting for?" he chirped.

I could only glare at the two of them while I groped for my socks and shoes. Five minutes later, we were in our rental heading towards Taskert's winery.

"What do you suppose Clement has to say?" Al asked.

"How about, 'I was the guy who shot out your tire and tried to plug your girlfriend,'" I offered.

"I'm not your girlfriend," Delinda objected.

With that, she sped up the Lexus even more, which in itself was impressive, seeing we were already moving at twice the posted speed limit. I counted it as a triple win for Delinda—driving up my blood pressure, testing the limits of the temporary spare, and arriving at our meeting at near-light speed.

"Okay, then if Clement didn't call to arrange a confession, maybe he has something more to tell us about Derek's murder," I said, tightening my death grip on the door handle.

A moment later, Delinda took the winery turnoff on two wheels and flew into the parking lot. Amazingly, the Lexus slid smoothly to a stop alongside a white Ford pickup truck, at which point I deemed it safe to open my eyes. Clement Wagner was standing there waiting for us. He looked like he hadn't slept since we saw him last.

I resisted the impulse to kiss the ground as I exited the car.

"Hey, what's so important you need to interrupt my beauty sleep?" I called out.

"This," Clement answered, reaching into the cab of his pickup. He pulled out a small laptop from the front seat. "It was Derek's."

"How did you get it?" Delinda asked.

Clement looked away from her as he answered. "We were more than just roommates…" He took a deep breath before continuing in a much softer voice. "We were married, but we kept it secret… I mean, even though folks 'round here consider themselves progressive and such, they're mostly farmers… You know how it is."

None of us replied as he woke the computer and punched a few keys.

"I found a bunch of emails on his laptop last night. Pretty sure he wanted them kept secret, even from me… But I knew his password."

Before he handed me the laptop, he opened up the email program and clicked on the "sent" column. There were three emails all addressed to Phillip Taskert. The subject line on all of them simply read: "I know."

I clicked on the last entry with Al and Delinda looking over my shoulder. The message was brief and to the point. "More $$, D."

"I think Derek was blackmailing Taskert," Clement declared. "That's why Phil killed him!"

"Maybe," I said. "When did you find out about this?"

Clement motioned towards the screen. "Not until I got into the computer. Up 'till then, I thought Derek's strained relationship with Phil was over the wine taint."

"Any idea how much money was involved?" Al asked.

"After I found the emails, I opened his last bank statement. We always kept our finances separate," Clement replied, wiping at his eyes. "Looked to be 'bout five grand every two weeks. That's why I got to goin' through his laptop to begin with. Other than me, he ain't got no family to settle his affairs."

"No relatives?" Al pressed.

"Not really. His folks disowned him after he came out… I was going through his email for contacts when I found those."

"What's this," I asked, pointing at the attachment icon on the final outgoing email to Taskert. It indicated the attachment was a picture.

"I don't know," replied Clement. "I tried to open it, but it needs a password…"

He clicked on it, and a dialog box came up requesting an access code.

"So, any suggestions?" I said, glancing over at Clement.

"Believe me, I tried everything…"

Delinda pointed one of her perfectly manicured nails at the screen.

"Try 'wineisfine,'" she suggested, spelling out the letters. "All lower case."

Clement did, and seconds after he pressed the enter button the unlocked picture filled the screen.

"Show off," I whispered.

Delinda allowed me a slight smile and a wink. I'd never tell her, but I love it when she does that.

"Wow!" exclaimed Clement. "That's crazy impossible."

He wasn't referring to Delinda's cracking the password in one go. Instead, his comment was directed at the photograph we were all staring at. It was a closeup shot of a bottle of wine.

"What's impossible?" I asked.

"That," Clement replied, pointing at the image. "The label says it's a 1945 Romanee Conti! But it can't be!"

"Why is that?" asked Al.

"The last known bottles were sold in 2018," drawled Clement as if that should be completely obvious to us. "Only 600 bottles were produced an' all of them are accounted for."

"Maybe that's one of them," I said. "But, why would Derek send that picture to Taskert?"

"'Cause that's what the blackmail was about!" Clement's voice grew louder. "The Taskerts got stuck with a bottle of counterfeit wine!"

I handed the laptop to Clement. "Are you sure it's a fake?"

"As sure as shit. No way on Earth that's real," he said confidently.

"Is a bottle of wine a motive for blackmail... And murder?" I asked.

"Hell, yes!" Clement exclaimed with an expression that clearly questioned my intellect. "The last two bottles of the '45 sold for nearly a million dollars! Whatever Taskert paid for that bottle, it was at least in the high six figures. He's probably fixin' to auction it at a profit."

"So, if word leaked the wine was fake, the Taskerts would lose a lot of money," Delinda said.

"Not to mention his reputation," added Al. "That's plenty of motive for murder."

"Goddamn it! I knew it! Taskert killed him!" Clement shouted angrily. "At first, I thought it was on 'count of the wine taint, but this here clinches it!"

"That might make sense, but then why kill him so dramatically?" I countered. "As much as I'd like to think Taskert is good for Derek's murder, it just doesn't feel right to me."

"Shit! How much more do you need?" Clement protested, thrusting the open laptop into my face. "It's all right here!"

"Calm down," said Al. "That's just a photo. And the emails aren't hard proof that Derek was blackmailing Taskert. Taskert could plausibly deny all of it."

Clement shook his head in disgust. "But, there's the money..."

"Yeah, Al's right," I interjected. "Taskert would just say the payments were a retainer or an advance on salary. Sorry, but there's no smoking gun here... It's all circumstantial."

"Maybe we should have a look down in Taskert's wine caves," Clement suggested. "I think that's where the picture was taken, and I have a good idea exactly where to start."

"So, what good would that do?" I asked.

"Well, for one thing, once I got up close, I could tell if that bottle of Romanee is real or not. I used to authenticate wine for the auction houses in New York before I came out here."

"How exactly could you tell?" asked Al.

"A couple of things... Like if parts of the label were embossed or not, and the type of printing on the cork. Stuff y'all can't see from the photo."

Delinda looked thoughtful. "What about the wine auctions here in Napa, Do you authenticate for them?"

Clement cleared his throat and appeared uncomfortable as he replied.

"No, Ma'am, I don't. Two years ago, when I first arrived in town, I applied to the brokerage house that runs the auctions out here. Unfortunately, the guy in charge and I have some ancient history between us."

"And," I prompted, "what would that be?"

"He used to work for the same auction house in New York as I did. He got me fired..." Clement cleared his throat again. "Supposedly, I missed a counterfeit bottle of Bordeaux."

Delinda gave him a probing stare. "Supposedly?"

"Well, here's the thing... I swear the bottle in question wasn't the one I inspected. But, the client who brought it back was a well-known collector. He also had purchased a whole lot of wine that year already. They weren't about to not give the guy his money back, an' somebody had to take the blame. That's the main reason I came out to the West Coast in the first place."

"Okay, I get it," I said. "But is it worth risking a breaking and entering charge? I've got my license to worry about."

Clement smiled and produced a set of keys from his pocket. "Nobody ain't asked me for these yet. Y'all got my permission to come in with me."

Arguing the fine points of law is not something I've ever worried about. I shrugged and glanced over at Al and Delinda. Neither of them voiced any objections either.

We followed Clement through the courtyard gardens to the giant iron-bound oak doors at the entrance of the tasting hall. The double doors were locked, and the yellow crime tape fastened to the potted trees on each side of the portal barred our way.

Clement ducked under the tape and used his key to unlock the deadbolt. He pushed open one of the doors partway, enough for us to squeeze through in a single file. Once we were inside, he locked it behind us and motioned toward the stairwell on the far wall.

As we descended the stairs, I noted the chain-link barrier at the bottom landing was locked shut, but Clement had a key for that one as well. After opening it and crossing the threshold, he lit up the tunnel with the switch on the rock wall.

He said, "A little ways down here, there's a tunnel that's closed off with a locked gate."

"I remember it from yesterday," I said. "Taskert told us that tunnel branch was dangerous and unstable."

"Yeah, so the sign says. And as long as I've been here, I've ain't never gone in there." Clement stifled a laugh. "Now, I figure it's the best place to start lookin'. Not sure how we're gonna get in, though. I don't have a key for that lock."

"We'll find a way," Delinda assured him.

You can count on that, I thought.

As I recalled from our tour, the chain-link fencing securing the entrance to the intersecting tunnel was substantial, reaching from floor to ceiling. As we approached, I saw my memory was accurate.

Beyond the fence festooned with danger signs, the tunnel was dark. The light from the main shaft we were standing in didn't reach more than several feet beyond the gate. It was enough, however, for me to make out the scratches on the padlock.

"Seems like this lock has been frequently used," I observed.

Clement came over to look and snorted, "So much for Taskert's bullshit explanation!"

"I think this is your area of expertise," I said with a sly glance toward Delinda.

Smiling, she walked up and took the padlock in her hand, and it fell open.

"It must have been unlocked," she declared.

"Sure," I replied, not bothering to hide my sarcasm.

"No, really," she insisted soft enough, so only I could hear. "It *was* unlocked."

Dismissing any doubts her revelation might have raised, I swung the gate aside, and we cautiously walked past it into the darkness. The flashlight app on my phone was adequate enough to illuminate the way ahead.

After about fifty feet, the tunnel narrowed, and we came up to a row of several A-frame caution barriers blocking the path. Each of them bore "Danger," and "No Entry" warning signs.

My light weakly shone on what appeared to be a solid wall of rock.

"Seems to be a dead-end," I observed.

Clement pushed one of the barriers aside.

"Maybe, maybe not," he said as he kept on walking.

Then he appeared to vanish from view.

"Come on," Clement said. "Around the corner."

Puzzled, we ventured beyond the warning barricades and immediately realized the tunnel intersected with another one at a sharp right angle. From where we had been standing behind the barriers, it had been impossible to see. In an abundance of caution, I shined my light over the rock walls. They appeared stable—certainly not on the verge of collapse.

"This way," Clement called, his voice echoing in the tunnel. "I think there's something back here."

With our phones lighting our path, we went another fifty feet. Here the narrow tunnel widened, and Clement motioned us to stop.

"Gotta be a light switch around somewhere," he said.

His phone lit up a small electrical box on the wall.

"Yeah, I thought so," he said as he opened it and threw the switch inside.

All at once, the space became filled with light from several rows of fluorescent lights that hung suspended on wires attached to the ceiling.

We now found ourselves in a squarish space filled with various items that I assumed weren't meant for prying eyes. Dominating the center of the room was a long table cluttered with empty bottles, corks, sticks of wax, and stacks of printed labels. A paper cutter sat at the far end of the table next to sheets of paper with more labels printed on them… In French. Nearby on a wheeled workstation was a computer and an all in one printer. Several tall racks of unlabeled and apparently empty wine bottles flanked each of the sidewalls. On one side of the back wall, an odd wooden door was the only visible feature.

"Well, well! Lookie here," Clement exclaimed, pointing to a couple of oversized bottles of wine on the table. "Shit! Now I get it!"

"Maybe you'll tell the rest of us," I said, putting away my phone. All I could see was that the bottles he was pointing to sported identical labels.

"This here," Clement announced, motioning to the items on the table, "is where they're counterfeiting wine!"

"So, these are fakes?" I asked.

I took a long look at the bottles. Not that it made any difference; I only saw that the wine was red, and the labels were in French.

Al read it for me. "1947 Cheval Blanc St-Emilion."

"Christ!" Clement exclaimed, shaking his head. "I got it all wrong! Iris and Phil weren't just buying and selling fakes. They were making them!" His eyes widened in disbelief. "These magnums can't be real… If they were, they'd be worth a quarter-million dollars."

"More."

In unison, we all turned towards the entrance to see Iris Taskert standing there, holding a pistol aimed in our direction.

I noted that Clement seemed even more surprised than we were at Iris's sudden appearance—if that was even possible.

"So, this is why you never opened the winery," I said.

Iris didn't answer my question. Instead, she waved her gun towards the rear of the space.

"Get back there... All of you," she ordered.

"You can't kill all of us," I protested, hoping I was right.

She smiled back at me, but there wasn't the least bit of humor in her expression. "Why not? Move, or I'll shoot you right now."

Iris herded us to the back of the space towards what I had taken to be a storage closet.

"Open it," she ordered, brandishing the weapon.

The door was sturdy, fashioned from a single slab of weathered oak. It was framed by rough-hewn wooden beams attached to the cave wall with crudely made black iron bolts. In contrast to the other recent improvements, the door looked ancient.

Al did what Iris demanded, sliding the latch, a thick, rusty iron bar aside and pulled the door open.

"Inside... Now!" barked Iris, and the four of us filed through the portal into the pitch-black tunnel.

The second we were all inside, the door slammed shut, followed by the sound of the bar being pushed into place. In the next instant, we all had our mobile phones back out, and our flashlight apps switched on.

"Shit!" Clement whined. "What are they going to do with us?"

Nobody answered. Naturally, I had some ideas on the subject, but I didn't think it wise to share them at the moment.

"I think this part of the cave was not on the list of their recent improvements," I noted as my narrow beam of light swept across the breath of the tunnel.

The earthen walls were black with lichen and mold. The ceiling was draped in dusty cobwebs left behind by whatever unlucky arachnids had found their way down here. From what I could tell, it seemed we were in more of an elongated hole than an actual tunnel.

It was also evident that before it became our jail cell, this small space had been used for storage. On either side of the door were stacks of cartons containing empty wine bottles, boxes filled with various types of paper, and sticks of colored wax. All of these items were placed close to the entrance. Clearly, no one had cared to go deep inside to retrieve any of the items stored here. What little room remained in these cramped quarters made it impossible to spread out, or to avoid rubbing up against the hoary walls.

"This isn't much of a tunnel," Al observed, as he ventured farther ahead where the shaft narrowed. "There doesn't seem to be any way out."

"Jesus! Jesus!" Clement moaned. "We're trapped here... until someone lets us out!"

"Yeah, unless we suffocate first," I offered light-heartedly, right before I tripped over something.

I focused my light onto the floor and saw I had stumbled over a body. I recognized it was Kaffee's bodyguard. From his wound, I concluded he had been shot through the heart. Even more notably, his unbuckled pants were gathered in a heap atop his shoes. Thankfully, he never got the chance to remove his tighty-whiteys.

To my very jaded way of thinking, the poor guy had been getting ready for a quickie. Although, instead of getting lucky, he got shot—with his pants down. When I worked the morgue in Iraq, I saw more than my share of dead bodies. With some authority, I could say this one didn't look as though he had been dead for very long.

"She killed him! Shit... I think I'm going to be sick," Clement said right before he threw up.

I turned to Delinda, who so far had remained silent.

"How about some genie stuff? Now would be a good time," I whispered.

The place smelled bad enough before Clement lost his cookies—now it was even worse.

"What makes you think I haven't been trying," she whispered back. "We're not alone down here."

Before I could ask what she was talking about, I heard a voice in the darkness—a child's voice.

"Help them... Help them, please! You must! You must!"

"How? Who should I help?" I replied, despite my growing dread, directing my phone's light ahead of me where the tunnel dead-ended. There I saw a small hole which would have remained imperceptible in the wall of black earth had not the child's hand been thrust through it. I watched in frozen amazement as it beckoned.

"Who are you talking to?" asked Al.

"Did you hear something?" Delinda whispered.

Clement was too busy retching to notice.

Ignoring them, I drew closer to the wall as the tiny hand withdrew. I found the hole and thrust my hand through it. At my touch, the surrounding dirt easily crumbled away.

"Hey! Look at this! I think it could be a way out!"

Al made his way over to where I was now digging at the wall.

"How d'you find that?" he asked.

"I'll tell you later," I replied. "I just hope it leads somewhere."

"Amen to that," Al said as he moved beside me and began clawing handfuls of dirt.

Clement stood aside silently, wiping his mouth with the back of his hand.

"Stand back, guys," Delinda said. "Give me some room."

Clement didn't move as fast as Al and I did. I reached over and pulled him back seconds before a large section of the back wall fell away, revealing more blackness.

"What the hell?" Clement coughed.

"She's a good digger," I offered.

I pointed my flashlight onto the opening. Although the beam illuminated nothing but dust motes, I took a step forward.

The two-foot drop to the rocky floor caught me by surprise, and I fell on my ass.

"Watch out for that first step," I warned. "It's a steep drop."

I held the light from my phone on the threshold of the entrance we had made until everyone was on the other side of the wall. The air was damp and stale, but far preferable to Clement's regurgitated breakfast. I cast my light about, and while it revealed little of the larger cavern we had escaped to, it was enough for me to confirm there was no child anywhere to be seen.

CHAPTER TWENTY

Napa Valley, California 1868

THERE WAS ONLY ONE bar in Napa, the Paseo Saloon, which was where Miles Russell and his riders were headed. They were all impatient to get back to town. The killing had been dry, thirsty work, and they eagerly looked forward to indulging in their second favorite pastimes of "quenching and wenching."

They rode their horses hard and were almost halfway there when death—bloody and silent—descended on them without warning.

The Harpies began their attack beginning at the back of the column, using the thick cloud of dust raised by the horse's hooves for cover. They swooped in with their razor-sharp talons, slashing their victim's vocal cords in the same moment they snatched them from their saddles.

Then, carrying their quarry high into the air, they shredded their bodies into unrecognizable bags of gory flesh. The riders ahead, unable to hear the futile gurgles of terror from their doomed comrades, remained ignorant of the carnage going on behind and above them. It wasn't long before the number of horsemen in the column was reduced by half without anyone suspecting that something was amiss.

Fate intervened when one man happened to turn back in his saddle in time to witness the rider behind him being ripped from his horse. Despite his horror, he managed to scream out a warning at the same time he drew and emptied his revolver.

More by luck than marksmanship, four out of his six shots found their mark, and Rosalee plummeted to the ground, crashing mortally wounded atop her dead victim. The lead projectile that shattered her brain was too much for even a legendary creature to endure.

"Noooo!" Merrilee howled, fury and anguish distorting her already hellish features.

The man who killed her sister had no time to reload his empty gun; his only recourse was to furiously spur his horse onward. It was a futile effort as there was no escape from the ferocious vengeance that hurtled towards him, nor from the hungering talons that tore open his back from shoulder to tailbone.

Alerted by the inhuman cries from overhead, the other riders turned to look behind them. Though it was difficult to see clearly in the clouds of dust, it was harder still for them to believe their eyes. The apparition that descended on them was a giant winged creature. It had the naked torso and head of a woman and the muscular, scaly legs and talons of an eagle. In a blind panic, the entire remaining column spurred their horses into a full run. Which, while facilitating their escape, made it almost impossible to aim their pistols effectively.

Merrilee, howling incoherently and berserk with grief, relentlessly swept among the horsemen with incredible speed—constantly maneuvering to avoid their shaky gunfire. Her raking claws rent bloody ribbons of flesh from both horses and men. Panicking steeds stumbled and tripped, crushing their riders beneath them or throwing them aside to meet death by iron talons before they could regain their feet.

What had begun as a renegade posse of twenty men was now reduced to eight, Miles Russell and Reg Putter among them. With a surprising presence of mind, Russell led his remaining men off the road and into a thick grove of trees. There, using the leafy branches as cover, they all began firing through the canopy indiscriminately.

With an angry roar of frustration, Merrilee broke off her attack, wisely retreating into the hills. She had regained enough composure to realize her thirst for revenge would have to wait. Now her first responsibility was to protect her and Rosalee's legacy—her egg.

* * *

Russell and his men waited for almost two hours before they dared to venture from cover. Still frantic with terror, they rode as fast as their horses could take them, glancing up into the sky every few seconds, fearful of another attack.

Emotionally spent, they finally reached the Napa City limits. Ignoring the curious stares that greeted them as their lathered horses, on the verge of collapse, stumbled down the main street. Desperate to seek shelter indoors, the men neglected to hitch their mounts. Having reached the Paseo Saloon, one of the few places in town that tolerated their business, they merely dropped the reins and hastened inside.

"Denton! Two bottles of Rye and eight glasses," Russell demanded hoarsely as he and his men slunk into chairs around a large round table. As always, they took no heed of the other patrons in the room who wisely took pains to avert their eyes. One didn't provoke the Russell gang.

Silently, the eight men worked their way through three more bottles before they were almost drunk enough to put the horrific events of the day behind them. After pounding down another shot, Russell called out to the barmaid he occasionally paid for sex.

"Hey Millie, come 'mere," he slurred. "I need some o' yer tender 'tentions."

The woman, who looked far older than her actual age reluctantly acknowledged his invitation. Russell's money was good, but she wasn't eager to abide any of his rough handling. Still, business was business, and things had been slow lately, so she feigned a warm smile and went over to sit on his lap.

"How ya doin' honey," she said as sweetly as she could manage. After all, she was a professional.

"Well 'nuff," Russell said, nuzzling his dirty, bearded face into her bountiful breasts.

"I see that," she replied, turning her head so that his fetid breath wouldn't overwhelm her.

She knew the man loved to talk about himself and that engaging him in conversation might distract him from pawing her so publicly.

"What'cha been up to, Sweety?"

"You wouldn't 'lieve me t' tell it," he said, pouring himself another shot of Denton's homemade rotgut. It burned like hell, but it got the job done.

"G' head an' try me Hon," Millie prompted with a forced giggle.

By this time, however, Russell was so deep in his cups it nearly was impossible to understand half of what he was saying. Even so, some portions of his slurred rantings caught the amused attention of other bystanders. Especially when he began to describe the encounter with the winged monsters he called, "She birds." But it came out of his drunken lips sounding more like, "Ree Bords."

Soon, his equally inebriated compatriots began adding even more unintelligible details of their harrowing escape. Naturally, they embellished their own acts of courage hoping to impress Milly, who was doing her best to appear interested.

Nearby patrons couldn't help but catch snatches of the loud, drunken ramblings, and were heartily amused that Russell and his gang were terrified of something so unmistakably imaginary. As preposterous as it was, the tale became a story worth retelling. As soon as the following day, word spread that the fearsome Russell gang had been scared witless by a bunch of flying "Rebobs."

It was dusk by the time Merrilee retrieved her sister's body and returned to what little remained of her beloved farmstead. The two-story clapboard farmhouse had collapsed into a charred, smoldering heap. Dolefully, she unfolded her muscular wings and used them to fan the smoking embers into flames for Rosalee's funeral pyre.

"The world of men will rue this day, sister!" she vowed in the old tongue while she watched Rosalee's corpse sputter into ashes. "This, I swear."

Later that night, Merrilee dared a flight before moonrise to deliver a letter to Martin Grayson's mailbox. In it, she wrote that she and her sister had narrowly escaped the fire and were moving to San Francisco.

She requested that in her absence, Grayson, in his capacity as Napa's notary and Tax Collector, place her property up for sale.

She left all the details in his hands, knowing it was highly probable the canny old merchant would purchase the land himself. She also left instructions for him to forward the proceeds from the sale to a San Francisco bank she had corresponded with in the past. The bank also had her power of attorney, so the legal transfer of title could be completed without complications. She was unconcerned about the relatively low sales price she had affixed to the property. Compared to the tremendous wealth she and Rosalee had brought with them from Greece, it was a mere pittance.

Within a month, the acreage had sold, and as she expected, Martin Grayson was the purchaser. In the meantime, however, she had never left the property. It had always been Merrilee's plan to dwell in secret, secluded underground. To that end, she took great care to conceal and repurpose many of the tunnels, ensuring they would remain undiscovered.

With that in mind, she had sealed off and enlarged many areas in the wine caves—entombing the remains of the dead and creating a safe haven for herself. The endeavor took a considerable amount of magic to achieve, but it afforded her both safety and privacy. Here, far from the eyes of man, she intended to build her nest and raise her hatchling.

Although Merrilee hadn't forgotten her promise, the reckoning could wait until after she brought her child into the world. Then, there would be plenty of time to avenge her sister, Mei-Ling, and all the rest.

Only weeks later, her intentions were crushed when Merrilee suffered another terrible misfortune. Suddenly, she grew sicker and sicker, and despite all of her frantic efforts, she birthed the egg well before it was ready. Although she used every device, both magical and otherwise, she could think of to save her unborn child, it perished before it could even take shape.

Whether her miscarriage resulted from the embryo's mixed human and harpy lineage—or from the magical and physical exertions she had expended while she carried it; the reasons for the tragedy would remain a mystery forever.

For days afterward, she couldn't cast out the nightmarish vision of the malformed egg and its remains from her thoughts. On the brink of losing her sanity, she found that summoning up the voice of little Mei-Ling soothed her restive mind. It was the only thing that would banish the torturous memories from her consciousness.

I love you, Auntie. I love you, Auntie.

But even hearing those words repeating over and over inside her head wasn't enough to bring her any meaningful peace. Consumed with bitterness and devastated by all she had lost, Merrilee's hatred towards mankind and those she deemed responsible for her misery burned hotter and brighter than all of Zeus's lightning bolts combined.

While her magic had yet not fully recovered from the trials of her failed pregnancy, she was still powerful enough to do what her vengeance demanded. The last of the Harpies would wait no longer.

CHAPTER TWENTY-ONE

Napa Valley. Present Day

MICHELENA PEERED UP AND down the sidewalk. Downtown Napa was smaller than she expected.

"Where to now?" she asked.

Anna looked down at the Navigation app on her phone. "First, we get something to eat. Then we'll call for a ride out to Partrick Road. That's where we'll find her... Probably by the graveyard."

"Are you sure?" asked Michalena.

Michalena had always admired Anna's fearless confidence, however, now that they were close to reaching their goal, she began harboring doubts.

"What will we do when we find her? I mean, how will we... You know..."

"You mean, how will we kill her?" Anna interrupted.

"Yes," Michalena said under her breath.

"We're going to drive a wooden stake into the bitch's heart."

"I thought that only killed vampires," Michalena replied.

Anna shrugged her shoulders and shot her friend a wicked smile. "I think it will work just fine... And, best of all... It will hurt... A lot."

Michalena nodded. "For Gia!"

"Yes... For Gia," echoed Anna. She motioned to the Deli Mart up the block. "After sandwiches, we'll head over to Home Depot. We're also going to need a hammer."

The ride-share driver who dropped the girls off at Partrick road found herself concerned for their safety. She was a grandmother who had recently begun driving part-time to fill the empty hours after the death of her husband and wasn't comfortable leaving them in a potentially dangerous situation.

"You know, we're out in the middle of nowhere," the driver warned. "Do you want me to wait?"

"No, we'll be fine, thanks," Michalena assured her.

"We're expecting to be picked up in an hour or so by my uncle," lied Anna, not as convincingly as she would have liked.

"You're not lookin' to find the Rebobs, are you?" asked the driver.

"No," replied Anna. "I don't even know what those are."

Knowing it was useless to argue, the driver replied, "If you say so, dear," before she reluctantly dropped them off at the side of the road, near the Partrick Family cemetery.

Over the years, the location had been a favored destination for those seeking the "Rebobs," the mythical, winged robot monkeys that were a longtime staple of Napa's local lore. If indeed, that was what they sought, they would have a long wait. To the ride-share driver's knowledge, no one had ever caught sight of fictional beasts—at least not in her lifetime.

The driver waited for several minutes after the two girls got out of the car, hoping they might change their minds. When that didn't happen, she drove slowly away, watching them in her rearview until she rounded a bend and they disappeared from view.

"I hope those girls know what they're doing," the driver said to herself.

Even before the vehicle was out of sight, the girls began mounting the roadside berm to start their trek through the woods. The air was redolent with forest decay, and the ground was thick with pine needles and other dead leaves that crunched underfoot as they walked.

They hadn't gone far before they happened on the old, overgrown Partrick Family cemetery. The crumbling headstones and the short, chain-link fence that surrounded them were all in advanced states of disrepair. It was apparent the graveyard had remained untended for many generations after the last Partrick family member had been interred there.

A thick canopy of tall trees darkened the glade in which the graveyard lay, casting eerie and foreboding shadows, even this early in the day. Nevertheless, Michalena and Anna didn't allow the ominous atmosphere to soften their resolve. Undeterred, they continued trudging onward in their search, alert for any signs of who—or what—they were looking for.

"Where is she supposed to be?" asked Michalena as they progressed through the heavy brush. "What are we even looking for?"

"That!" answered Anna, motioning to the steep rise ahead.

What she was pointing out could be easily missed, for it was almost invisible, shaded by a dense stand of tall oaks and masked by a tangle of wild vines. Even so, Anna's sharp eyes found the edges of a dark hollow amidst the scraggly brush on the hillside.

"What is it? A cave?" Michalena asked breathlessly as they drew nearer.

"That's where they said Momo would be hiding," Anna declared confidently. "I read it in a blog."

"Are you sure?" Michalena shivered. The air was much cooler here for some reason.

"Sí, por supesto. Look up there!" Anna directed, pointing farther up the hill.

Michalena didn't see it at first, as the well-camouflaged parabolic antenna was artfully concealed in the jumble of bushes carpeting the top of the hill.

"So, that's how she gets on the internet," she said, squinting for a clearer view. "By satellite!"

Anna nodded in agreement as she lifted the hammer they had purchased earlier out of its plastic bag. She began walking up the slope, casting her eyes about, searching for a stout stick from among the many that littered the forest floor. Moments later, she found one suitable for what she ultimately had in mind.

Cautiously, she climbed the rest of the way up the hill, looking around for the hollow she had spied. She was about to give up when she spotted it once more. She drew close enough to see that behind the snarl of overgrowth was a patch of darkness that was neither dirt nor rock. Using her stick, she pushed the curtain of tangled vegetation aside.

"Come on!" Anna whispered as she carefully entered the black maw of the opening she had revealed. Somewhere, far off in the trees, a crow cried out ominously.

Michalena shuddered as the echo of the bird's guttural rattle died away. Then, hoping they weren't making a terrible mistake, she followed Anna into the darkness.

CHAPTER TWENTY-TWO

Napa Valley, California 1868

IN THE DAYS SINCE their harrowing experience with the deadly Shebirds, Miles Russell and the remaining vigilantes had exhibited a morbid, yet well deserved, fear of open spaces. Weeks of sleepless nights and recurring nightmares had also taken an enormous toll on them. Three of the survivors had apparently fled town, vanishing without a word to their comrades. Another had committed suicide by leaping off the Napa River bridge into the cold and fast-flowing water. Two more were judged to be a danger to themselves and others and ended up involuntarily committed to the infamous Napa Mental Hospital for an indefinite stay.

Of the eight men who had escaped death since the massacre at the Harper's farmstead, only Miles Russell and Reg Putter remained. Neither was left unscathed by the experience. Rarely venturing outdoors, they spent their waking hours inside the Paseo Saloon, drowning their dread with Denton's rot-gut whiskey.

"You feller's gotta go," Denton informed them late one afternoon. "Your tab's unpaid, and I ain't gonna serve you on credit no more."

"Shit, Denton! Ain't we been good customers?" Russell slurred.

"Not if you don't pay! I heard you owe Miss Milly too!"

"Aw, Come on!" Putter argued. "We'll find some money!"

"Well, as soon as you do, y'all can come back," countered Denton. "Until then... Git!"

Left with no choice, they struggled out of their chairs and quit the premises.

"Any ideas?" asked Putter as they stumbled out front to where their horses were hitched.

Out of nowhere, a thought crept into the fringes of Russell's mind. It made no sense to him, but he felt an unexplainable urge to ride up to Partrick Road. He didn't see the point to it, because other than the Partrick's small family farm, there wasn't much else out that way.

"I'm headed out to Partrick Road," Russell answered slowly.

"How funny is that?" chuckled Putter. "I was thinkin' the same thing!"

As they rode, they seemed relaxed and oblivious to their surroundings for the first time in a month. That in itself was unusual, for lately, neither man ever went out of doors without continually looking up at the sky. But on this occasion, they leisurely rode from town, seemingly without a care in the world. Unconcerned with anything other than guiding their horses along the trail, they traveled well past the Partrick farmstead. They didn't pull back on their reins until they came to the edge of a thick stand of Oak and Pine where the trail ended. There, both men dismounted and stood staring at each other with blank expressions.

"What the hell! Where are we?" Russell barked in bewilderment.

"I have no idea," contended Putter, equally confused. "It's like I just woke up or somethin'!"

"What are ya doin'!" yelled Russell in alarm as he watched Putter draw his revolver.

"What are you doin'?" echoed Putter accusingly, seeing that Russell had also drawn his weapon.

Before either of them could say another word, they both began firing their weapons. Only feet away from each other, there was no way they could miss, although at the moment, they had no control over their actions. Equally strange was neither of them felt any pain as the bullets exploded into their flesh.

Russell and Putter emptied their revolvers into each other, leaving their midsections as red as a Harpy's wrath. From her vantage point high in the trees, Merrilee watched impassively, working the magic that held the men tightly in her thrall. Only after she heard the hammers click uselessly on empty chambers, did she release them from their enchantment. The results were exactly what she hoped for.

Simultaneously, Putter and Russell began screaming as the harrowing pain of their gut wounds finally reached their brains. No longer in the sway of Merrilee's spell, they fell to the ground writhing and bellowing in unimaginable agony. For an hour they endured their suffering, as Merrilee held back death's sweet release with her magic. It was unfortunate, she thought, that even her considerable power wasn't enough to sustain their tenuous hold on life as long as she would have liked.

Even after watching her victims die in the most horrible fashion she could devise, she felt hollow. Their deaths weren't enough to slake her burning thirst for revenge, nor could they keep the visions of all she had lost from clouding her brain.

I love you, Auntie. I love you, Auntie.

Now, imagining the strains of Mei-Ling's calming voice wasn't enough. She needed more than that. Much more. Perhaps it was a sign that her sanity had slipped too far from her grasp because what she was considering amounted to pure madness. Once the idea of resurrecting those who had been so cruelly taken had entered her mind, she could think of nothing else. Her compulsion to achieve that end was stronger than the enchantment she and her sister had visited on Henry Watkins.

In centuries long past, she might have implored Aïdes, God of the underworld, to release all of their souls—but after mankind had ceased to worship the old gods, he had fled with the rest of his brethren to other realms of existence. Instead, she realized it fell to her to devise other means. There were ancient practices that she was aware of, such as the spells of nekromanteía that Origen of Alexandria used. His incantations were potent, but he and those who followed in his footsteps lacked a critical ingredient—the blood of an immortal. So, where others had failed, she would not.

In the days and weeks following her decision, Merrilee meticulously assembled and prepared everything she required for the resurrection rites. Sacred Mirrha wood was obtained from Ethiopia and shipped to the port of San Francisco before being delivered to a vacant summer cabin in Napa. For the ritual sacrifice of flesh, she stole a baby goat from the Partrick's farm. The required ceremonial instruments were already at hand—part of the treasure she and her sister had brought from Greece—a silver chalice, and a golden dagger, both relics from the temple of Hera.

Finally, on the night of a new moon, everything was in place. Inside her lair, she lit the Mirrha wood in the pit she had dug for the fire. She waited until after it burst aflame before she opened a vein on her arm with the sharp point of the small, gold dagger. With impatient anticipation, she watched as her blood dripped into the ceremonial goblet. Only when the cup was filled, did she will the bleeding to stop, for she knew to summon the dead required a significant offering. Then, putting the vessel aside, she seized the baby goat. Holding the terrified animal high above the fragrant, burning Mirrha, she slit its throat and without waiting for it to stop struggling, dropped it into the fire pit.

With a loud burst of red and blue flames, the kid instantly exploded into tiny, floating ashes, as if it had been but a piece of paper. Then, as Merrilee pronounced the incantations, she slowly emptied the silver vessel of black ichor over the fire until it sputtered and belched black, noisome clouds of noxious smoke. Finally, she invoked every last shred of her magic to compel the spirits of Mei-Lei, her sister, and even her unborn child to come forth.

The result was nothing like she had imagined. After the last word of the spell had escaped her lips, there was a flash of blinding light. The odious stench of her burning blood was replaced with the electric odor of spent lightning. The clouds of smoke grew thicker, filling the lair and swallowing the light of the fire, plunging the cave into darkness. Then, rising amid the smoke were three indistinct shadows. Giddy with triumph, she thought she recognized the foremost shape.

"Sister," Merrily entreated in the ancient tongue, "I bid you return to the world of the living."

Rosalee replied, her voice harsh and sibilant with anger.

"Fool! Do you know what you've done?"

Rosalee's forceful and unexpected response turned Merrilee's jubilation into uncertainty, but she had not come this far only to fail.

"Yes... I have broken every natural law, so that we may all be rejoined on the mortal plane!"

Rosalee's voice grew even more wrathful. "Sister, you have unwisely overestimated your power and your sovereignty over that which is not yours to give. We cannot cross, and by summoning us, you have doomed us to wander in-between life and death."

"Impossible!" Merrilee protested in horror. "I have parted the curtain between death and life so you may pass into the world of the living!"

"No. There is no curtain, only a trap. Are you foolish enough to think Aïdes would have left his world unguarded?"

"It matters not! My power is greater than his!" Merrilee shrieked. "You will see... I will prevail! Come to me, I command you!"

"You are mad, sister!" Rosalee's voice began to fade away, growing softer with every word. "Your hate has robbed you of all reason..."

The smoke began to thin, and the apparitions within it waned dimmer and dimmer until they were gone. Then, she found herself alone with only cold ashes in the fire pit and the strains of her sister's rebuke ringing in her ears. Still, she was not to be deterred.

"Sister! Child! Mei-Ling!" Merrilee called out repeatedly, demanding a response. But the shades paid no heed to her exhortations and did not answer.

Merrilee was emotionally spent. Chastened by her failure, weakened from blood loss, and her magical exertions, she still summoned the strength to spread her wings in defiance. If all she had left was rage, then she would let it define her.

"Now, you will be doubly avenged!" she screamed, her voice echoing throughout her lair. "I will not rest… Not until the last child of man is no more! Only then will we all know eternal peace!"

CHAPTER TWENTY-THREE

Napa Valley. Present Day

"THIS CAVERN IS HUGE," Al declared. "Looks like we've stumbled into an undiscovered portion of the caves."

He was standing next to me on the other side of the opening Delinda had made, pointing his light straight up. The dim beam of his phone light barely illuminated the ceiling above us, and our combined lights revealed the space was at least the same distance in width. Straight ahead, beyond the range of our lights, there was only darkness.

"I don't think goin' this way is gonna lead us out of here," Clement declared as he made the short hop to the ground.

"Better than waiting for Iris to come back and finish us," I reminded him.

I hadn't mentioned to either Al or Delinda about how I discovered our escape route, nor did I voice the troubling question that still puzzled me—which was why Iris didn't shoot us when she had the chance. Ghost child aside, this entire scenario wasn't adding up, but I couldn't put my finger on what exactly was bothering me.

While I turned all of this over in my mind, we continued slowly into the inky blackness. The barely adequate light from our mobiles created only a small bubble of illumination around us. So, I didn't see what I stepped on until I felt and heard it crunch. The sound distracted me from my disquieting thoughts, immediately directing my attention and light down to my feet.

"Hey, Somebody left their glasses down here," I said, bending down to pick up the wire-rimmed spectacles, or more correctly, what was left of them.

"I doubt if they're coming back for 'em," Al quipped.

"Look over here," Delinda said. It wasn't a suggestion.

She was twenty paces ahead of where we were, and her light was shining on what appeared to be a rusty, antique wood-burning stove.

"Someone was living down here," she added.

"Not just someone," I said, sweeping my beam of light over to my left, where it revealed rows of rotted wood and canvas cots. "A bunch of some-ones."

"I wonder why anyone would want to live underground," Delinda mused.

I was going to ask her why anyone would live in a clay vessel for a few centuries but thought better of it.

"Who the hell cares," muttered Clement.

He was clearly uninterested and seemed to be less in the moment than the rest of us. I chalked it up to the stress of our current situation. In the meantime, Al had made his way over for a closer look.

"Maybe these folks had no choice," he ventured.

"Why?" I asked. "Do you suppose they were hiding?"

"That's one answer," Al replied as he bounced his light off of a dozen wooden trunks. Over time, they had split apart, spilling mounds of moldy and rotting fabrics onto the cave floor.

"Could be we found a little underground city," he added.

Farther ahead, we found other items that confirmed Al's supposition. Day-to-day implements like cups and dishes, though all were mostly shattered as if haphazardly crushed underfoot. Here and there were more personal items, like a hairbrush or the remnants of a hand mirror.

I caught up with Delinda. "What do you think?" I asked.

"It's not so much what I think," she answered. "It's what I feel. And it's not good."

"Well, we can't stop here," I pointed out. "And I'm sure going back isn't a good option either."

Suddenly, Al's yell of surprise pierced the oppressive silence. I hustled over to him, eager to know what could spook a guy who has purportedly seen it all. When I reached his side, he was standing there, his grim expression revealed by my mobile. I moved the thin beam of light from him over to where he was shining his. Our combined beams painted a swath of light over a long line of human skeletons lying face down on the dirt cave floor, reflecting eerily off of the bleached, white bones. I looked around for Clement, sincerely hoping he wasn't going to upchuck again, but I didn't see him.

"Great Zeus! They were all shot execution-style," Al observed.

He was right. Every skull displayed a similar jagged hole that could have only one source. A bullet—from point-blank range fired into the back of the head. This was murder, pure and simple. Worse, judging from the sizes of the skeletons, many of the victims were children. A sensation like an electric shock ran up my spine as our lights played over the carnage.

"Horrible," Delinda whispered as she joined us in surveying the dead. "Just horrible."

"She led me here," I said, pointing to a small skeleton. "She wanted us to find her… And them."

The rag-doll clutched to her chest was unmistakable. Her skull, almost completely shattered by the bullet that killed her, had wisps of black hair clinging to it. The decaying shreds of fabric dangling from several of her ribs were from the dress the apparition had worn. Whoever had done this unspeakable crime was indisputably long dead, but knowing that did little to diminish my anger.

"Looking at those," said Al pointing to the numerous heaps of shredded straw. "Lead me to believe these are bodies of Chinese Coolies. That's all that's left of the conical hats most of them wore. My guess is these folks tended the vineyards and dug these caves." He shook his head sadly. "Fitting that the word, 'Coolie' was derived from the Chinese words: Ku Li, meaning, Bitter labor."

My light hadn't moved from the body of the little girl.

I said, "I know that's her… I recognize the doll. The spirit was holding it every time she appeared."

"The one that said, save them?" asked Delinda.

"Yeah," I replied. "But, I take it we're way too late."

"What? Are you suddenly an expert on spirit pronouns?" Delinda chided softly. "It's possible she was referring to someone or something else."

I shrugged. "Okay, but right now, we're the only ones that need saving."

"That spirit sought you out for a reason," she insisted.

"Me? What makes you say that?"

"You seem to have developed a knack for attracting these kinds of events," Delinda replied with a canny smile. "Who knew?"

"I will venture a guess you might have some idea," I countered, tapping the scar on my cheek.

"In any event," she said, "You are the key."

"Wonderful!" I huffed under my breath. Then louder, so Delinda could hear me, I asked, "The key to what?"

"I'm sure you'll find out in due time," she offered blandly. "That's how these things work."

"Great," I groaned. "That wasn't in my copy of the manual. Oh, and before I forget, I need to ask, why is it I saw the spirit, and you didn't?"

"I'm not sure," Delinda replied thoughtfully. "I've been wondering about that myself."

More good news, declared my inner voice, dripping with sarcasm. Sometimes, I can't even refrain from wisecracking to myself, although at the moment, there was nothing funny about any of this. Shamed by my own shallowness, I finally tore my eyes away from the remains of the little girl.

"Hey, where's Clement?" I queried, now aware of his absence for the first time.

"I thought he was right behind us," Al remarked, casting his light about.

"So did I," Delinda said. "Maybe he went back."

"What?" I was incredulous. "Why would he do that?"

The three of us searched, turning our lights in every direction. We called his name several times but got no response.

"Well, he might have slipped by us," Al proposed. "Do you think he might have gone up ahead?"

"Perhaps, but we should keep moving," Delinda advised. "If he's moved on in front of us, we'll find him eventually."

"Maybe, but the dust on the ground up ahead looks undisturbed," I observed. "We're the only ones who've been down here in years."

We continued onward through the cavern. Our puny phone lights weren't powerful enough to penetrate the gloom much farther than a few yards in front of us, making it appear as if there was no end in sight.

"You know, I wonder why Iris didn't just shoot us in the first place," Al mused. "She had no qualms about offing Kaffee's bodyguard."

"Yeah, that's also been bothering me," I agreed. "Along with how easy it was for us to get into the phony wine workshop."

"I just assumed Delinda undid the padlocks," replied Al.

"No," Delinda said. "I told Mark at the time, I didn't. They were all unlocked."

"That's way too coincidental," Al remarked. "Don't you think?"

Before I could answer, Al stopped in his tracks.

"Hey, look at this!" he exclaimed, shining his light on what he had discovered.

Delinda and I caught up to him, curious to see what had drawn his attention. He was staring at the remnants of a bird's nest, one fashioned from wattle, sticks, and straw. Although much of it had dried and decayed into dust, it looked as though it was originally a good four feet in diameter. Entangled within the heaps of dried wood were bits of unrecognizable dander and tiny flakes of shell fragments.

"What kind of enormous bird makes its nest underground?" I mused.

"Only one comes to mind," Al replied.

After a long pregnant pause, I said, "Well, are you going to tell me?"

"Remember our conversation at dinner?" he said.

"You're not seriously referring to a giant chicken, are you?" I joked, conjuring up an image of the coq au vin Al had ordered the night before.

"No. I was referring to the Harpy. You know, the one you told me about."

I hoped it was too dark for anyone to see me standing there in open-mouthed surprise.

"Come on, Al," I objected. "Isn't that way too much of a coincidence?"

"Not really," interjected Delinda. "It's like I've said before, you seem to attract all sorts of supernatural events."

"Lucky me," I muttered.

"Could be you've happened on the trail of that Mama you were talking about," Al added.

"That's Momo. And no thank you, please. Can we concentrate on getting out of here first? I'm feeling the need for a tall glass of something alcoholic… Other than wine."

"Momo? What's that?" Delinda asked.

After a deep sigh of resignation, I explained the entire story to her. The crazy internet presence, the missing girls, and the news that they were last seen searching for the mythical internet persona in nearby Oakland. When I was finished, Delinda remained silent. I knew that even if I could see her expression in the dark, it wouldn't reveal much.

Finally, she said, "I think those girls are here."

"How is that possible? They're supposed to be on a bus home!" I protested. "Are you implying Momo is somewhere close by?"

She frowned. "Something is. Something very ancient and powerful…" Delinda paused and closed her eyes for a moment. When she opened them, she added, "And very dangerous."

"That's comforting," I snarked. "Anything else we should know?"

For fifty years following her revenge on Miles Russell and his men, and her ill-fated attempt at necromancy, Merrilee seldom ventured from the safety of her lair. She had patiently waited until all who might remember the Harper sisters and their farm were either dead or gone. Only then did she dare to revisit the world of man.

Adopting her human guise once more, she rented a small house in the hills above where her vineyard still grew and lived unnoticed. During those years, her hatred for all of mankind continued to fester. On occasions when her bile became too much to bear, she took to the night skies seeking opportunities to wreak havoc on those unfortunate enough to travel the rural back roads.

In the daytime, she lived a reclusive life, interacting with others as little as possible. She took great pleasure in reading the local newspaper, which chronicled her handiwork—the occasional missing person, or the chance sighting of the flying creatures the locals referred to as 'Rebobs.' While she did not understand how the legend evolved to include descriptions of winged robot monkeys or other outlandish explanations, she still took a perverse pride in being part of Napa's folklore. After all, she thought, in modern times more people read the Napa Register than Apollonius Rhodius's Argonautica.

With the advent of radio in the 1930s, and later with television, Merrilee was able to study her nemesis in greater detail. Communication technology offered her the opportunity to reflect on how little mankind had changed over the years despite the advances of the modern age. The bigotry, the wars, the pettiness of politics, the promotion of violence, their polarized and fractured societies were constant reminders of how unfit man was to rule this world.

Indeed, over time, it became much more apparent that humans were utterly apathetic, even about threats to their own existence. It was incomprehensible to her how they could blithely ignore the obvious dangers while they continued to spew poisons into the air and water. Had Zeus and the other gods not abandoned the world centuries ago, the human race would have been deservingly wiped from the face of the planet. Now, that task remained to her.

Despite her bitterness and disgust for mankind, she followed their advances in technology with great interest. Grudgingly, Merrilee marveled at the accomplishments brought about in the modern age—

and contemplated how she might exploit them for her own ends. Decades later, the answers she was searching for came with the arrival of the computer era and the internet.

She became fascinated with digital tech and thought it might be possible to meld it with magic, weaponizing it to extend her reach. With that in mind, she decided to return to her hidden underground lair, where she could work in secret. Money was no object, so she had no difficulties gathering whatever electronic or digital products she wished to study and refine.

Merrilee spent every waking hour keeping pace with each advancement in those related fields. Then, applying them to her continual and methodical experimentation in hopes it would bring her closer to her ultimate goal. Her first trial run using the internet was a resounding success. One that had drawn its inspiration from an unlikely source.

One night, she had taken to the air shortly after dusk, only to have a chance encounter with a group of oriental visitors who were sightseeing near the old Partrick Cemetery. No doubt they had come in search of the legendary Rebobs, and Merrilee was more than happy to accommodate them, though not in the way they had anticipated. Initially intent on venting her wrath on the group, she turned away at the last moment, allowing the group to glimpse her flying overhead.

Reluctantly, she had concluded it was in her interests not to kill them, wisely reasoning the act would create a threat to her solitary existence. Instead, she used a powerful compulsion to make them forget what they had seen. Her magic, as powerful as it was, still wasn't infallible, and not everyone's memory was erased entirely.

One of the Japanese tourists was a sculptor who, only months afterward, created a distorted likeness of her from a dream—or so he thought. By accident or fate, Merrilee happened on a photograph of the sculpture online and realized the image was the perfect vehicle for her first internet experiment. And thus, ironically, Momo was born.

Her engagement with the world wide web was the culmination of a long learning curve and many failures. In the end, Merrilee finally achieved the result for which she had hoped. Combining magic and technology was no easy feat, and despite being relatively crude, her results surpassed her wildest expectations.

Her reimagined likeness, imbued with a potent enchantment had—in contemporary parlance—gone viral. Momo worked exactly as she designed it to, casting the seeds of her revenge to every part of the globe. Impressionable young minds proved easy targets for the magic she had embedded in the pictures and words. Merrilee was gratified by both the death toll and the fact it took almost two years before internet service providers acted to lock Momo out.

Empowered by that success, she redoubled her efforts to master other aspects of digital technology. Now, she was on the verge of something far more ambitious. A recent technology had emerged, one that promised her the opportunity and the means to unleash even greater destructive magic.

Merrilee's hatred of mankind had grown stronger, fueled with every scrap of knowledge she acquired. Her anguish and loss remained fresh in her mind as if she had fallen victim to man's misdeeds only days before. Her unquenchable thirst for vengeance drove her to master dozens of computer programing languages and other related skills.

Even if her computer skills hadn't been combined with powerful magic, the techniques that enabled her to inject the Momo curse throughout the worldwide web bordered on genus. And soon, even that would pale compared to what she now had in mind.

With the wealth she garnered over so many years, nothing was out of her financial reach. It enabled Merrilee to continually update her underground laboratory with the latest hardware and software as soon as it became available. Now, she had nearly everything she would need to complete her most ambitious opus. Within the next few hours, the final component she required to set her plan into motion would literally appear in the sky.

Several days ago, a Silicon Valley startup launched several hundred satellites into space, intending to bring internet access to every corner of the Earth. Once they finally achieved their designated orbits, all the satellites would engage their links to begin two-way transmissions. When that step was completed, the interconnected network would provide Merrilee with the means to blanket the planet with a newer and more potent magic. One that would be immeasurably more effective than Momo ever was. Thousands of children would die, and millions more would feel the same pain she had endured for so long.

Few people realized the relative ease with which a satellite can be hacked—especially if the hacker was as gifted as Merilee was. The instant the low-orbiting transceivers went live, she would inject the code that would place them under her control. Over the past several weeks, she had prepared and assembled the software and hardware required and was poised to strike. As she waited, every passing second before the satellite net came online felt like an eternity to her.

Then, with only minutes remaining until the penultimate moment, Merrilee suddenly became distracted. The sensation was unmistakable. Someone was coming. Her preternatural vision effortlessly pierced the darkness, revealing the two human females who had found their way into her lair. The weak beams of light from their mobile phones did little to illuminate their surroundings and served only to disclose their youth to their immortal observer.

As they drew farther into the tunnel, one girl whispered, "Diós! This place is filled with electronics!"

Her light Hispanic accent held a measure of innocence that reminded Merrilee of little Mei-Ling. So much so, that it almost weakened her resolve. That impulse vanished with the other's reply. Her accent was similar; however, her tone was harder, more worldly, and held no innocence at all.

"Well, what you would expect? It's fucking Momo! Let's find the bitch and get out of here."

Merrilee had to suppress a desire to instantly gut both younglings like the small deer she routinely hunted for food. Instead, she waited patiently, like a spider in a hidden web, clinging unseen to the roof of the cavern. Once the two young girls were nearly underneath her perch, she swooped down without warning to land directly in their path. One of the girls screamed in terror, while the other raised the wooden shaft she was carrying intent on thrusting it into the Harpy's breast.

The Harpy made only the slightest gesture with her hand, and the wooden spike fell from Anna's nerveless grasp. Michalena's unfinished scream froze in her throat. Then, in the merest blink of an eye, both girls were staring blankly straight ahead—powerless to do anything else. Merrilee was entertaining several amusing possibilities to seal their fates when another, now-familiar sensation crept past the edge of her consciousness. More intruders were coming.

CHAPTER TWENTY-FOUR

WE HEARD THE ECHO of a scream from up ahead in the darkness.

"That didn't sound like Clement," I said unnecessarily.

Delinda and Al both nodded their agreement. I started to move, but Al grabbed my arm.

"Wait!" he cautioned.

"For what? Somebody's in trouble," I insisted. "We gotta go."

I'm not one to tear off fearlessly towards the unknown, but instinct had taken over. Playing my mobile's thin beam of light in front of me to avoid stumbling, I forged otherwise blindly ahead. So much so, I wasn't sure if Al and Delinda were on my heels.

Twenty yards ahead, the tunnel curved abruptly to the left. I rounded the corner only to find myself at another intersection. I stopped, out of breath, unsure of which way to turn. Then, materializing out of nowhere, there she was again—the dead Chinese girl. She pointed to the left, but before I could take off in that direction, I heard Delinda's voice behind me.

"I saw her too."

I turned to see Delinda, not even breathing hard. Al's beam of light drew closer as he ran up to join us. He was as winded as I was, but he signaled we should keep going with a wave of his hand.

We pressed on wordlessly as the tunnel straightened and narrowed before it spit us out into another enormous cavern. The dim light radiating from clumps of iridescent fungus that dotted the walls and ceiling—together with the illumination from other, more unlikely sources made the size of the space apparent.

On the far wall, a dozen computer monitors were placed side to side on a long table that faced several racks filled with computer gear and other kinds of electronic equipment. I only had seconds to take in the unexpected tableau before the thing came down directly in my path.

The form was straight out of a nightmare, though it was one I had seen before. I was looking at Momo—in the flesh—glaring at me with eyes as black as a banker's heart. I felt like I was being pulled into those two black pits as if someone had tied a rope around my consciousness and was trying to drag me into oblivion. The scar on my cheek was burning painfully as the pressure in my head continued to build. I realized Momo was directing her power at me, trying to blast my brain into pieces. Then, just as I thought the pain in my cheek could grow no greater, it suddenly stopped, and the sensation in my skull ceased as inexplicably as it began. In that same moment, the look in Momo's eyes transformed from malevolence to frustration, and then to anger. Evidently, because of the bits of genie condo in my face, things hadn't gone the way she expected.

If the wings were any indication, then Al was right—Momo *was* a Harpy, and an ugly one to boot. I only hoped I lived long enough to tell him so. The odds of that got slimmer as the Harpy screamed something I couldn't understand and rose into the air above me.

Good timing has never been my strong suit, just ask my creditors. Nevertheless, I dove for the floor face-first as Momo swooped in for the kill. A rush of air swept across my back as her questing talons missed me by mere inches.

The flying nightmare roared in rage as she swerved around for another try, intent on eviscerating me. Unwilling to part with any of my internal organs, I rolled out of her path in the very moment her iron-black claws scraped the ground where I had been.

"You don't believe in manicures, do you?" I yelled, leaping to my feet and racing for cover behind a rack of electronic equipment.

Apparently, harpies, like genies, have no sense of humor. Unamused by my flippant remark, Momo alit only several yards away from me, her ugly face twisted into a scowl.

I risked a quick glance around and saw Al standing frozen and unseeing in his tracks. Whatever had kept me from falling under the

Harpy's spell hadn't done the same for him. Delinda was nowhere to be seen.

"You will die for that insult!" Momo hissed in an icy voice that reminded me eerily of my ex-wife.

"I hope not," I mumbled to myself.

I resisted an impulse to apologize for showing up unannounced, but before I could finish the thought, Momo waved her hand, and the steel shelves between us were struck by an invisible force and swept away. With a feral snarl, she shot upwards from the ground, and I staggered back, buffeted by the powerful turbulence from her wings. Then, without the slightest hesitation, she launched herself at me. This time there was no cover to be had. The fallen equipment rack lay to one side, and the cavern wall was behind me. In a useless gesture, I put up my hands to cover my face, expecting the inevitable impact and the slashing claws. It never came.

I lowered my hands to see what miracle had intervened to save me. It was the little Chinese girl, translucent, and hollow-eyed, floating between me and certain death. At her appearance, the Harpy had halted her attack in mid-air, hovering and seemingly as confused as I was.

The little girl's gaze wandered from me to Momo before she spoke. "He will save us," she said in a voice barely above a whisper.

"No, child," Momo replied. "It is too late."

"No, Auntie. He must save us all," the little girl insisted. "It's his destiny."

The Harpy's features softened somewhat, the bleak hatred vanishing momentarily from her face.

"You are mistaken, little one," she said sadly.

Astonished at the monster's sudden transformation, I somehow felt sorry for her, if only for a second or two. My instinct told me the spirit's intervention was merely going to delay my demise. Suddenly another female voice forcefully echoed through the cavern.

"It's true, Sister. His fate is entwined with all of ours."

I looked around for the speaker and saw it came from another harpy, but this one, like the little Chinese girl, was also a spirit. Aside from the way it addressed Momo, the familial resemblance was unmistakable. Clearly, I had gotten myself into the middle of a family affair. From my experience with human domestic situations, I knew they rarely ended well.

"Impossible!" Momo angrily shook her head. "His only destiny is to die!"

Her words and the dramatic change in her expression suggested her opinion regarding my fate might prove more accurate. Without waiting to see what came next, I scrambled towards one of the equipment racks that still remained upright. I expected her to come right at me, but she didn't. Instead, she circled up and around. Then, she flew towards me again, using the distance to redouble her acceleration.

Still running, I tripped over something and landed face down on the ground, out in the open. Momo didn't slacken her speed, plowing through the floating spirits as if they were clouds of smoke, her talons fully extended. I was, as they say—toast.

Then, appearing from nowhere, Delinda was between us, holding a sphere that glowed like a small sun. With only feet between them, Delinda hurled the glistening ball of luminescence at the Harpy as if she were pitching in the playoffs.

The gleaming missile struck Momo full-on, knocking her out of the air and onto the ground, where the circle of light continued to expand, enveloping her in white-hot incandescence. With a shriek of rage, Momo struggled to her feet and shook off the light in dazzling rivulets, like a dog shaking itself dry.

Now, even more enraged—if that were even possible, the Harpy rose high into the air, furiously beating her featherless wings. She launched herself at us head-on and then suddenly banked left, coming at Delinda from the side. The unexpected angle of the attack caught Delinda off guard. I had seen the feint and reacted in a way that was more reflexive than well-considered.

I rushed forward and smashed into the winged horror, head down, shoulder first—just like I was taught before they kicked me off the freshman football team.

My timing wasn't perfect—which came as no surprise to me, and I only delivered a glancing blow. While it didn't entirely stop Momo's headlong rush, it was enough to knock her off course, causing her to miss Delinda and instead smash into the cavern wall. I careened backward faster than an arcade pinball but remarkably remained on my feet.

I ran to Delinda's side, as the Harpy, seemingly none the worse for wear, renewed her onslaught—bounding back into the air with a maddened scream. She sped to the far end of the cavern, then arced around, gathering more momentum as she used every ounce of her strength to propel herself towards us. With a sinking feeling, I realized there was no way to avoid what would happen next. I threw my arms around Delinda, who surprisingly didn't resist, and prepared for the worst. This was the first time I had ever held Delinda like this—except in my dreams. For that instant, time seemed to stand still.

Death was only seconds away when an abrupt, psychic shock tore me apart from Delinda. I became acutely aware of separate presences as they manifested themselves inside me, channeling the power and strength of their combined emotions. In the scant moment that remained of my life, I sensed their anger. I felt their sadness, and, most of all, their love.

I became overcome with a peculiar and unfamiliar sensation, one I was unable to process—but I knew something portentous was about to happen. What happened next still remains unclear to me, because my consciousness fled my body, crowded out by the spirits that possessed my body.

I heard afterward that Momo was flying too fast to stop, but I had a vague sense there was more to it than that. Perhaps she had anticipated the outcome and either welcomed or resigned herself to it. Whatever the reason, she collided with whatever it was that had emanated from my body at full speed—an irresistible force striking an immovable object.

I felt nothing. I only heard myself say in a voice that wasn't mine, "We love you, Auntie."

Abruptly, I snapped out of my dreamlike state. I was myself again, and after my vision cleared enough to regain a measure of situational awareness, I approached Momo where she had fallen.

"I... I wanted to avenge all of you," she whispered hoarsely.

I knew she wasn't talking to me. Momo lay on the cavern floor, wings shattered, body broken. Streams of her black blood fed the dark pool steadily spreading underneath her.

Take my word for it, you can't have a cadre of spirits play house with your body without absorbing some measure of understanding.

I said, "Your hate nearly doomed their souls for all eternity. This was the only way they could be free."

"Forgive me," the Harpy pleaded.

Standing there, watching as her life ebbed away, I knew it wasn't me she was addressing.

"We love you, Auntie. Now, you can be at peace." Mei-Ling's soft voice grew fainter with each word.

"Yes," Momo replied, so softly I could barely hear her. "Forever."

Al, now free from the magic that had restrained him, rushed over. The Harpy, nearing the end, murmured something in a language I didn't understand, but Al nodded and replied in the same tongue as Delinda and I looked on.

Whatever he said seemed to give her a measure of comfort in those last seconds before her eyes dulled, and her body quivered, stiffening with a final shudder.

None of us spoke for several long moments afterward until I asked, "What did she say, Al?"

"She asked me if she would ever find forgiveness," he replied solemnly.

"And, you said?"

He looked at me and exhaled a pent up breath. "I told her Zeus was a merciful God."

I going to say it was more than she deserved, but I held my tongue. Instead, I turned to Delinda.

"Thanks for conjuring up those spirits at the last minute. Forget everything I said about cheap genie magic."

"That wasn't me. It was you and the spirits you attracted," she asserted, not even bothering to gift me with a raised eyebrow.

"Me? You're joking, right?"

She locked her eyes with mine and said, "It was all you, Mark. You drew them to you and channeled their power... Just like you did in Palm Springs."

"Really? Is that supposed to be a gift?" I said. It was less of a question than a complaint.

"I'd say so," Al replied. "Saved our asses, didn't it?"

"It's your power," Delinda continued. "So, embrace it. It's a part of you…" She paused, still staring at me with her jade green eyes." As much as you are a part of me."

Equally stunned by what she told me and the way she said it, I was at a loss for words. Nor did I have the opportunity to search for any owing to the soft whimper that drew everyone's attention to the other end of the cavern.

"Help us! Please," sobbed a young female voice.

At the other end of the cave, two girls were lying on the ground. Their ankles were bound, and their arms were tied tightly behind them.

"You stopped her!" rasped one of them in a thick Hispanic accent as we drew closer. "She was about to bewitch the whole world!"

"To do what?" Al asked as he went to work untying her.

Delinda was kneeling at the side of the other girl. I watched the ropes fall away at the slightest touch of her hand.

"Her magic was going to make every kid on Earth kill themselves!" insisted the girl Delinda had freed. Her accent was lighter, and I recognized it as the voice that had cried out for help.

"She wanted us to watch while she infected the internet with her magical tech before she killed us," added the other grimly. "If you hadn't interrupted her, she would have done it!"

"Anna? Michalena?" I ventured.

"Yes! I'm Michalena," answered the girl who had cried out. "How did you know?"

While I should have been gob-struck by this incredible coincidence, I didn't allow myself that luxury. Frankly, once you've hosted a mess of assorted spirits, survived a few close calls with vampires, resurrected shamans, and the occasional rare mythical beast, there's not much left that can surprise you.

"Mark!" Al hollered from the other side of the cavern. "Get over here! Fast!"

I hustled over to where he stood studying one of the brightly lit computer monitors. He was pointing to a red progress bar on the screen labeled "upload." It was more than halfway to the end and was incrementing with every passing second.

"If that's what I think it is, then we haven't stopped anything at all!" I exclaimed.

"Suggestions?" Al blurted as the bar grew nearer to completion.

I knew enough about computers to realize smashing the display wouldn't accomplish anything. I grabbed the wire connected to the back of the monitor and quickly determined where it went. It was plugged into a black, cylindrical computer I recognized as a high-end Macintosh computer.

"Whatever you're going to do, do it now, Mark!" Al yelled. "We're almost out of time!"

I yanked out the power cord and held my breath. Behind me, an alarm began to sound.

"You stopped the transmission," Delinda declared as she rushed over to where I was standing, power cord still in my hand. "But, not the Harpy's magic!"

"What does that mean?" I asked, noting her worried expression.

I followed her eyes and saw the rows of boxes tethered together with thick cables. They were starting to glow fire-engine red, becoming brighter as we watched.

"She digitized and stored her enchantment, and now it has nowhere to go," Delinda explained quickly.

I didn't have long to reflect on any of this; my scar suddenly began to burn.

"That's bad, right?"

"Oh, yes!" Delinda blurted, "We need to leave now… Right now!"

Her warning was punctuated by a low rumble, as one of the glowing boxes split open, followed the others in fast succession. I couldn't see what was coming out of them, but the ground started to shake violently, and pieces of the cavern's roof rained down around us. The rumbling and shaking grew more and more intense as larger pieces of the ceiling began to fall.

"This way out!" Anna screamed as she and Michalena began to run.

We followed them as they darted into a narrow tunnel on one side of the cavern, hoping they knew where they were taking us. As fast as we fled, it became evident we might not be able to outrun the tunnel's imminent collapse. Dark, roiling billows of dirt and dust began overtaking us, making it nearly impossible to see. It was looking more likely than not that we weren't going to make it.

"Keep going!" Delinda shouted over the combined roar of the convulsing ground and falling earth. "I've got this!"

I stopped in my tracks and turned to see Delinda's silhouette dimly outlined in the thickening clouds that were enveloping her. Her arms were extended straight up as if she were supporting the roof of the shaft.

"Don't stop!" she commanded emphatically, her voice booming above the crashing gouts of earth and rocks falling around us.

I felt Al grab me roughly by the arm. He pulled me behind him as more of the tunnel's roof continued to shower down, threatening to bury us underneath the falling rubble. Self-preservation spurred me on, despite my unwillingness. Stumbling, I allowed Al to drag me along until we finally emerged from the mouth of the shaft—above ground at last. Almost as if it was waiting for us to escape, the tunnel gave way. Seconds later, tons of collapsing earth and rock had erased the cave entrance in an explosive belch of dirt and dust.

Al still had a grip on my arm. He and I stood there—wheezing on dust and looking around for any sign of Delinda. The girls were sitting on the ground a few feet away, out of breath and exhausted from their ordeal.

Still gulping air, I freed myself from Al's grasp. I wiped away the moisture that had suddenly appeared below my eyes and rushed back to the solid wall of earth and stone where the entrance had been. In desperation, I clawed at it uselessly, until I felt Al's hand on my shoulder.

"She bought us the time we needed to escape, Mark," he said softly.

I couldn't reply. My mouth was dry with dust, and my throat was too tight to voice the words I was searching for.

"She's dead, isn't she?" one of the girls said as she rose to her feet.

"No one could live through that," agreed the other.

Al remained silent. With an effort, I forced my eyes away from the hillside and saw we were in the midst of a thickly wooded area. Intertwining branches from the tall California Live Oak trees and Ponderosa Pines shaded the dense detritus of the forest floor from the noon-day sun. Other than the pile of rocks and fresh earth on the hillside that marked where the cave's entrance had been, there was no other landmark to be seen.

"This way," Anna declared, peering at her phone. "We go downhill to the road."

The girls quickly regained the visible path of trampled underbrush they had left earlier in the day. As I trudged along behind them, I grudgingly admired their dedication. Regardless of whether the girls were fearless or merely foolish, few grown men would have attempted to undertake what they had.

I kept pace, trancelike, as we plunged through the tall, dry brush, putting one foot after another, all while trying to keep my thoughts from unraveling. It was all I could do to keep from being overwhelmed by my last glimpse of Delinda. The sight of her being swallowed up by the tunnel collapse was etched onto my optic nerves —like an afterimage from staring too long at the sun.

Until we passed out of the trees into a group of weedy clearings that comprised the grounds of an old, untended cemetery, I had lost all track of time. I was only partially aware as we threaded through and around the randomly placed sections of crumbling granite headstones sprouting from the loamy forest floor like broken teeth.

"We're almost there," Anna assured us as we passed through a rusty ruin of a waist-high chain-link fence. "The road is just beyond the gate up there."

"Hey, I think we've finally got cell service," Al said, looking at his phone.

"I'll call for a pickup," I said, grateful for an opportunity to concentrate on something other than Delinda's last moments.

Even if we didn't know exactly where we were, the app on my phone would send our GPS location to the ride-share driver. I launched the app to summon the ride. Besides being informed our driver would arrive in fifteen minutes, the map showed we were on Partrick Road.

"How far away from the winery are we?" Al asked.

I zoomed out on the map. "About a mile as the crow flies."

I looked over at the girls. Whatever adrenaline had kept them going was gone. They looked like I felt—deflated and exhausted.

"Anna, Michalena… I think it's time we get you home," I said. "Your families are worried sick about you."

Both of them nodded numbly. Like Al and I, their clothes and faces were grimy with dust and dirt.

I handed over my phone to Anna and said, "Right now, I think you should call your folks to tell them you're safe and on the way home. All right?"

"Sí," Anna answered. "We got what we came for."

Michalena nodded. "We're sorry about your friend."

"Me too," I whispered too quietly for them to hear.

CHAPTER TWENTY-FIVE

MY SENSE OF LOSS had overshadowed any urgency I might have felt to call Reeves and Feinstein. Besides, my first responsibility was to the girls we rescued. While there wasn't anything that could bring Delinda back, I knew exactly what she would have expected of me.

Once we arrived back at the resort, we went directly to my villa, where all of us cleaned up as best we could. Afterward, Al and I escorted the girls to the bus depot and bought them tickets for the trip home. As we were leaving, Michalena surprised me with a kiss on the cheek.

"You saved us and avenged our friend. I will never forget," she said.

"Yes," added Anna, "We are grateful, as I'm sure my brother will be. The Garcias never forget our friends... Or our enemies."

A chip off the old block.

I used my mobile to hail another ride for Al and me to return to Taskert's winery. I told Al what I had in mind, but he had something else he wanted to discuss before I made the call to the Napa PD.

"What you did in the cave was pretty impressive..." Al said.

"Not impressive enough to save Delinda," I replied glumly.

Al put his hand on my shoulder. "You know, Mark, I've seen plenty of magic in my day," he began. "Black, white, and in-between... Only one thing's stronger than all of it."

"Yeah? What's that."

"The most powerful force in the universe... Love."

I'm sure he caught my expression of utter disbelief before I said, "You've seen too many Disney movies, Al."

"You can't deny it," he argued, smiling, "You defeated the Harpy by channeling all of it: The love of a child and a sibling that transcended death. But you know what set it in motion?" He didn't wait for me to answer before he said, "You did. And I have to believe your love for Delinda had a lot to do with it."

I knew he meant well, but at that moment, it was the last thing I wanted to hear.

"It doesn't matter. It's all meaningless now that she's gone," I retorted sullenly. "I'm done with magic and all the rest. It's Bullshit."

Before Al could say anything else, my phone buzzed, announcing the arrival of our driver.

Once we got into the car, I decided it was time to reach out to detective Reeves. I bounced around in the Napa PD's phone system for a few minutes before I finally got through.

"Yeah, Tonnick, what is it?" Reeves said brusquely.

I got right to the point. "Iris Taskert threatened us with a gun, and maybe she's already killed someone."

"What?"

Figuring I had his undivided attention, I went on. "And, there's also a counterfeit wine operation down in the caves…" I waited a beat before I added,

"That's where we found the body."

"Whose body?" Reeves pressed.

"Kaffee's bodyguard," I answered.

"You can substantiate this?" he challenged.

Despite my dramatic presentation, the detective sounded doubtful. Good thing I saved the best for last.

"Yeah, I can, and believe me, that's not all. Once you get down into the wine caves, ignore the danger signs, and keep going. Beyond the last set of barricades, you'll find the counterfeit workshop. There's a wooden door down there that looks like a closet. Open it, and you'll see the dead body. Oh, and there's a hole on the back wall of that same tunnel leading to an ancient section of the caves… Where you'll find the remains of twenty or thirty people."

"Really? And you think Iris might have killed them too?"

From the sound of his voice, I could tell my credibility had become stretched to the limit.

"Hardly. These are skeletons… It could be they're more than a hundred years old. We found them while we were escaping from the tunnel Iris locked us up in."

"If you say so," Reeves muttered, followed by a loud exhale. "Where are you?"

"On our way to the Winery."

"We're there already," said Reeves as he clicked off.

"That's strange," I said, addressing Al, "they're already on scene."

He nodded in acknowledgment but remained silent until we turned off the highway onto the side road leading to the winery.

Then he said, "Mark, you've gotta have faith."

I shook my head. "Right now, I'm fresh out."

Al was not to be deterred. If nothing else, he set about derailing my pity party by distracting me with more questions.

"Okay, then help me out here," he continued. "I'm having trouble understanding why Iris killed Kaffee's bodyguard."

I hated that he had resorted to that tactic, but I couldn't help myself. I guess my brain is just wired that way.

"I'm also having a problem with that," I admitted.

Al did a poor job of hiding his self-satisfaction at bringing me back into the moment.

"Well, then who *did* kill the guy?"

"I get what you're trying to do, Al, but you won't make me feel any better by asking questions."

"Okay, don't feel better."

"Fine, I'll play," I conceded with a loud sigh. "Let's assume Mr. Muscle was the one who shot out our tire on the highway. Plainly, he was ex-military, and let's also assume he was enough of an expert marksman to hit the sidewall of a tire on a car doing eighty plus. But then, afterward, this same expert marksman aims at Delinda and hits Kaffee instead.

"Remember how shook up he was when we saw him at the hospital? He knew he didn't miss his target. Whoever put him up to it was either angry he hit Kaffee by mistake, or concerned that he was unnerved enough to tell his story to the wrong people."

"So, Iris and Phil are behind all this?" asked Al.

"I thought so for a while… But after Clement disappeared on us, I began to realize that everything he told us was a lie."

"All of it?"

"Yeah," I replied. "Every single word was pure, unadulterated bullshit."

Fifteen minutes later, we were back at Taskert's winery, standing in the parking area. As the old baseball guy once said, it was "déjà vu, all over again." For the second time in so many days, the lot was overflowing with police and emergency vehicles.

"Did you miss me?" asked a familiar voice behind me.

Instantly, my legs turned into Jello, and Al had to grab me to keep me from hitting the ground.

I couldn't decide whether to be overcome with joy—or totally pissed off. I decided to settle for something in between.

"Delinda?" I sputtered. "How?"

"You shouldn't need to ask," she said smugly.

"I told you to have faith," said Al, grinning broadly.

Although he'd probably beg to differ, it was clear Al was just as relieved as I was.

"Damn it, Delinda! You might have said something!" I protested, my voice growing louder with every word. "Like, I'll be back… Something! Or did you enjoy screwing around with my head!?"

She looked taken aback by my tirade. Her reaction surprised—and unnerved me.

"I'm sorry," I said far more softly. "It's just…"

"Mark," she began slowly, "There was no time. I thought you would figure it out…"

She was right; I should have known. If bullets passed through her harmlessly, why worry about a few hundred tons of rock and dirt?

I shook my head. "All right, I get it... Just promise me you'll never do that again!"

She tilted her head slightly and gave me a warm smile. "I'll try."

I felt the elephant leave—the one that had been sitting on my chest. I could breathe again. I could think again.

"Al, I'll deal with you later!" I taunted, wagging a finger at him in faux anger.

Without giving him an opportunity for a comeback, I made my way over to the nearest uniform.

"Get a hold of Reeves or Feinstein and tell 'em Mark Tonnick's here. I'm positive they'll want to talk with me."

The cop eyed me carefully. "Wait here," he said before walking off into the courtyard.

A few minutes later, he returned with detective Feinstein.

"You really know how to pick your clients, Tonnick," the detective said, shaking his head.

I ignored his dig and asked, "So, did you arrest her?"

"No, we didn't," the detective replied tersely.

"Why not?" Al asked.

"Because she was dead when we got here an hour ago... Shot. The hospitality manager found her and called it in."

"Lissette," Delinda stated.

"Yeah, she came into work and found the body," Feinstein confirmed.

"Any idea when she was shot? Or who shot her?" I asked.

"We're working on it," said Feinstein.

"So, where's Phillip Taskert?" I interjected, asking the obvious question.

Feinstein coughed up a humorless laugh. "That's what we'd like to know. Right now, I want you and your friends to stick around. Reeves is still down in the caves, and I'm sure he'll want to be here when you make your statements."

"So, did you find the counterfeiting operation and the old remains?" I prodded.

"Yeah," he answered grudgingly. "We're leaving all of that for the State Police to sort out. We've got enough on our hands already."

Feinstein left us to meet the guys who were pulling two empty gurneys out of the ME's van.

"You saw Clement's truck is gone," Al pointed out while the three of us watched them unload the van.

"I sure did," I replied. "Which confirms he got out of the cave."

"So, why did he just leave us there?" Delinda asked.

"Because he didn't know what else to do," I replied. "Whatever he had planned went sideways the moment Iris locked us all up. Like I told Al, Clement was lying through his teeth about everything."

Delinda nodded. "That makes sense. I would have never thought Derek was gay."

I had also remembered how the winemaker looked at Delinda when she was introduced—not that you ever know. His gate could have swung in both directions.

"Yeah, but he needed to get us down in those caves somehow," I agreed.

"So, you're convinced Clement led us into a trap," she said, glancing at me and then at Al.

"That's how it's looking to me," I replied. "It was a setup."

"So, how did Iris fit into all this?" Al interjected.

Before I could answer, detective Reeves strode up. He was wearing latex gloves, and I saw his knees were marked with dirt from the cave floor.

He looked at us crossly. "Why is it that whenever any of you show up, a shit-storm follows closely behind?"

"None of this is our fault," I asserted. "The last time we saw Iris, she was alive enough to threaten us with a gun."

Reeves's expression darkened. "Be that as it may, she's been dead for at least two hours. After you called, we searched the wine caves and found the dead body exactly where you said it would be… Along with what appears to be the murder weapon."

"Which murder weapon?" I asked. "The gun that killed her, or one that killed Kaffee's bodyguard?"

"Won't know until forensics runs ballistics," Reeves conceded.

"Okay, but you must have some idea who killed her," I pressed.

Reeves nodded. "It's not looking good for the husband. We haven't been able to find him."

"I also suggest you question Clement Wagner," I began. "He called us here to meet him this morning and took us down into the caves. Coincidently, he led us right to the counterfeit wine operation before Iris appeared and locked us all up at gunpoint. If we hadn't been able to dig our way out, who knows what would have happened!"

"Any idea where is Clement now?" Reeves asked.

"None," I answered. "Somewhere along the way, he gave us the slip." I paused to let that sink in before I added, "Oh, and by the way, If you found any upchuck near the body, it belonged to him."

Reeves's eyes narrowed. "Feinstein will want to thank him for that. He stepped in it before I did. We'll get Wagner's statement too… As soon as we find him."

Al nodded. "What about the phony wine?"

Reeves looked puzzled. "What wine? We didn't find any wine, counterfeit, or otherwise. Just a bunch of fake labels and empty bottles, along with other stuff that might be used in counterfeiting."

Delinda, Al, and I shared a three-way double take.

Al cleared his throat and spoke. "Detective, there were two bottles of 1947 Cheval Blanc St-Emilion down there when Iris ambushed us. Clement insisted they were counterfeits."

"They weren't there," claimed Reeves as Feinstein walked up. "We conducted a thorough…"

Reeves was interrupted by Feinstein, who pulled him aside.

"Wait here," advised Reeves after he and his partner conferred out of earshot. "We've got a few more questions."

After they walked further away, both detectives engaged in an animated conversation.

"Hmm, Iris ends up dead, and the wine we saw is missing, along with Phil Taskert and Clement Wagner," I remarked to Al and Delinda. "Draw your own conclusions."

Al said, "Do you suppose Clement doubled back and took the wine?"

I paused, running the events through my mind. I answered, "That's a possibility. He could have easily done that while we were distracted."

Delinda nodded and asked, "So, could Clement have killed Iris?"

"I'm not sure," I conceded. "But I'll bet a case of tequila he's in the middle of all of it... Right up to his red neck."

Al didn't say anything, but Delinda nodded again in agreement.

While Clement certainly might be capable of murder, he didn't strike me as being smart enough to concoct the convoluted explanation he used to lead us into such a complicated trap. My gut told me someone else was pulling the strings.

"Once we finish giving our statement to Napa's finest, we should have a chat with Richard Kaffee," I proposed. "I'm looking forward to seeing his face once we tell him his investment wine scam has been blown."

CHAPTER TWENTY-SIX

DELINDA HEADED THE LEXUS over to the hospital at her usual break-neck speed. For the second time today, I prayed the rental's temporary spare was up to the task.

"How do you want to handle this?" Delinda asked as she swerved around a large, slow-moving recreational vehicle with only inches to spare.

"Why don't we start by asking him how he's feeling… Then, go for the throat."

"Subtle… Is that something you learned in Private Eye school!" she teased.

"Oh yeah, I was top of my class," I quipped without bothering to mention most of my academia was accomplished online. "It's safe to assume he's involved in the wine fraud thing, and maybe murder. He and Taskert have likely made millions bilking investors."

"I figure he'll just deny everything," Al interjected. "He'll blame everything on Taskert, and claim he's another victim of the scam."

"He can try, but I'll know if he's telling the truth," said Delinda.

I didn't doubt that for a New York minute. A genie's sensibilities were far and away more reliable than a polygraph. Too bad that our timing wasn't nearly as good. We arrived at the hospital only to discover they had released Kaffee an hour before we got there.

"That might end up working in our favor," I ventured as we returned to the Lexus. "If we talk to him at home, there'll be no interruptions from nurses or doctors."

Naturally, Delinda knew the way to Kaffee's house, and as expected, got us there in record time. His property was located on a narrow, winding road several miles after it branched off from the main highway. A long, gravel driveway led to an immaculately restored craftsman style home distinguished by a half dozen wide steps that led up to an elevated front porch. A pair of ornate, Romanesque, white columns flanking the entrance gave the place a decided plantation vibe.

When we pulled into the driveway, an unmarked police vehicle was already parked in front. I slapped my hand on the dash and swore.

"Damn it! We missed the window! I'll bet Reeves and Feinstein are grilling him as we speak."

"An' more than likely, they aren't going to share any of their info with us," Al remarked.

Before Al could finish his pronouncement, Kaffee's front door flew open, and both detectives emerged. They did not look pleased as they made their way down the stairs.

"I think you're wrong, Al," Delinda smiled. "They can't wait to tell us everything they know."

The two cops were ready to get into their cruiser when they suddenly stopped and turned in our direction. Delinda rolled down her window as they walked over. On their approach, my cheek began to itch.

"Nice to see you again," Delinda said sweetly.

"Nice to see you, too," Reeves replied.

Besides the fact that his polite greeting was totally out of character, Reeves's voice also lacked both the disdain and impatience I had grown to expect. Both detectives had the same glassy, faraway look in their eyes. Whatever magic Delinda was working, I was all for it.

She made a small, nearly imperceptible motion with her hand.

"So?" she asked, as though we were all sipping lattes at Starbucks.

Reeves broke out in a visible sweat as his words came out in a rush.

"Kaffee denies knowing anything about the phony wine operation. He insists he was also a victim. He claims that besides arranging for Taskert's wine collection to be sold at auction, he even purchased some himself. On our way out, Kaffee said he intends to sue Phillip Taskert for everything he's got."

"What about the attempt on his life the other night?" I asked.

Reeves and Feinstein stood there as if they hadn't heard my question.

"What about the attempt on his life the other night?" Delinda repeated. The slight humor in her voice was plainly for my benefit, but this time Feinstein answered.

"He's convinced Taskert was behind the shooting and his wife's killing too. Over the last few days, Kaffee thought Taskert was becoming unhinged… Even accused him of having an affair with his wife. An assertion, by the way, Kaffee denies. From our perspective, Taskert has all the classic motives for murder… money and revenge."

"Thank you, detectives, you've been very accommodating," Delinda said before she rolled up her window.

The men had walked halfway back to their car when they suddenly stopped in their tracks. From their confused expressions, I'm sure they couldn't remember why they were still yards away from their sedan.

"Well, that was a novel way of getting an update," I remarked.

"I thought you might appreciate that," she smiled.

Al shook his head. "How was that helpful? I'm more confused than ever!"

"Actually, now things are becoming clearer," I said. "Consider: Kaffee has been angling to take over Taskert's winery, buying out everyone's shares… Aside from Ashton's, of course. If Taskert goes down for murder, Kaffee's got a clear path to a majority ownership… Nice and clean."

"What about Lissette? You said she also owns a piece of the winery," Delinda interjected.

I didn't get to reply, because my mobile began to ring.

"Tonnick," I answered.

Carlos Garcia said, "Hey, I want to thank you, Man."

"You're welcome."

"I can't begin to tell you how happy I am," he stated.

I had to stop myself from laughing. The guy's voice had no emotion in it whatsoever.

"Good to know," I acknowledged. "One thing, though, would you mind seeing that Michalena gets home okay?"

"You got it." There was a long pause before Carlos asked, "Anna said you killed Momo... Is that true?"

"Yeah."

"Muy bueno."

That was all I got before he abruptly clicked off.

Another satisfied customer.

We waited until Reeves and Feinstein drove off before the three of us mounted the steps to Kaffee's front door. The doorbell had a built-in security camera, so Delinda positioned herself directly in front of the lens before she rang the bell. A moment later, Kaffee opened the door with his arm in a sling and a broad smile on his face. His smile swiftly faded as soon as he saw Al and me standing behind Delinda.

"Well, I'm certainly glad you came, my dear," Kaffee said, visibly disappointed she had not come alone.

"I remained at the hospital last night until they said you were okay," Delinda said, returning his smile. "All of us wanted to see how you were doing. Is it all right if we come in?"

His smile returned, if somewhat forced, as he opened the door wider and waved us inside. "Please, make yourself at home."

The front door opened directly into a spacious front room, furnished sumptuously in a style that strongly suggested it was the work of the same interior designer that had outfitted his winery. Everything appeared clean, modern, and very expensive.

We filed in and sat down next to each other on a long, overstuffed leather couch as Kaffee took a seat across from us in a matching recliner.

"The police were just here," Kaffee began. "They said Iris is dead... Along with my security man, Gustave. Very sad."

"Our condolences," Delinda said. "I suppose they also spoke to you about the counterfeit wine?"

"Yes, they did," said Kaffee. "I'm still having trouble believing Phil and Iris would be involved with that sort of thing, but I suppose anything's possible... Especially when so much money is concerned."

While he was talking, I observed him carefully. Kaffee was avoiding direct eye contact with any of us while he professed his ignorance. It didn't take a jaded guy like myself to know he was being less than truthful. With that in mind, I decided to yank his chain to see what fell out.

Very deliberately, I asked, "So, you... The wine broker... and the auctioneer, had absolutely no idea that the wines you were auctioning off were fakes? Seeing you've represented yourself as both a collector and a wine expert, I find that hard to swallow."

I enjoyed watching the abrupt transformation of Kaffee's demeanor. He went from calm to crazy in less than a nano-second.

"You've got a helluva nerve! To come into my house and accuse me of a crime!"

"Oh, you think that's bad?" I prodded shamelessly. "My theory is that you, Iris, and Phil were in it together, ginning up fake wine. And when Ashton sent us up here to investigate the winery, all of you panicked. That's why you sent your bodyguard to shoot out our tire on the highway. And, when that failed, you had him take a shot at Delinda."

"That's absurd!" Kaffee sputtered, growing red in the face. "I'll sue you for slander!"

His loud protest only fueled me on. "Go ahead and try!" I challenged, pushing back with a louder voice than before. "And you want to know what else? I think your man, Gustave, bought a bullet because he missed Delinda and hit you instead!"

That must have struck a nerve.

"Get out! Get out now!" he yelled, rising from his recliner in apoplectic rage. "All of you!"

"We'll go," I said calmly. "But this isn't over by any means... I promise you. Once we find Clement and the missing wine, we'll have all the proof we need."

That got his attention, and he suddenly dialed back his outrage enough to ask, "What do you mean, missing wine?"

Thankfully Al stepped up to provide the details. Even if I remembered the name on the bottle—which I didn't—there was no way I'd be able to pronounce it.

Al said, "Before Clement took off, he disappeared with two three-liter bottles of fake 1947 Cheval Blanc St-Emilion,"

All the fire left Kaffee as he sunk limply back down into his chair.

He said, "Those weren't fakes. Those were real!"

Now it was my turn to be surprised. "Real?"

"Yes," Kaffee ran his hands nervously through his hair. "I acquired them two years ago. They're worth about a hundred and thirty-thousand dollars apiece."

"Are you positive?" I asked, now as surprised as he was.

Kaffee took a deep breath and nodded.

"I saw they were missing last week."

"If that was the case, why didn't you report them stolen?" I pressed.

Kaffee didn't answer. Instead, he pointed to the front door and ordered, "I think you all need to go now."

Al motioned to Delinda and me, and we followed him outside. The curtain of Kaffee's front room window wasn't drawn closed all the way, affording me a partial view. The moment the door shut behind us, he pulled out his mobile. Inside my brain, another piece of the puzzle slid into place. The answer had been in front of me from the very beginning.

"So, what now?" Al asked as we crossed the driveway to our rental.

"I think we need to find Lissette and have a conversation with her… Before the cops do."

"Of course, you think she was in on it," Delinda stated.

To her credit, there wasn't a trace of snark in her voice.

"To tell you the truth, I don't see how she couldn't be," I answered.

CHAPTER TWENTY-SEVEN

DELINDA HAD DRIVEN HALFWAY back to Downtown Napa when my phone rang.

"Mark."

Lissette O'Hannon's breathless brogue was barely audible above the road noise from our rental's temporary spare tire.

"We need to see you right away!"

"We?" I replied. I had stuck a finger in my other ear so I could hear her more clearly.

"Yes, Phillip and I... We gotta talk, 'fore he turns himself in."

"So you know the police think he shot Iris, right?"

"He swears it's not true!" she insisted. "Come right away! Please!"

I memorized the address she gave me and repeated it to Delinda as I rang off. She nodded and immediately turned the car around and headed back to the highway. I was under the impression genies don't need GPS directions, but Delinda's navigation app was already programmed to our destination.

"Neat trick," I said admiringly. "I didn't even see you pick up your phone to enter it."

Delinda shot me a glance implying it was beneath a reply. In return, I gave her a mock salute. Perhaps it was only my imagination, but it seemed to me that our relationship, if you can call it that, was finally on the mend. Despite being comforted by that thought, I resumed my white-knuckled clutch on the door grip as Delinda tore off to Taskert's location. A few miles later, we turned off the main drag onto a frontage road in the small town of Saint Helena.

At first, I wondered if Lissette had directed us to her residence, but quickly realized that wasn't the case. She was smart enough to know the cops were probably keeping an eye on it, but even so, I was surprised when the navigation app announced we had reached our destination.

"Is this it?" Al asked as Delinda pulled into an empty strip mall parking lot.

There were three storefronts. Two of them appeared empty, and the third reminded me of Mrs. Krentzman's mini-mart. Its interior was dark, and a closed sign was prominently displayed in the front window.

"We're at the right address," she confirmed.

"Figures that Taskert would be hanging out in a liquor store," I added.

"It's a wine shop," corrected Al. "Look at the sign."

There were red block letters across the glass double doors that read: Saint Helena Fine wines.

"You're right," I conceded as we all got out of the car. "Still, it's not much of a distinction."

I tested the entry door with a gentle push and found it unlocked. I looked over to Delinda, who shook her head. If she hadn't unlocked it, then someone was apparently expecting us. I only hoped we weren't walking into another trap. I pushed the door open all the way, and we warily entered. The interior lights were off, but the afternoon sunlight filtering through the windows revealed nothing but dancing dust motes. We were alone. No cashier, no customers.

"Hello?" called Al. "Anyone here?"

"Yes," came Lissette's cautious reply from the rear of the store. "D'ya think you were followed?"

"No," I called out confidently. At the speed Delinda was driving, a tail would have been easy to spot. "Where's Taskert?"

"Here, with me in the backroom," Lissette answered.

We hastened to the far end of the shop to a set of black, double doors, each with a small, round glass porthole. I pulled the leftmost one open, and we entered the storeroom. Lissette was sitting on one of the haphazardly stacked cases of what was presumably wine, while an extremely agitated Phillip Taskert paced impatiently.

"I'm glad you made it, Tonnick," Taskert said. "I'll get right to the point. I need to hire you and your team… To clear me."

"I'm not sure that will work," I replied. "It might be a conflict of interest."

"Bullshit!" he retorted angrily. "Ashton had you come up here to help me. So help me, damn it! I'm innocent!"

"Of what?" I countered. "Innocent of wine fraud? Innocent of murder?"

Taskert was having none of it. "Don't be an asshole! I didn't kill my wife… I swear it. And, there is absolutely no way either of us would be involved in pedaling phony wine."

"How is that possible?" asked Al. "When we stumbled onto the workshop, Iris locked us up at gunpoint!"

Taskert shook his head rapidly. "You got it wrong… If she did what you say she did, she had a good reason. We didn't need to fake wine. We had our own collection to sell, and I know for a fact every single bottle was genuine. I'll let you know right now, she was a highly respected businesswoman. So much so, that other collectors sought her out to broker their wine at our auctions."

"So, was it possible that she and Kaffee were running the scam without your knowledge?" I asked bluntly.

"No goddamn way! We were both very careful about that. Clement Wagner authenticated and verified the provenance of every bottle we put up for auction. He's an expert… Supposedly one of the very best!"

"Supposedly?" Delinda repeated, punctuating her comment with her classic arched brow. "So, you just took his word on it?"

Taskert took a deep breath and exhaled loudly before he answered.

"There wasn't any reason not to. Clement used to authenticate wine for auction houses in New York. Derek, our winemaker, checked with several of them and assured us we could rely on Clement's expertise. I don't understand how we could have gotten it so wrong!"

"Oh my god, Phil!" Lissette suddenly blurted out. "I did na want t' tell you, but I'm sure Iris and Derek were having an affair… Coulda been all their doin'. An' whoever killed him, killed her!"

"What?" All of us said at the same time.

Between Derek and Kaffee, the late Iris Taskert was a very busy woman, at least according to gossip.

Taskert turned to Lissette. "Are you sure? I know Iris and I were having our ups and downs… But Derek?"

"I'm so sorry, Phil. But that's what it looked like t' me."

Delinda, Al, and I looked at each other. From the looks in their eyes, I knew they were thinking the same thing I was. Lissette's assertions alluded to a motive that might implicate Phil in both murders.

"There could be other reasons for Iris and Derek's murders," I said. "If Derek and Clement were running a con, secretly making the counterfeit wine at the winery, then tainting the wine would make sense. Since they had access to every bottle and barrel of wine, it would have been easy to do. It was a brilliant but risky play to keep you preoccupied with the contamination issue… Misdirecting your attention and making it less likely that you'd stumble onto their hidden operation... Which was literally right under your nose."

"So, are you implying Clement killed Iris?" Taskert asked.

"My take on it is that Iris somehow found the secret workshop in the caves," I answered. "And on the morning Clement lured us down there, she was probably already inside the winery… Waiting to see who showed up."

"But, she locked us in the tunnel too," Al objected, clearly not convinced.

I shrugged. "Maybe Iris thought we were in on it. She saw the storage closet at the last minute and decided to lock us in there while she called the cops… Which, also leads me to believe she didn't know the bodyguard's corpse was hidden in there."

Since I had everyone's attention at this point, I went on. "Someone other than Iris killed Kaffee's bodyguard and stashed him there. I'm also convinced that whatever Clement had in mind for us, didn't include him being locked up with us, let alone our discovering the body."

"So," Delinda said. "Why did he get sick to his stomach?"

"I'm guessing nerves," I speculated. "Things weren't going as planned, and he was beginning to panic."

"Then, what do you think he was expecting?" Al asked.

I had a hunch, but I wasn't ready to share it, so I only said, "I'm not sure, but Iris suddenly appearing screwed up whatever he had in store for us. That might explain why, after we found a way out, Clement doubled back. Maybe he got Iris to unlock the door... There was a struggle over the gun, and he managed to shoot her. In any event, I'm convinced he escaped from the locked tunnel somehow and hightailed it out of there with the four bottles of wine."

"Four bottles?" said Al, looking confused. "We only saw two."

"Yeah. We only saw one set of bottles, but there were two sets," I replied. "The fake ones were out on the table, but the real ones were hidden somewhere else in the workshop."

Seeing Taskert's puzzled expression, I added, "The authentic ones belonged to Richard Kaffee. I think Clement took them to reference when he made his copies."

"So, you believe I didn't kill Iris?" Taskert interrupted.

I shrugged. "It doesn't matter what I believe, it's all about the evidence."

Lissette left Taskert's side and drew closer to me and gave me one of her 'come hither' smiles.

"What canna we do 'bout it?" she asked sweetly. "We canna let Phil take the blame for something he didna do."

I snuck a quick glance at Delinda to see her reaction. I was rewarded with a flash of disdain that instantly evaporated into an unreadable expression.

I nodded in agreement. "Phil, you need to hire an attorney and make arrangements to surrender to the cops. Hiding out like this makes you look guilty as hell. Lissette, you'll also want to retain an attorney. This is going to get messy."

"What will you do?" asked Taskert.

"We're going to track down another lead," I replied.

"All right. Whatever it takes," Taskert nodded. "Just find who really killed my wife!"

We left the building and got back into the car.

"So you think when Iris unlocked the door, Clement shot her?" asked Al.

"He didn't kill Iris," I replied.

"Now, I'm confused," Al countered. "You just as much said he did!"

"Yeah, maybe. I didn't want to show all of my cards," I said. "I'll explain after we have a conversation with Clement Wagner."

Delinda started the car and drove out of the parking lot as Al gave me a questioning look via the rearview.

"I'd like to see you pull off that trick," Al said. "Where do you suppose we'll find him?"

With a slight shrug of my shoulders, I replied, "Where else? With his partners."

Forty minutes later, we were parked a short distance away from Kaffee's place, where we could view the house without being seen from the property.

"So, you think Clement will come back here?" Al asked.

"Hell yeah," I responded. "If he's going on the run, he'll need cash, and he knows Kaffee's good for it. In any event, it's a cinch Kaffrey'll want his wine back."

Al nodded his understanding, which was good since I was flying entirely by the seat of my pants. I was beginning to doubt my instincts when nearly an hour later, Clement Wagner's pickup truck rolled into Kaffee's driveway, rewarding my intuition.

"Looks like you had it right," Al said. "We should call the cops."

"We will," I replied. "But first, I think we should go up and have a talk with Kaffee and Wagner."

I had just begun to open the car door when another car roared up the road, quickly making the turn onto Kaffee's property. It was Lissette's Honda Accord.

Delinda inched the car closer so we could get a better view of what Lissette was doing. As soon as she parked her car, the Accord's trunk popped open. Lissette got out, looking up at the house to see if anyone had noticed her arrival. She exited her vehicle, keeping her attention focused on the building, as she quietly shut the car door.

Confident no one inside was aware she had driven in, she pulled a red, plastic gasoline container from the trunk, before easing it shut without a sound. Plainly, she had no intention of advertising her presence.

"I don't think she has Merlot in there," I said sarcastically.

Lissette quickly mounted the steps to the porch, where she held the container out of sight behind her back and rang the doorbell. Moments later, Kaffee opened the door. He looked surprised, yet waved her inside unhesitatingly. Lissette entered, but Kaffee never had a chance to close the door behind her. In all probability, the muffled gunshots we heard had a lot to do with that.

"What now?" asked Al.

My scar began to itch.

"Now, you can call the cops," I said. "I'm going up there."

"Not without me, you're not," Delinda declared.

It was pointless to argue with her; besides, she was already out of the car. The two of us sprinted the length of the long driveway to the foot of the porch steps and dashed up to the open front door. There, we found ourselves face to face with Lissette. At the exact moment the smell of gasoline reached my nostrils, I saw the small automatic pistol in her hand.

"I had t' do it!" she sobbed. "They were gonna kill me!"

I looked past her into the house. Kaffee and Clement were sprawled on the floor of the front room, lying motionless and bleeding all over the white, designer rug.

"Yeah, that's why you doused the place with gas," I said. "Give me the gun, Lissette… It's over."

The sudden change in her expression was striking. Her voice went from a little girl in distress to full-on desperate housewife in an eye blink.

"It is, for you!" she snarled, bringing up her weapon and leveling it at the two of us.

I quickly put up my hands, and Delinda did the same.

"By the time they put out the fire an' find your bodies, I'll be on a plane t' the Caymans."

Her maniacal smile sent a chill up my spine, and since she knew I didn't carry, my only option was to stall—and hope for a miracle, or genie magic, whichever happened first.

"So, did you kill Taskert, too?" I asked, aware we had left the two of them together.

"Na. Phil's more valuable as a patsy thanna corpse."

I had to admit, that was a smart move. She probably left enough breadcrumbs behind to make him look good for Clement and Kaffee's murder too.

"So, Taskert never suspected a thing, did he?" I said. "I take it you, Clement, and Kaffee were the ones behind the wine fraud scam. But I have to ask… Why kill your partners?"

Lissette Sneered. "Trying t' buy time isn't going t' work for ya, Mark."

She pulled the trigger, but there was only a loud click as the weapon misfired. I flinched, although I anticipated the outcome when my scar began to itch. Lissette's eyes narrowed as she tried several more times with the same result.

"They don't make 'em like they used to, do they?" I chided, hoping I didn't sound as relieved as I felt.

With a string of curses, Lissette threw the gun at my head. While I dodged the weapon, she made a dash to maneuver around me. Big mistake.

Delinda had already planted herself directly in Lissette's path as she charged forward, head down, intending to bowl Delinda over. Instead, Delinda calmly raised both hands, palms forward. I watched in amusement as Lissette flew backward as if she had collided with a vertical trampoline. She landed with a loud crack—the back of her head ricocheting off the hardwood porch.

"I hope that hurt," I commented under my breath.

Al came rushing up the steps a few seconds later.

"I see you didn't need my help," he noted, looking down at Lissette, who was groaning as she began to regain consciousness.

"You'll need these," Delinda said, handing me a set of LAPD regulation handcuffs.

I ignored the fact they seemed to appear out of nowhere.

"Nice you come prepared," I complimented as I pulled Lissette's arms behind her back and snapped on the cuffs.

"Did you expect anything less?" Delinda smugly replied.

"Not really," I answered, rushing into the house, leaving Lissette to Delinda's not-so-tender mercies.

Kaffee was gone, but Clement, by some miracle, was still clinging to life—if only by a thin thread. Before I pulled out my phone and dialed 911, I tore a piece from his T-shirt and balled it up, stuffing it forcefully into his chest wound.

The cops were just arriving as I got off the call. Three black and whites, followed by the detective's unmarked Crown Vic were skidding into the driveway.

Reeves was the first one to reach the top of the stairs. He saw Lissette sitting on the porch in cuffs, under Delinda's watchful glare, and me, through the open front door, standing over Clement, applying pressure to his wound. Before he could say a word, Feinstein bounded up behind him.

"What the hell happened here?" Feinstein shouted, looking at Reeves for an explanation.

"I was about to ask the same thing," Reeves said.

Despite the detective's questioning stares, I smiled and motioned to the dazed and disheveled Lissette. Her fetching baby blues were also fixed on me, lustrous with murderous intent.

"The lovely lady there is responsible not only for the carnage here, but several other killings," I began.

I pointed to the automatic lying where it had landed after nearly hitting my head. "You'll find her prints on it, and there's no doubt ballistics will show it fired the bullets in Richard Kaffee and Clement Wagner. And, I'll bet you double or nothing, it will also turn out to be a match for the ones that wasted Kaffee's bodyguard. Oh, and she killed Iris Taskert, using Iris's gun, which she planted to frame Phil Taskert."

Reeves looked at Lissette and then back at me. From his expression, I could tell he wasn't pleased being late to the party.

Feinstein appeared confused. "Mind telling us why?"

"Not at all," I began. "Lissette, Clement, and Kaffee were all in the counterfeit wine operation together."

"Hold on!" interjected Reeves. "I thought you said Iris was responsible for that."

"I jumped to the wrong conclusion," I admitted. "Yesterday morning, Clement called us over to the winery intending to lure us into a trap. Originally, he schemed to take us down into the caves where he and Lissette would make us disappear, like Kaffrey's hired muscle, once and for all."

"Really? Why did they think they could get away with killing all of you?" Feinstein scoffed.

"I'll get to that," I promised. "But, that plan went down the toilet... Because what neither of them suspected, was that Iris had discovered their secret workshop and immediately realized its purpose. That's why on the morning Clement guided us down there, Iris was waiting to see who would show up."

Reeves's brow furrowed as he listened until they nearly met in the center of his forehead. "So, why pull a gun on you?"

"Because when Iris saw us with Clement, she couldn't assume we weren't also in on it. That's why she locked all of us up together... Out of an abundance of caution. Naturally, she didn't know that was where Lissette had stashed the bodyguard's corpse."

"Hold on!" interrupted Feinstein. "Why did Lissette kill Gustave in the first place?"

"Only one explanation comes to mind," I explained. "Gustave, like a lot of ex-military guys, probably suffered from PTSD... Occupational hazard. And he was rattled after he shot Kaffee by mistake. When we saw him at the hospital, he was clearly shaken... So, it's not much of a stretch to assume Lissette decided he had become a liability and thought it was time to get rid of him."

"That's a pretty big assumption," Reeves argued.

I raised one hand to halt his objection and said, "Let me finish... So, after Iris locked us in the cave, she rang up Lissette, assuming she was at home. But she wasn't... Lissette was already on the winery premises, preparing to ambush us once Clement got us underground. So, when Lissette got Iris's call about finding Clement and the three of us red-handed in the secret workshop, she had to change her course of action. Instead of showing up with Phil and the police, as Iris expected, Lissette surprised her, disarmed her, and shot her with her own gun."

"Okay, do you know how crazy this sounds?" Feinstein protested. "You still haven't explained why Lissette thought she'd get away with killing all of you!"

"Before Iris threw a monkey wrench into her plans, I think she intended to pin all of our murders on Clement," I replied. "After he helped dispose of our bodies, he'd have pangs of remorse and commit 'suicide.'" I framed the word with air quotes before I added, "Leaving a detailed note behind, of course."

Before either of the detectives could respond, Delinda added, "But, that plan went out the window the moment Iris called Lissette. Imagine her surprise after she shoots Iris and then opens the locked door inside the workshop only to discover we weren't there."

I nodded. "Instead, she finds only Clement, who had doubled back while we were looking for a way out. Then, with us on the loose, Lissette had to rethink everything. With the counterfeit operation blown, and us out of reach, her only option was to frame Phil for Iris's murder… And the wine fraud."

"There's no doubt Lissette encouraged Taskert to go on the run," Delinda offered. "She wanted him to look guilty."

I chuckled and added, "I'll bet you found Phil… Anonymous tip, from a female caller by any chance?"

I saw my answer in Feinstein's face before he replied.

"Yeah," Feinstein admitted. "We picked him up twenty minutes ago."

"Phil was going to be the perfect fall guy for the killings, at least long enough for Lissette to get out of the country," I continued. "Because now that their wine scam was blown, they were going to have to close up shop, and she was eager to cash out.

"But she wanted more than just her share. Neither Kaffee nor Clement ever suspected she intended to double-cross them. As you can see, she was about to torch the place when we came along."

While I was talking, Feinstein had donned a pair of latex gloves to pick up Lissette's gun from where it lay at the bottom of the steps.

"So where's the money, then?" he asked as he slid the weapon into a plastic evidence bag.

I didn't have the answer to that question, but Delinda, who had been staring intently at Lissette for the last few seconds, did.

"Bitcoin," answered Delinda confidently, holding up Lissette's phone.

I hadn't seen it in her hand before this very moment and tried not to look surprised.

Lissette reacted to this with an angry howl. "Fuck you! Fuck you!"

Her profane outburst and twisted expression of rage confirmed Delinda's supposition, at least to my satisfaction. Once again, genie magic proved to be a PI's best friend. I beamed in appreciation as Delinda continued her explanation.

"As a safeguard, the three of them split the key token for the blockchain account where they kept the profits into three pieces. It was supposed to keep them all honest since they needed the entire code to access the account. Lissette had suggested this, of course, but only after she had secretly acquired the entire passcode."

The expression on the faces of both detectives was priceless. I'd take double or nothing they would lookup "Bitcoin" on their phones the minute they got back in their car.

Before either Reeves or Feinstein could ask Delinda for the source of her information, she added, "You'll find the encryption key on her phone. The numbers, 54321, will unlock it."

"What the fuck are you, Bitch!?" Lissette screamed, followed by another string of shrill curses.

I stood there in admiration with a big smile on my face. I wanted to add something like, "Don't piss off the genie, or she'll turn you into a poisonous toad." But, I held my tongue, reasoning that for all intents and purposes, Lissette was halfway there already—metaphorically speaking.

"What about Derek?" Reeves asked, scratching his head. "How did he fit in?"

"That puzzled me at first," I answered. "But, once I decided everything Clement told us was a lie, I arrived at the conclusion that Derek, along with Clement, were the ones tainting Taskert's wine. Kaffee probably paid them to do it, because he had plans that went beyond just the wine fraud deal. But, once Derek realized how much money the counterfeiting operation was generating, he wanted in on it too. That's what he and Clement were arguing about on the day we met them."

"So, you think Lissette killed him too?" Feinstein pressed skeptically.

"No, I think after we left them, their argument escalated, and Clement ended up strangling Derek. Maybe he didn't mean to kill him, but it was too late. He probably called Lissette, who was running errands for Taskert. She not only provided him with an alibi, but she was smart enough to have him disguise the cause of death by mutilating Derek's neck with the chain and hanging him from the chandelier to further muddy the waters. That whole 'cursed castle' thing was a red herring."

I didn't add my assumption that somewhere along the way, Taskert had shared Bruce Ashton's penchant for the supernatural with Lissette. It would have been natural for her to capitalize on that bit of information, if for nothing else than to misdirect us even more.

Feinstein helped Lissette to her feet, guiding her out of the way of the paramedics scrambling to get into the house. If Clement survived, he'd probably have more to add, but I was sure I had most of it right.

While the detectives began Mirandizing Lissette, Delinda, Al, and I walked back to our rental.

"That was an impressive show of deductive reasoning," Al said, adding, "Sherlock Holmes couldn't have done better,"

"Thanks, Al," I said, wondering if Al had ever run into Arthur Conan Doyle. I made a mental note to ask him some time as I added, "I can't take all the credit, we did it together."

"We do make a good team, don't we?" Delinda declared, expressing it as a matter of fact.

"Yes, we do," I agreed. "I'll try not to screw it up."

"Apology accepted," she declared, smiling.

I was about to challenge her on that point, but Al read my expression and interrupted me before I could get fired up. As I had come to expect, his tone of voice revealed nothing of that intent.

"Why contaminate the wine as a distraction? After all, they might have found somewhere else to base their operation."

I exhaled in frustration, as I realized there was nothing to be gained from fighting Delinda over having the last word. Instead, I answered Al's question as we all piled back into the Lexus.

"Kaffee had more than one objective in mind when he had Clement and Derek sabotage Taskert's wine. Mostly, it was to keep Taskert from opening the winery, which served two purposes. Kaffee knew it would be a powerful motivation for Taskert to sell his wine collection for cash flow. He planned to bleed Taskert dry, so he'd have to sell out eventually. And, as a bonus, Taskert's own collection was authentic and lent more credibility to the auctions, which also included slipping in a few fakes. Apparently, Clement was a much better wine forger than he was a cellarmaster. His work in that regard was quite good.

"Ultimately, the wine fraud was a lucrative, although temporary byproduct of Kaffrey's real objective. He was well on his way to taking over Taskert's winery and assumed it would be in his hands before the secret workshop could be discovered."

"But, why would Kaffee want to own a winery with a dubious reputation?" Al asked. "After all, word was bound to get out as to why the winery failed… It might have never recovered from that."

I laughed. "I don't think Kaffee was interested in the winery per se. He had other plans for the land and the facility. He figured he had the political and the financial juice to turn the Napa County Council around on the pot thing. He already had more than enough grapevines on his other properties and was determined to cash in on what he saw as California's newest and most profitable business… Cannabis production. When we came along, it screwed up Kaffee's brilliant plan. The last thing he expected was for Ashton to become involved and launch his own investigation."

"Kaffee already was a very wealthy man," remarked Al, ignoring our rate of speed as Delinda tore back out to the highway.

"Yeah," I agreed. "But for guys like that, nothing is ever enough," I replied.

"Human nature?" Delinda mused. "Not that I'd know."

CHAPTER TWENTY-EIGHT

BY THE TIME WE finished making our formal statements to the Napa PD downtown, it was early evening. No doubt encouraged by a little genie magic, the detectives allowed us to watch from the video booth as they interrogated Lissette. Almost as soon as it began, Lissette thoughtfully provided the cops with a complete confession. Besides admitting to the murders, she also revealed other details, most of which validated many of the conclusions I had shared with the detectives.

Reeves and Feinstein seemed surprised at Lissette's willingness to unburden herself, but I wasn't. When the interview first began, Lissette declined to speak until Delinda started inscribing subtle gestures in the air with her fingertips. Then, detail after detail poured out of Lissette's mouth in a torrent despite her expressions of alarm and bewilderment.

While nearly everything Lissette told me the night she came to my villa was a total fabrication, a few things were true. Her grandfather was in the hospitality business in Europe. That being said, she had neglected to add he had a thing about collecting empty wine bottles from his establishments. After she met Phil and Iris and discovered how lucrative the wine business was, Lissette thought about all of those old boxes of bottles sitting in her barn, some of which held very costly wines back in the day.

Soon after she arrived stateside, she discovered Clement had an encyclopedic knowledge of rare and collectible wines. While trying to get into her pants, he shared with her the fact he had briefly dabbled in counterfeiting wine in New York. While cultivating that relationship, she had her empty bottles shipped to Napa, where Clement chose the best candidates to refill and re-cork. Now all they needed was a way to sell them.

Clement and Lissette then approached Kaffee, who had already enlisted Derek and Clement to make sure every ounce of Taskert's wine was dead on arrival. Kaffee recognized the profit potential in their scheme, but was initially hesitant—that is until Lissette convinced him to get on board. Sex was a significant factor, but Kaffee also saw it as another way to undermine Taskert.

I was also proved correct as to why Lissette murdered Gustave, AKA, Mr. Muscle. As I assumed, the guy had been utterly unglued by what he saw the night he attempted to shoot Delinda. He swore to Lissette that he didn't miss the shot. He saw through his night-vision scope that the bullet appeared to pass harmlessly through Delinda's forehead with a puff of smoke before striking Kaffee, who was standing behind her.

When she heard that, Lissette became convinced Gustave was unraveling mentally. She had to be sure he'd never bring that up with his PTSD therapist. To that end, Lissette lured him down to the wine cave with the promise of sex. Then, while the poor guy was busy unfastening his trousers, she shot him.

It was a very enlightening and, dare I say, entertaining couple of hours. Lissette's confession, along with Clement's testimony—assuming he survived his injuries—would ensure the murderous Irish beauty would spend the rest of her days behind bars. No Lucky Charms for her.

Afterward, we had a long conversation with Bruce Ashton on the phone, detailing everything that had happened. When the dust finally settled, he would own the majority of shares in Taskert's winery, for whatever that was worth. Thankfully, it was his problem and not ours. We ended the call with him inviting us to spend the night at the resort before we started back to LA. By the time we rang off, it was almost eight PM, and so out of convenience, the three of us agreed to revisit the restaurant where Al and I ate the previous night.

The eatery was much busier than it was the last time we were there, and even the overflow area was full. Despite that, we were seated promptly because somehow, Delinda had a reservation. Again, I was not surprised. Genie magic can be extremely practical in certain circumstances.

When I opened the menu, I was amused to find it was substantially the same as the night before—despite the claim it was printed daily. More proof you can't believe everything you read, including the label on a wine bottle.

Al and Delinda started with a glass of club soda, and I ordered a double Hendricks martini. When the waiter returned with my cocktail, he offered us the wine list.

"I've had enough wine to last me a while," I remarked.

Al laughed, and Delinda gave me a warm smile.

"One thing I have to know, Mark," Al began. "What made you suspicious of Lissette?"

"Besides the fact she feigned interest in you," Delinda slyly interjected.

I shook my head in resignation and returned her smile.

"I have to admit, I didn't think she was involved at first, but my perspective began to change after the night she came to see me... Burning scar and exploding wineglass aside. After I began to suspect that Clement was up to something shady, I remembered Lissette indirectly had asked me if I carried a gun. In retrospect, now I know she wanted to make sure we were defenseless since she originally planned to ambush us in the caves."

"If it hadn't been for Iris getting in the middle of things, who knows what would have happened," Al said.

Delinda took a sip from her glass and stated, "Fate works in mysterious ways, doesn't it."

I caught her meaning. "Yeah, if she hadn't locked us into that tunnel, we wouldn't have stumbled onto Momo, and stopped her from infecting the internet." I neglected to add, "and nearly getting killed in the process."

"Or discovering an ancient massacre, and saving those girls," Al stated.

"And, some long-suffering souls would have never been freed," Delinda added.

"Oh, which brings up something I've been meaning to ask," I said, addressing Delinda as I polished off my cocktail. "Down in the caves, what exactly did Momo slam into? I'm sure you noticed I wasn't all there at the time."

"Do you really want to know?"

"I wouldn't have asked if I didn't," I replied.

"Do you know what 'ectoplasm' is?" she asked.

"Isn't that the gooey slime in the Ghostbusters movies?"

She smiled and said, "I think you answered your own question."

I looked around for our server. I needed a refill. "You're right, I really don't want to know."

Al seemed to be paying no attention to our conversation, and since I was eager to change the subject, I spoke up.

"Hey, Al, are you with us?"

At the sound of my voice, he refocused and replied, "I was thinking about why Lissette called to tell us where Taskert was hiding."

I considered that for a moment before I said, "I think she had gotten to the point where she couldn't dissuade Taskert from reaching out to us. Plus, she had no choice since she needed him alive. You have to admit it was a smart move on her part. Lissette rightly figured out that once Kaffee got Taskert's winery, she'd be at risk of becoming another loose end. That's why she decided to strike first and disappear with all the money. By the time the Napa PD sorted it out, she'd be long gone."

"I hate to think she might have gotten away with it," Al stated somberly.

"Oh, I don't think that was ever a possibility," Delinda said with a knowing smile.

Genies.

The food came, and I couldn't help but steal several glances at Delinda, who was delicately going to work on her salad.

"Do you really need to eat?" I asked.

"No," she replied. "But I enjoy it. It reminds me of when..."

Her voice trailed off before she finished the sentence.

"So, you weren't always a genie?" I guessed.

Her reply was so soft, I barely heard it. "I don't wish to talk about that."

"Understood," I said, just as quietly. Delinda wasn't going to give me any details, and I knew better than to press.

Al, still running interference, quickly changed the subject. "Well, it looks like Bruce will make sure that Taskert's winery will be back in business very soon."

"Yes, but Taskert will probably be drowning in litigation on account of the wine fraud thing," I speculated. "The lawyers will make a fortune, and Taskert might have to start wearing his own wine barrels."

Delinda shook her head gently and laughed. "I actually doubt anyone will complain. Most of those who were swindled will never admit they were taken in. They'll open those bottles at functions where they can bask in the glory of such rare and expensive extravagance."

"What happens when they drink that stuff?" I asked.

"Delinda's right," Al chortled. "They'll either pretend the wine is magnificent, even if it's not."

"What if it's total crap?" I pressed.

Delinda's wry smile broadened into a full-on grin. "Easy... They'll claim it turned in the bottle."

I looked at her and grinned back. "You know, you're right. And, if they make it look like it's no big deal, their friends will even be more impressed."

She took another bite of her salad. "People are such funny monkeys."

I had no intention of arguing that point.

After dinner, we walked back across the street to our resort and said our goodnights before we parted ways to our respective villas. Instead of going directly back to mine, I found a bench near a small, marble fountain to gather my thoughts. Delinda continued to weigh on my mind.

"Mark, can we talk?"

Startled, I turned to find Delinda sitting on the bench beside me. Naturally, I wasn't aware of her presence until she spoke.

"Sure," I replied, trying hard not to look as surprised as I felt. "What about?"

"About you and me. I owe you a better explanation."

I thought it through carefully before I replied. "No, you really don't. In fact, I think we're both better off if we just keep on the way we are."

"I'm glad to hear you say that," she said. "Because we really don't have a choice."

"At least for now," I offered, smiling weakly.

"At least for now," she echoed. "Goodnight, Mark."

"What?" I called after her as I watched her walk off into the gathering moonlight. "Aren't you just going to vanish into mid-air?"

She looked back at me, beautiful, radiant—every man's dream.

"I'm not giving you the satisfaction," she replied with a wide grin. "No more magic tonight!"

I went back to my room, with the hope I would see her again in my dreams.

The next morning we all got into the Lexus, and I prepared myself for the white-knuckle drive back to Oakland. To my astonishment, the speedometer never got past ninety—which I considered to be a gesture of good will. She still took every opportunity to pass every other car we encountered—but you can't have everything.

When we boarded Ashton's private jet for the trip home, I commended her for keeping my blood pressure within normal limits on the trip back.

"I wasn't thinking about you, Mark. I was only worried about the temporary spare," she said blithely.

"Well, thanks anyway," I said.

"Don't get used to it."

CHAPTER TWENTY-NINE

A WEEK AFTER WE returned from Napa, I decided to begin an investigation of my own. One which brought me to downtown Los Angeles. My destination was a bookstore on East 8th Street that was located in a part of the city which made my stretch of Sunset Boulevard look elegantly upscale by comparison. I made the trip owing to my conversation with Bruce Ashton the night before. When I discussed what I had in mind, he recommended that I pay the place a visit.

"It's been there practically forever," he had informed me.

Coming from him, that was quite a reference since the Circle of Solomon buried in the palm of his right hand makes him practically immortal. Also, in the same conversation, he insisted I park my company car several blocks away in a commercial lot and walk the rest of the way. As I made my way down East 8th, I understood his concern.

With several exceptions, nearly all the storefronts on the entire block were shuttered. The windows and doors of the shops that managed to remain open were fortified with various types of ironwork. I supposed it was necessary because despite the air of desolation and abandonment the district conjured up, it nonetheless teemed with activity. Out of necessity, I resorted to walking in the street since swarms of homeless and their makeshift tents and shelters crowded the sidewalks and curbsides. As I passed, a few met my eyes, and I smiled back, refraining from any judgment, as there was a time I had come very close to joining their ranks.

There, but for the grace of the genie, go I.

The building that housed the bookstore was one of the old masonry types that had been retrofitted with steel rods intended to hold them together in an earthquake. Each of the letters on the large front window had initially been painted in gold and thinly outlined in black. Now, the lettering was chipped and sun-faded to where the outline and the lettering had become almost indistinguishable. "Cutter's Rare Books," it read, and behind the grimy glass I could see piles of books cluttering the shop's interior.

Wondering how anyone could find anything in there, I pushed open the equally grimy glass door, which struck and rang the small brass bell hanging from the doorframe. Assuming customers were scarce, I expected to see someone scurry hurriedly to the front of the store to meet me—but that didn't happen. I glanced around, noting that, as one would expect, the walls of the shop were entirely comprised of overstuffed bookshelves. I threaded my way through aisles of tomes, many that were piled chest-high until I reached the counter. Unlike the rest of the place, the countertop was clean and uncluttered except for the service bell, which I pressed twice.

"Can I help you?" came the voice behind me.

I turned immediately and saw the greeting came from a man who looked just as old as most of the books in the store. His sudden appearance startled me, and I supposed my expression made that plain.

"Sorry if I gave you a start," he apologized in a tone that was both sincere and yet tinged with humor. "I was back here sorting through some volumes of Chaucer, and I became so absorbed in Troilus and Criseyde that I didn't hear you come in."

"No worries," I offered, not having a clue as to what he was referring to. "I'm only hoping you'll have what I'm looking for."

"And what would that be?" asked the man, whom I presumed was Mr. Cutter.

"Something on the djinn... Or efrits, as some call them."

The man looked at me strangely for a moment before he replied.

"Occult fiction, then?" he asked with a smile.

I smiled back and answered, "If that's all you have, then I'm sorry to have wasted your time."

"Ah, I see... So, what are you looking for precisely? Historical accounts? Qur'an, Talmudic, or Biblical references? General information?"

"I'm not sure," I admitted. "Bruce Ashton sent me here. He said you would be helpful."

The man nodded and motioned towards the back of the store. He was rail-thin and wore a white short sleeve shirt unbuttoned just enough to reveal his sleeveless undershirt underneath. His dark blue slacks were neatly pressed, though dusty around the knees from kneeling on the floor. A shock of pure white hair framed his pale, wrinkled face, which appeared untouched by the sun. Not an unusual attribute for someone who had spent his years engaged in indoor literary pursuits. It was his pale blue eyes that held my attention. They shined with a remarkable youthful vigor that lit up his whole face.

"I'd be delighted to help you in any way I can." He paused to introduce himself. "I'm Ian Cutter. Bruce Ashton and I go back quite a long way."

In return, I introduced myself before he led me through the piles and bins of books that crowded every available space in the store. As we ventured deeper into the shop, I realized the place was far larger than I had thought. Once we neared the back wall, I followed him around a tall bookcase into a hidden nook that held even more stacks. The books here appeared much older, judging from the condition of their bindings and the layer of fine, white powder that covered them.

"Since Bruce sent you, I assume you'll be looking for in-depth studies on the subject," Cutter declared.

Before I could answer, he pushed several books aside from one of the stacks, raising billows of dust.

"Mr. Tonnick, do you read Latin?" he asked, holding out the book he had picked from the pile.

"No, unfortunately," I replied, keeping a straight face. One good look at me should have answered that question.

"Too bad," he commented, sounding more sincere than not. "Then, this one will have to do."

Ian Cutter ignored the new cloud raised up by the book he pulled from the middle of an adjacent stack. It was clearly very, very old. The spline was hanging on by a thread, and the pages were yellowed with age. He opened it with considerable care and read the title page.

"'Spirits and other curiosities of ancient Megiddo,' by Ludwig Christoph Hellwig. Translated from the German, in 1750 by Eugenius Philalethes. The prose is archaic and a bit dense, but it's quite definitive, especially in the area you inquired about."

He held it out to me, and I gingerly took it into my hands. The leather cover and binding were cracked, and I was afraid the book was going to break apart.

"I don't think I can afford this," I said, staring blankly down what was clearly a rare and ancient first edition—most likely the *only* edition.

Cutter cackled dryly. "No charge. I'm indebted to Bruce, and my sense is that you may find what you're seeking in these pages. If memory serves me, you can skip over the first seven chapters to the section on King Solomon."

"I'll bring it back when I'm done," I offered. "What I'm after is very… Specific."

Nodding, he said, "I wish you success in finding what you're searching for." Then he paused to study me for a moment before his expression changed to concern. "But I also should warn you… You might not like what you find."

"Maybe," I replied. "Nothing comes without risk."

"True, young man, however, while you should never fear knowledge, you must always be wary of where it might take you."

Despite his ominous warning, I thanked him and watched as he carefully took the book from me and placed it into the paper bag he plucked off a nearby shelf.

An hour and a half later, I was back at my desk, delicately leafing through the brittle pages under the watchful auspices of Ruby, my self-appointed, feline protector. Ludwig Christoph Hellwig, the original German author, had thoroughly researched the subject of djinn, genies, and related creatures. It was a slow read, causing me to speculate the original German prose was just as ponderous and impenetrable as the English translation. After deciphering several dozen pages of old English text where the letters s and f were recklessly interchanged, I plodded through many legendary backstories. Only then did I discover the two items that piqued my interest.

First, Solomon may have been a legendary king, but for all that, he died a beggar. He came to that end because he had the misfortune of both believing his own press and supremely pissing off the divine powers. The main reason he shot to the top of God's shit-list was that he apparently contracted with a demon to build his temple at Jerusalem. The result of that unholy pact, according to the author, was supposedly how the djinn came to be.

The second item of interest, harked back to what Delinda had told me some time ago as to why it was impossible for us to have any physical relationship. She said I was flesh and blood, and she was smoke—inferring that all of her kind shared the same attributes. While that was consistent with what I read, other details were puzzling and contradictory. Legend holds that after the temple was built, Solomon turned on the djinn, banishing them all to who knows where—clearly in breach of contract. But from what I come to know, the author may have been mistaken on several counts.

If indeed, Solomon made the genies disappear, then he missed one—at least that I know of, and if that was the case, he might have overlooked more. And, while Delinda might be a lot of things, a demon certainly isn't one of them. Nor is she someone who would know much about construction. So as far as I was concerned, Hellwig's origin story didn't ring true. Not that I blamed him, considering he hadn't the advantage of first-hand knowledge.

Because Solomon supposedly lived a thousand years before the birth of Christ, there are no contemporary written accounts of his life. All we know about him comes from stories passed on through oral history and woven into religious literature. So, everything Hellwig gathered regarding his subject was based on apocryphal accounts.

Having said that, later on in the same chapter, Hellwig described another ancient rumor, almost as an aside. He recounts this tale in a mere paragraph as if it almost wasn't worth retelling. In it, King Solomon's long life and magical powers are ascribed to four relics he found as a young man; items that supposedly fell from the sky.

Next, the author went on to dismiss the story entirely and writes he only mentioned it in the interests of completeness. In the early eighteenth century, when the book was written, the idea that magical tech could have fallen from the stars was not nearly as compelling as dealings with deities and demons.

Hellwig, aside from giving the passage short shrift, leaves the nature of those four objects to the reader's imagination. Three centuries later, I realized that those items had to be the circles that granted Solomon, and the others who came to possess them, near immortality. I knew of three Circles of Solomon from my first case with Ashton, involving Al and a psychopathic immortal named Malthus. Except for Ashton's circle, which was still embedded in his palm, the other two had been destroyed.

If indeed, four circles had come into Solomon's possession, then new questions came to mind: What happened to the fourth circle? Where had the circles come from in the first place, and for what purpose? I pondered these as I replaced the book into the paper bag and tucked it away in a drawer. I was left with no answers, more questions, and the beginnings of a major migraine.

I poured a couple of fingers of Don Julio into my empty coffee cup and looked over at Ruby, who was curled in a furry ball on my office couch.

"So, do you think there's a fourth circle?" I said out loud. "And that it might have something to do with Delinda?"

Ruby cracked her eyes open and replied with a silent yawn.

I finished my shot of tequila and answered for her. "Yeah, me too."

The cat went back to sleep, and I refilled my cup wondering how I would go about solving a mystery rooted so deep in the past. I considered ringing up Delinda and simply asking her. At that very instant my mobile played the ringtone I had programmed for her. The first few bars of "Friend Like Me" from Disney's Aladdin.

"Please, don't!" Delinda said, even before my lips could form a greeting.

"I was just about to call you," I replied, not at all surprised by her timing—she was a genie, after all.

"I know you were."

"Of course you did," I agreed, before cutting directly to the chase. "So tell me, where is the fourth Circle of Solomon?"

There was a brief pause before Delinda spoke.

"I'm the fourth circle," she answered slowly, "Which is why you must not pursue this any further."

"Why is that?" I asked, "I want to know."

"Because you might destroy us both."

There was a tinge of fear in her voice, something I had never heard before.

"Delinda…" I began, but she had already hung up.

I put some kibble in Ruby's bowl and cleaned out the cat box, as Delinda's words played back in my head. Naturally, I had no intention of heeding her warning.

Ruby jumped off the couch to inspect her dinner and my less than thorough sifting job. I took her soft meow to be a reminder to me that curiosity killed the cat.

"You know I never listen," I told her.

A Note From the Author

Thanks for reading, and I hope you've enjoyed this book as much as I enjoyed writing it. If so, I'd like to ask you to take a few minutes and review this or any of my other works on Amazon.

For independent authors, your reviews and comments are our lifeblood. Whether you loved it or hated it, your opinions are a significant factor in influencing and informing other reader's decisions.

Thanks in advance,

Steve A. Zuckerman

If you have any suggestions, I'd love to hear from you.

Steve@djinnandtonnick.com